PEOPLE'S REPUBLIC

A Novel By
Kurt Schlichter

ISBN: 978-1539018957
ASIN: B01M0H7WQZ
Version 012217

PRAISE FOR
PEOPLE'S REPUBLIC

Kurt Schlichter's People's Republic *is a surreal, fast-paced journey through a dramatically different America but less than a generation away: a flag with fewer stars, crack-shot Mormons, "militant climate change deniers," trendy genericism, cat tacos, iPhone 16s, "the border in Kentucky", rote protests, "Harry Reid International Airport" and eerie new definitions of "red lies", "Indian country" and "the border wall with Mexico." Violent, imaginative, full of mordant humor and dark, gritty details, you won't want to live in this* People's Republic…*but you'll feel a chill as you wonder how different our real future will be.*

Jim Geraghty, Author of *The Weed Agency* and *Heavy Lifting* and Columnist at *National Review*

The dystopian, Orwellian picture of an America gone mad in People's Republic *sounds too frightening to ever come true -- until you realize that the leftism behind that dystopian picture has destroyed societies the world over. Read this chilling book and learn the true cost of leftist policy.*

Ben Shapiro, Radio Host, Author of *True Allegiance*, and Commentator

My friend Kurt Schlichter — attorney, Army vet, and compelling writer – has written a thought-provoking action thriller set against the backdrop of a shattered America. If you are trying to make the case to your politically disengaged friends about the dangers of the growing attacks on the rule of law, People's Republic *is Exhibit A.*

David Limbaugh, Author of *The Emmaus Code: Finding Jesus in the Old Testament* and Columnist at *Townhall.com*

People's Republic *is a well-written, action-packed political thriller that cleverly shreds progressive hypocrisy in a multitude of ways. Kurt successfully did what our mutual friend Andrew Breitbart advised that conservatives do: Get out there and compete in the world of popular culture!*

Dana Loesch, Author of *Hands Off My Gun: Defeating the Plot to Disarm America* and Radio/*BlazeTV* Television Host

They say conservatives are terrible storytellers, but Kurt Schlichter destroys that stereotype in his new novel People's Republic *and issues a dire warning about the future of America. But do not fear, we can still change course and this page turner will embolden the country to take action and do so.*

Katie Pavelich, Fox News Contributor, Author of *Assault and Flattery: The Truth About the Left and Their War on Women*, and editor at *Townhall.com*

The fast paced action of a Brad Thor thriller blended with a dystopian future worthy of Orwell. Kurt Schlichter's People's Republic *is a roller coaster ride through a post-election Hellscape that will leave you wanting more.*

Cam Edwards, Author of *Heavy Lifting* and *NRANews* Television Host

So, what's the worst that could happen?" So say the folks who don't pay much attention to politics, candidates, elections, courts. The real answer is: Lots you don't want to think about, unimaginable things that come out of nowhere. Schlichter puts a whole flight of Black Swans in the air --each of them plausible-- and the result is a riveting, page-turner, and a demand from Schlichter for...more.

Hugh Hewitt, Author of *The Queen: The Epic Ambition of Hillary and the Coming of a Second Clinton Era*, Columnist and Syndicated Radio Host

Reading Kurt Schlichter's description of a future People's Republic of North America reminded me of my 1987 visit to East Berlin but without the Cold War charm. His novel is a timely warning of what could happen to our Republic if our Constitutional norms are abandoned and the vitriol of our political discourse continues to increase. A retired Army Infantry colonel, who deployed to hot spots himself, Schlichter brings the brutal violence, long stretches of tedium and gallows humor of combat to life on his pages. People's Republic *is a fast-paced thriller that will almost certainly end up on the big screen.*

Robert C. O'Brien, Author of *While America Slept: Restoring American Leadership to a World in Crisis* and U.S. Diplomat

People's Republic *by prolific author Kurt Schlichter is a must read for all who care about the future of our currently rapidly deteriorating nation. The fast paced, dark, deadly, all too realistic actions of former special operations soldier Kelly Turnbull makes it a book you will not be able to put down.* People's Republic *is a frightening but realistic portrait of what our nation may well become if we cannot reverse the current destructive trends destroying our constitution and our society.*

William V. Wenger, Writer and Colonel (Retired), Infantry, United States Army

In his previous book, Conservative Insurgency, *Kurt Schlichter reexamined what it was to be an American surrounded by grilled steaks, alcohol and weapons. His new effort,* People's Republic, *peeks into the not-too-distant future and shows Americans*

not only how to kill that meat themselves, but how to annihilate despair. It is powerful, gripping, and priced to change your life.

Stephen Kruiser, Comedian and Columnist

I can't wait to see Lin-Manuel Miranda make a musical out of this!

Tony Katz, Radio Host, Commentator and Blurb Legend

ACKNOWLEDGEMENTS

Many people helped make this novel possible. Not that I am attempting to shift blame should it turn out to be a raging dumpster fire of jumbled words and stupid ideas – in that case, the fault is entirely my own.

Always first is hot wife Irina Moises, who was there from the beginning. Actually, not from the beginning – I would not let her read it at first, but she eventually became the first reader and my primary advisor on whether I was veering entirely off the rails. Without her hard work and support, this book never would have happened.

Kellie Jane Adan again joined in to proofread the entire manuscript, for which I am immensely grateful. She is a heck of a writer – check out her latest book *The Method*.

Thanks also to Drew Matich, Brad Essex, and Jimmie Bise, Jr., for their takes! Also, to all those who read the sample chapter and provided feedback – thank you!

The amazing Salty Hollywood turned my very basic idea about a cover into the remarkable cover you now see. Thanks, Salty!

And, of course, I want to thank radio studs Larry O'Connor, Tony Katz, Dana Loesch, Hugh Hewitt, Derek Hunter, Ben Shapiro, Cam Edwards and Cameron Gray. There are others too. Their support brought me to a wider audience despite the risk to their own careers.

Folks like Michael Walsh, Robert O'Brien, Owen Brennan, Stephen Kruiser, Adam Baldwin, and John Gabriel talked through the scenario with me even if they didn't know it. Thanks for the input, suckers!

Two gentleman who have since passed on inspired me to do this work. One is Andrew Breitbart, whose reaction when facing the cultural gatekeepers of the left was never to ask to be let inside but to simply scale the wall without permission. The other is Captain Daniel Deaton, United States Navy, who became a friend through social media and provided me with much valuable feedback on my fiction from the perspective of a guy who had been there and done that. Any officer the NCOs adored as much as they did CAPT

Deaton had to be squared away. I wish both of them were still here, but we are richer for having known them.

And finally, there is noted author of real literature Kenny, who drank many a beer with me back in J3 talking about how we would write our own books someday. Remember: I don't like fiction, I can't use fiction. Brochures – now that's where it's at!

There were many others whom I may have overlooked. Thank you too!

And, of course, I want to thank every single one of my Twitter followers (currently 71,000+) for being so very, very #caring.

Kurt Schlichter

PREFACE

This novel is not an eager fantasy of a future that I or any other sane person wants. Rather, it is a warning. It, or something very like it, could represent America's future if we continue down the path we have embarked upon. And we must reverse that course before it is too late. We still can – if we choose to.

The key feature of a democratic republic is less that each participant has the capacity to win than that each participant has the capacity to lose and accept that loss. They can lose gracefully because they believe they have been heard, that the system is fundamentally fair, that it is not rigged. So when they lose, they accept their loss and continue to press for their preferred candidates and policies through the existing system. Chaos, violence, upheaval – while not unknown, even in recent decades, these are entirely foreign to a healthy United States of America.

The idea of ending the system, of truly disrupting the status quo, does not arise in a healthy democratic republic. But I fear that our Republic is no longer healthy. In fact, I fear that there is an elite distinguished both by its cultural and political progressivism and its geographical concentration in the cities and on the coasts that is seeking to disenfranchise the rest of the population by altering the rules that competing interests have, until now, played by.

There was a time when politicians did not seek to win the presidency by the thinnest of margins over 50%, where the President was the President of all Americans, where he (or she) did not encourage his supporters to "reward our friends and punish our enemies." He (or she) did not label millions and millions of Americans as "deplorable" and "irredeemable."

There was a time when presidents did not attempt to escape the legitimate input of Congress through executive decrees and appeals to unelected judges who all seem to have graduated from the same dozen liberal universities. There was a time when the media prodded and poked every candidate and leader, instead of targeting only the opponents of their preferred candidates.

There was a time when reasoned debate was possible, where an opponent's argument was honestly framed and debated on that basis instead of misrepresented and the points raised ignored in favor of personal slanders and cheap snark. Remember that if you read a critique of this novel accusing me of hoping to see the future *People's Republic* depicts.

These norms, laws, and customs, along with our Constitution, are what holds our country together. But these are also the very things that our cultural elite attacks, undercuts and weakens. After all, these are obstacles to their power; they are *meant* to be obstacles to rule without restraint. They are designed to be employed by other citizens to check and balance those who would rule without accountability, without the need to consider the other half of the population.

When the norms, laws, and our Constitution are ignored for short term political advantage, those who would do so likely imagine that it is merely an expedient measure, that somehow, down the road, we will return to normal again. But it is not that easy. It is not that simple. You cannot expect that your opponent will placidly continue to abide by the old rules even as you reap the advantages of the new ones. If you push and push, eventually there will be a push back. There will be a reaction, and we may not be able to control it. Because when you change the rules, you change the game. And when you change the game, it might not be into a game you are prepared to play and win.

This novel explores what might happen, how the forgotten half of America might react, if we choose to change the rules. But we can also choose not to throw away the greatest, freest nation in the history of mankind.

And I pray we do.

1.

"Stop talking."

The young man in the passenger seat wisely did as he was told, but he kept loudly breathing in short, shallow puffs. He was scared, as he should be. Kelly Turnbull, behind the steering wheel, was merely ready – his breathing slow, but deep and steady. Turnbull stretched out the fingers of his right hand, his shooting hand. He felt the pressure of the sixth gen Glock 19 in his belt. He mentally ran through the motions – left hand on the door handle, pushing it open, swinging out onto his feet as his right hand retrieved the pistol, bringing his hands together to grip it, taking aim, and rapidly putting two 9 mm hollow point rounds into the faces of each of the three gangbangers now staring at them from the crosswalk.

The gangsters decided to keep walking – there weren't many cars to jack anymore out on the roads outside secure sectors, but something about this guy told them that the cost benefit analysis of potentially grabbing a working ride versus dealing with the hard case in the driver's seat was not going to work out in their favor. Even dirtbags have intuition, and they prudently obeyed theirs.

The light turned green – naturally, one of the few working traffic lights left in Los Angeles had to be right there – and Turnbull pressed the gas. The Dodge was nearly 20 years old, but it still ran fine – Turnbull had made sure of that before he bet his life on it.

He had gone east right through this same part of Pico with his parents a thousand times as a kid, running errands, shopping, eating out. Most of Los Angeles was prosperous then, not just the parts behind the fences and the guards where the rich people now partied while everyone else fought over scraps.

On those drives – everyone had a car back then and you could always find gas – his dad used to listen to talk radio, before all radio came under the "fairness" guidelines and morphed into straight up propaganda. The shrunken media here – you didn't need a lot of outlets when they were all spewing the same thing – merely regurgitated the government policy *du jour*, with a healthy dose of hate for the enemies within and without. The villains were always the same – the religious, the hardworking, the liberty-minded, the ones who refused to kneel. And especially bad were the ones *over there*, on the other side of the border, in the red.

Turnbull distinctly remembered being right on this very same block listening to KABC radio and hearing about how the country was about to collapse if the big banks didn't get bailed out. That was late 2008, right before Obama was first elected and things really started heading downhill. Turnbull was what then? Twelve, thirteen?

Most of the small businesses that had lined Pico were long gone, some boarded up, others just abandoned when the owners fled east – they were usually referred to as "worms," the ones who were beneath contempt for rejecting the paradise that progressivism offered. Now piles of trash lined the sidewalks, and a few people squatted in the urine-soaked doorways, glaring at those lucky enough to have cars. A few blocks north, running parallel to Pico, was the southern part of the wall that blocked off the Westside Sector from the rest of the city. These derelicts lurking in the ruined buildings along the road were just some of the people being walled out.

Inside the Sector, there was order and prosperity. But here, not so much. Here, graffiti helpfully informed passersby about the local gangs in charge of each little bit of turf. On this block, it was the Pico Deuce 40s. And up above it all, the billboards cheered the big gang that was in charge of everything. The blues.

The people who had been trying to kill Kelly Turnbull since the old United States broke apart.

They certainly loved their propaganda. One billboard looming over an abandoned coffee shop offered a picture of a bunch of unsmiling, multi-ethnic children with their fists raised into the air. Superimposed across their chests were the words "FREEDOM FROM HATE IS TRUE FREEDOM. REPORT HATEMONGERS, DENIERS AND SPIES TO YOUR PEOPLE'S BUREAU OF INVESTIGATION!" In the lower right corner lurked the People's Republic of North America's rainbow flag, or at least one version of it. The flag kept changing as one group or another agitated to add its color to the mix, or to move its color to some position of greater prominence; the billboard had to be six months old because the flag had changed twice since. This month, the color of the top stripe was orange; who or what group orange represented Turnbull neither knew nor cared.

After the United States split up, they called the half that inherited the two coasts a "People's Republic," choosing the same hoary old cliché every medal-bedecked Third World butcher had grafted onto his country's name in the 1960s and '70s. The political/media elite resurrected the term as yet another jab at the hated bourgeois primitives who remained in the now independent blue states; it was a much more benign provocation than the various political pogroms and cultural assaults that followed. The blue elite was determined to grind the faces of their opponents into the dirt, even as most picked up and left until the blockade stopped the migration. Labeling their new country a "People's Republic" was just one more way to do it. Take that, nobodies.

Of course, it was not *the* People's Republic, but only *some* People's Republic. And, in fact, it was not much of a republic at all. The blue elite had always felt that when the people have a voice, they often say the wrong thing. So, unrestrained by ancient parchments, they gagged those unworthy of input into their own governance – a group conveniently consisting of everyone not within the blue elite.

But none of the people cared much about what the elite was calling the country anymore. Its name was really the least of their problems. They were too hungry to care about the liberty they had lost. It was no longer freedom they were concerned with but survival. Reds, blues – what did it matter if your kids were crying because you didn't have the ration coupons you needed to get them some dinner?

Turnbull glanced left through his window and observed a long line snaking out of what had been a Ralphs supermarket back twenty–some years ago. Now it was a "People's Market," with trash blowing across its nearly empty parking lot. The people in the queue looked like something out of an old photo from the Great Depression – gray, tired, sullen. There were always lines outside the secure sectors whenever Turnbull came over, but this time something was different. The crowd's mood, even viewed from a passing sedan, seemed unsettled, tense, angry. A fistfight over a place in the queue broke out; everyone simply stared as two ragged men pummeled themselves into bloody heaps for priority in purchasing three cans of generic beans imported from Argentina.

13

"The store must have food today," said his passenger. "You really don't have food lines in the Flyover?" He was skinny, like everyone else who wasn't elite, and maybe 17 years old, the kid of some rich guy back in Kansas City whose wife made off with him to leverage a divorce settlement and who got caught behind the border when the PRNA decided to shut it down for good. Daddy was willing to pay Turnbull's price to get him out, an especially hefty one because mommy would certainly raise the alarm, and there's nothing the People's Bureau of Investigation liked better than catching an infiltrator. What the PBI did to infiltrators – "spies" – was distinctly unpleasant.

"Don't call it 'Flyover.' That's going to be your country soon. It's called the United States of America."

Of course, now there was no flying over it any more – the PR claimed it was the US that shut down the air corridors from the western blue states to the eastern blues, but that was a lie. They just didn't want anyone to see what was happening in red America, even from 35,000 feet.

After a moment, the kid asked, "Will I really have to join the Army?"

"Only if you want to be a citizen. Now stop talking."

In the first years after the Split, there were refugees moving in both directions as people picked a side, but soon the flow from red to blue became a trickle and from blue to red a torrent as their left wing policies, freed of conservative obstruction, began to bear the bitter fruit they always did wherever tried. Determined not to import the same political pathologies that had ripped apart the old United States, Congress, now sitting in Dallas, amended the Constitution. If you had not been an adult living in the red at the time of the Split and you wanted to vote, to be a US citizen, you had to earn the right with a tour in the military carrying a rifle.

There was no alternative service. No reading stories to juvenile delinquents. No scam make-work gigs for rich kids who didn't want to soil their hands. You put on camo and served, and you only got citizenship if you discharged honorably after your two years—or you got shot sooner.

The car shuddered and jerked; another pothole. But there was one nice thing about driving in the impoverished Los Angeles of 2034 – the near total absence of traffic. Thanks to gas being rationed,

14

when it was available to the non-elite at all, people were finally obeying the urban planners who for decades had wanted them out of their cars and into public transportation.

There were plenty of buses–wheezing, dirty buses driven by unionized drivers who answered to no one and ran on their own personal schedules that bore only a glancing resemblance to the optimistic ones the transit authority published. Near the intersection of Pico and Livonia Avenue, Turnbull was nearly sideswiped by a bus driver who felt no need to signal as he wheeled his rickety vehicle away from the curb and into traffic. On its side was a fading, tattered banner depicting an angry woman of ambiguous ethnicity, naturally with her fist in the air, under the superimposed words "WOMYN WILL SMASH SEXISM, RACISM AND DENIAL!" It was remarkable how a nation so focused on rooting out what it called bigotry under various labels always seemed to uncover more and more of it lurking inside itself.

Their destination was not far now. Switch out the car, siphon the gas, get on the freeway, get as far east as possible and make the crossing into Arizona on foot. His mind ran through the checklist again; food, water, clothing for the hike. All good. Travel passes with carbon offsets accounted for, good to go. He had paid enough for them. Blues always talked a good game about being progressive, but they all had their price.

His weapons? Ready to rock, if need be. Hopefully, there would be no need. Not that shooting blues made much difference to him – his time in Indian Country had disabused him of any illusions about the value of human life in the People's Republic. Avoiding trouble was solely a matter of convenience. It was simply easier to avoid a fight if he could. This trip should be a milk run, but with everything falling apart, who knew. It was always worse every time he came back, but this time it was a whole new level of bad. He had almost got caught in a mini riot in Santa Monica surveilling the kid before grabbing him. Better to have superior firepower and be safe rather than sorry.

In all of Turnbull's life, he had never once regretted being too well-armed. Never once.

Now an electronic noise derailed his train of thought.

Da-da-da-da-da.

Turnbull's head swiveled right. "Are you fucking serious?"

15

"I'm sorry," stammered the kid, digging inside his jacket for his cell phone.

Da-da-da-da-da.

"I asked you if you had a cell. You said 'No.' By that I foolishly inferred that you didn't have a fucking cell phone."

"I forgot," the kid replied miserably. Turnbull made a mental note to always search his package. Trusting civilians not to be stupid was a bad bet.

The kid looked at the caller ID. "It's my mom."

"Don't answer it," Turnbull said. He assessed what he could do to undo this screw up. He settled on a plan.

Da-da-da-da-da.

"Give it here, genius." The kid handed the phone over and Turnbull rejected the call.

"Now roll down your window." The kid complied and Turnbull glided the Dodge to a stop in front of a packed bus stop. "What's the unlock code?"

"Uh, one, two, three, four."

"Of course it is," Turnbull replied, and then he yelled over his passenger out to the puzzled riders waiting at the curb.

"Who wants a free phone?"

The riders stared back, their faces thin, their clothes ratty, unsure, unwilling to move. Was this some trap? After a few moments, a young Hispanic woman stepped to the window.

"Free? I'll take it."

"The code is one, two, three, four," Turnbull said, tossing her the device. She caught it, smiled, and stepped back as the Dodge headed down Pico again. Hopefully, she would lead anyone following them on a merry chase across the length and breadth of the Los Angeles public transit system.

"Why did you do that?" the kid asked, petulant. "It's got my address book! I don't even know my mom's number. I just hit the favorite!"

"You understand you can't talk to your mother, right? You get that she's going to report you're gone and that we're fugitives and that that phone could track us, right? Geez, are you really that stupid?"

The kid's eyes welled with tears. Apparently mommy had never let her magical unicorn child in on the fact that he was a numbskull. Turnbull pitied the kid's drill sergeant, assuming the kid had the stones to volunteer.

"We have to lose this car." Turnbull turned off Pico south on a side street. "Now listen, you do what I say when I say it. Do you understand?"

"Yeah," said the kid, petulantly.

"Okay, any more surprises for me? Any other cell phones, personal computers, trackers, smoke signalers, anything on you?"

"No."

"Good. Like I said, you just do exactly what I tell you when I tell you and in a couple of days you'll be in the red and wondering why your mother ever brought you to this shithole."

The neighborhood between Pico and the 10 Freeway felt abandoned, as if everyone had just vanished and nature had started to reclaim it. The buildings were decaying, and the yards had gone feral in the rows of houses liberated from their owners in the wake of the Split. Green weeds sprouted from cracks in the asphalt. Someone had left a broken couch on the sidewalk, and someone else had set it on fire.

And in the midst of all the emptiness were more lies. There was another billboard, brand new but stuck incongruously in a deserted neighborhood. This one depicted a smiling young blonde woman, well-fed and happy, and therefore likely a fantasy. "I LEFT TEXAS AND TYRANNY TO COME HERE! BE GRATEFUL FOR YOUR FOOD AND FREEDOM!" And in the corner, yet another version of the rainbow flag. The top stripe on this one was mauve. Turnbull had no idea what race, ethnicity, or personal lifestyle choice that tint represented either.

After a few moments and a couple turns, they reached a forgotten commercial area. Turnbull parked the Dodge on a quiet street in front of a tan Ford Taurus from the mid-2010s. He said a silent prayer of thanks that it was still there after 12 hours. The Taurus was a bit beat up too, but the engine was still good. It would do the job. Turnbull used the key remote to unlock it.

"Grab my duffle and put it in the back seat of the Ford. Then get in the car and sit there. Don't open the bag. I'm going to siphon out the gas from this one to fill the Ford's tank. Should take me maybe 10 minutes. Don't do nothin'. Don't touch nothin'. Don't say nothin'. Just sit there and wait. Got it?"

17

The kid nodded, and they got out of their respective doors. The kid opened the Dodge's back door and dragged a large olive drab duffle bag with a zipper across the top off of the back seat and onto the cracked sidewalk.

"This is really heavy," the kid said, hefting it over his shoulder.

"Why are you still talking?" asked Turnbull, scanning the area. Nothing but old gray industrial buildings, largely abandoned. It's hard to manufacture without raw materials. He went to the trunk and popped it; it held two empty plastic jerry cans and a siphon rig.

There was movement down the street. Turnbull stepped out from behind the trunk. About 50 yards out was a scraggly man on an ancient bicycle, plastic bags full of what appeared to be salvaged junk swinging from the handlebars. He was probably in his fifties, dirty, with the look of a druggie.

Oh, great.

"Uh, sir? Sir?" shouted the rider, coming closer, now maybe 20 yards out. "Sir, could you spare –"

"No. Move on."

"You look like you got some extra –"

"Move on."

The rider stopped perhaps 30 feet away, straddling his bike frame in the empty street.

"Why you so selfish? I know you got stuff. I just want a little."

From behind, the kid leaned his head out. "What's going on?"

"Get your stupid ass back in the car," Turnbull snarled over his shoulder, then returned the bum's stare.

"Move the fuck on, right now."

"This is my street and you can't just come here –"

Turnbull sighed and pulled back the left flap of his jacket, revealing his pistol.

"I'm counting to three…"

The rider remounted his bike, muttering.

"You think you can come onto my street and run me off? Motherfucker, I'll show you what's up." He turned in a lazy half circle and pedaled away back where he came from.

Awesome. This guy would be back in a few minutes with his pals, or worse tip off the People's Security Force that there was some guy with a non-government piece for the reward. Narcing out formerly lawful gun owners was a traditional profit center for lowlifes after the Split. They got a few bucks and the gun owners got stuck in the prisons the new government had emptied of real criminals.

Turnbull grabbed the empty cans and siphon and shut the trunk. There was no time to salvage the gas remaining in the Dodge. The Ford had half a tank, about enough to ride the 10 Freeway out to near Palm Springs. Unless they got ultra-lucky and found a station with fuel to sell before then – fat chance – he'd have to figure something out there to get them the rest of the way to the border. He would burn that bridge when he came to it. Now it was time to go.

After loading the cans in the Ford's trunk, Turnbull got into the driver's seat and turned the ignition. It started, and he offered a sigh of relief. They accelerated down the street; there was no sign of the bum.

He went east several blocks, and at La Cienega, Turnbull turned right. He knew that up ahead was a freeway entrance, just a little ways south. And gas stations. At least there used to be.

"Keep a lookout in case there's a gas station open," he instructed his passenger.

"Like that one?" The kid was pointing. Parked in front of what had been a Shell was a white van, and snaking from the pump to its gas tank was a hose.

"No way," said Turnbull. Usually a station that got a fuel resupply would have fifty cars lined up out into the road. Weird. Something was not right. But they needed gas. He turned off the road and pulled up behind the van. The van's driver smiled.

"Hey there."

"Hey there. They got gas to sell?"

"Well, no. This here's a little bit of marketing. *I* got gas to sell, though. In back here." He motioned to the van. "How much you need?"

"How do you know I'm not a cop?" Turnbull asked.

"You don't look like a cop," the entrepreneur replied.

"And how do I know *you're* not a cop?"

The seller smiled. "Do I look like a cop? Three hundred bucks a liter. How much do you want?"

"Nah. Pass. Thanks."

"Two-fifty."

"Nah, I'm not feeling like being an economic criminal today." Turnbull pulled around and past the irritated van driver and onto the street.

"What's he doing?" asked Turnbull.

"Who?"

"That shithead. Look back, tell me what he's doing."

"Looks like he's on the phone."

"Fuck me. Okay, we just need to get to the freeway. It's maybe two minutes."

"I thought we needed gas."

"We do. Except if he's not a cop, he's working with the cops, or that van was full of guys to rob us the second I flashed some cash, or best case, the gas in his cans was half water. Whatever his scam was, it was too good to be true."

A beat-up black and white cruiser from the People's Security Force slowly pulled in behind them from a driveway of what used to be a luxury car dealer. Written across the rear quarter panel were the words "Diversity Is Our Strength," except the "v," the "u," and the "S" had peeled off.

"Di ersity Is O r trength."

For just a moment, before the light bar came alive with blue and red, Turnbull had hoped that the appearance of the cruiser was just a coincidence. But it really didn't matter. Whether they were working with the guy at the gas station or whether they just wanted to relieve a citizen of a working car, there was no escaping a confrontation.

"Oh shit, oh shit," whimpered the kid.

"Put your window down."

"What?"

"Put your window down all the way, put your seat back, and do not say a fucking word or I'll kill you myself."

Turnbull pulled over to the curb in front of an abandoned saloon. There were people milling about, and they had seen this little police drama unfolding in front of them before. No one paid much attention. Hassling people is what the PSF did.

The blues' cruiser stopped maybe 20 feet behind them and idled for a moment, but not long enough to run his plates. Both occupants got out, approaching by moving up each side simultaneously in some semblance of the proper tactical template for stopping an unknown driver. They did not seem afraid or even cautious – they were almost arrogant as they came forward. Turnbull could not get a good look at the one on the passenger side, but in the mirror he could see the neck tats of the one moving up on his side. The PRNA was still hiring the cream of the crop, Turnbull noted.

The People's Republic had decided that it needed to run the police force centrally, and it incorporated the local sheriffs and police departments into a national police force originally called the "People's Internal Security Squads." When it became obvious that acronym would not work, it became the PSF – the People's Security Force.

Cops were key villains in the left's rogue's gallery, and most police officers and deputies quickly saw the writing on the wall and left, heading to the red states before the borders closed. That left just a few professionals to address a lot of crime from freed prisoners and the refugees fleeing the welfare reforms in the red states. They flocked to the blues, where the People's government doubled benefits in an effort to fight inequality and racism, as well as, apparently, individual initiative and fiscal stability.

In re-filling the ranks, the People's government decided to prioritize "diversity," and evidently dirtbags constituted an important part of society that was previously shamefully underrepresented in law enforcement. The People's Security Force long ago abandoned hiring standards, and they trained to somewhere lower than the lowest common denominator. But that was sufficient for the People's Security Force's primary task of bullying hungry, cold, disarmed subjects. The People's Bureau of Investigation was a different story – the government ensured the PBI had the best of everything – but these PSF patrolmen were neither trained nor equipped to take on a professional.

Yet they were still dangerous. They both carried holstered, battered Berettas from back when their organization was still known as the LAPD.

"Where's your ID?" the one at his window demanded. The other parked himself at the kid's window, framing himself nicely.

21

"Got it here," Turnbull handed over a very expensive fake he had prepared by his guy in Houston. The name on the card was Charles Schooley. He lived in the Western Sector and had a Privilege Level of "7," a number that indicated he was not quite untouchable, but normally you would not mess with him. Apparently, today was not normal.

"You tried to buy illegal gas back there."

"He offered it to me. I turned him down."

"You calling him a liar?"

"I'm just telling you what happened."

"You think you can come out here and do whatever you want? You think you're special? I don't give a fuck about your PL. You're no fucking 7. I know you bought this shit. You think you can buy everything? And who the fuck is this little bitch with you? Your butt boy?"

"I'm just trying to drive home, okay?"

"Get the fuck out of the car." From the corner of his eye, over the terrified kid, Turnbull could see the cop's smiling partner cup his earphone. Turnbull could make out a few words – "about sixty seconds to your 20, over."

One minute. All right. So now it's going to go how it's going to go.

"I'm getting out," Turnbull said.

"Hurry up," said the cop, never having been taught, or not remembering, to stand back and put some space in between himself and the suspect.

Turnbull shut his eyes for a moment, ran through his plan, and then opened the door slowly, pushing it all the way out. The cop stepped back just a bit, but not far enough. Turnbull stood up to his full 6'3" height deliberately and smoothly, doing nothing to spook them until his left hand shot back, grabbed the cop's utility belt and pulled the stunned thug forward and around into the "V" between the door and the body of the Ford. As Turnbull drove his full weight into the pseudo-cop to pin him, he drew the Glock with his right hand and swung it into the passenger compartment. It roared twice inside the car, the hollow point rounds streaking over the kid and into the chest plate of the other pseudo-cop's body armor. The pseudo-cop staggered back and fell, the 9 mm bullets pounding his chest plate like sledgehammers.

22

Turnbull pivoted and brought the pistol out and up under the pinned one's chin. The pinned one felt it and knew he was screwed, but his self-critique ended a half-second later as Turnbull put a round up through his jaw, tongue, and soft palette into his brain. The pseudo-cop sagged and collapsed like a bag of warm, wet meat.

Turnbull's ear rang as he moved around the back of the Ford to the sidewalk – the tinnitus blurred the kid's terrified howling. The other cop was lying on his back and twitching like a roach, waving his arms and legs as he tried to catch his breath instead of drawing his own weapon. Turnbull casually killed him with two rounds to the face, then turned and opened the passenger-side's rear door.

Thirty seconds. Replacing the Glock in its holster, he unzipped the duffle bag, pulling out the modified M4, leaving its suppressor in the bag. He wanted noise. There was a Magpul mag in already, and a parallel mounted spare – you could see both were full of 5.56mm rounds through the smoky plastic.

Forty seconds. People were watching now up and down the street, but Turnbull's focus lay elsewhere. He walked back into the road past the idling cruiser with the black carbine in his right hand, yanking back the charging handle with his left. He let it go, slamming a 5.56 mm round into the chamber. Locked and loaded.

Using his thumb, through pure muscle memory, he set the selector switch to "Auto."

Fifty seconds. The back-up cruiser appeared ten seconds early, rounding the corner expecting to assist on an easy score. From their angle, the scene before them was unclear – that lump on the street by the Ford was merely a lump and would be for a few more seconds until it came into focus.

But they didn't have a few more seconds. Turnbull shouldered the carbine and fired a long burst – seven or eight shots – into the driver's side of the car. The roar was horrendous; he wanted it loud to disorient his targets and to discourage others from intervention. Golden brass spurt from the ejection port like a fountain, and white geysers of pulverized glass danced across the blues' windshield. He could see shadowy jerking and thrashing inside the passenger compartment.

The cruiser wobbled and pulled right, toward the curb. Turnbull unleashed another burst, this time on the passenger side. Another string of craters erupted across the windshield in front of the

23

passenger. The cruiser went up on the curb and slammed into a telephone pole. Turnbull fired two more long but controlled bursts as he approached, weapon high, and then he squeezed off a third burst. It was cut short as the weapon ran dry. Without pause or even a glance, he dropped the mag from the well using the thumb button, reinserted the loaded mag clamped to its side, and hit the bolt release. The bolt slammed a fresh round into the chamber.

By then he had reached the brutalized, smoking cruiser, his weapon high and ready. The blue cop in the passenger seat was bloody, but still gasping and trying to sit up. Turnbull put a burst in his head and then another in his partner's. Then he turned back to the Ford as onlookers ran and shouted.

All Turnbull heard was ringing.

Tossing the carbine in the back seat, he got behind the wheel and turned on the ignition. The kid was crying; his ears were still roaring from the two rounds Turnbull had fired inside the passenger compartment.

Time to move. Every PSF thug on the Westside would be inbound when word broke that four of their own were down. That might just clear his path out of town.

It was not far to the freeway, and from there to home. Turnbull pulled out in traffic, and in his mirror saw the locals already scavenging the bodies.

"You killed them, you killed them!" the kid was screaming. Turnbull hit the gas and the Ford accelerated.

"Stop talking," he said, but the kid couldn't hear him.

2.

From the 97th floor of the Lone Star Tower, you could see Dallas sprawling out in every direction all the way out to the horizon and beyond. The city was a living thing, humming, alive, with people on the sidewalks and cars filling the streets and freeways. To the north, the New Capitol complex was gleaming in the sunlight. The New White House lay a mile away at the other end of the Mall. This was the nerve center of the United States of America, version 2.0.

Turnbull did not feel much more at ease here than on the other side. But then, no one was trying to kill him here, so there was that.

Still, he openly carried a Kimber 1911 .45 for his long trip into town. Security took his phone downstairs, but made no attempt to disarm him. You don't mess with a man's weapons in the USA. That's how fistfights and civil wars start.

He could feel the heat outside radiating through the windows; the air conditioning was cranked. Turnbull sipped his coffee and took a seat at the conference table, back to the window and, as always, facing the door.

This had better not be a waste of his time.

The door opened and Turnbull recognized the first guy to walk in – George V. Ryan, looking every bit like the kingmaker he was. Tall, handsome, probably 55ish. Usually when you saw him he was on TV standing behind the President. His suit probably cost as much as Turnbull's ranch.

The next guy was a young man, good shape, probably recent military judging by the hair and his general demeanor. There it was, the red star pin on his jacket's lapel – he'd earned his citizenship with military service. The young man looked a little like Ryan – probably his son.

And a third man entered, smaller, wearing a cryptic smile, looking like he knew things you didn't. Turnbull knew him well, and it figured he'd be wrapped up in this somehow.

"Hello, Clay," Turnbull said. Clay Deeds nodded and took a seat across the table.

"Hi, Kelly. You look good for a guy everyone on the other side is looking for."

"Oh really? Now why is that?" "Somebody waxed four People's Security Force thugs in LA last week. My sources tell me not one of them even got a shot off."

"Probably militant climate change deniers. Those guys are super bad news."

"Clearly. That was you, wasn't it?"

"Me? Of course not. No way," he replied. "So, do they have my name?"

"No. Just a vague description and a blurry security camera photo of some big scary guy. But you'll be happy to know you've inspired a whole new round of internal security arrests. Apparently you're not a loner. Apparently, you're part of some giant conspiracy to undermine the legitimacy of the People's Republic."

"I try to make a difference. But like I said, I totally don't remember anything like that. Now, why did you interrupt my recuperation and drag me into town today?"

"You're always charming, Kelly. Let me introduce Mr. George Ryan. *The* George Ryan. He's got a proposition you need to hear."

Ryan stepped forward while Turnbull stood, and they firmly shook hands. Turnbull sat back down. Ryan stood for an awkward moment, assessing his guest.

"You know me, correct?"

"I know *of* you. I know you're rich and you're powerful and you have really nice offices near the top of the tallest building in North America. I don't know why I'm here, though I am enjoying this coffee and the view."

"Well, Mr. Turnbull, you are correct that I am rich and powerful and that these are nice offices, and I'll take your word on my secretary's coffee, but none of that really means anything to me right now. I have a problem, and Mr. Deeds tells me you are the only man who might be able to solve it for me."

"Clay says a lot of things. You need to watch what Clay says. He's a spook and sometimes you can't be absolutely sure whose side he's on."

Clay simply smiled. "Just to be clear, I'm on the United States' side. You might not always see that at the time, but in the long run that's my side."

"Uh huh," replied Turnbull.

Ryan went on. "Mr. Deeds tells me you were Army. Afghanistan before the Split. Other places. You helped grab Ft. Hood during the Crisis. Fought in Southern Illinois and Indiana, Indian Country, behind the lines, organizing and leading guerillas. Other places."

"I did my part."

"You were part of Operation Megiddo."

"I don't know anything about that," Turnbull said, glancing toward Clay with a frown. "That would be totally classified and anyway, I read that the Israelis took out the Iranian nukes all by themselves. Your researchers shouldn't believe everything they read on the internet."

"Of course," said Ryan, continuing. "Now, you grew up in California, so you know it well. After the Split, you made a lot of runs back over the line before you left government service – well, *official* government service – and started doing runs on your own. You cross over and bring people out for money."

"Well, we all have to eat. And I'm not an office kind of guy."

"No, you are most definitely not an office guy, Mr. Turnbull. I've just scratched the surface on your record. You're quite impressive. You are also clearly the best at extracting individuals trapped inside the People's Republic and now I need you to use that skill for me. Right now. In the next 48 hours."

"Go back in right now? See, that conflicts with my calendar. I have a lot of nothing scheduled in my immediate future."

"It has to be now."

"Mr. Ryan, I just came out less than a week ago. You just heard Clay mention that they're looking for me. I survive doing this work by not pushing my luck. Don't go in or out the same way twice, and put in a little time between runs."

"We don't have time to delay, Mr. Turnbull. Tell me, what was it like over there this last run of yours?"

"It was a mess and getting worse. Less food, less fuel, more cops. People were angry. It's falling apart. The whole house of cards is collapsing."

"Yes. We've been expecting this for years. The People's Republic is imploding, Mr. Turnbull. While we in the US doubled down on what made America great, they doubled down on the blue state socialism that split the country apart. And exactly what we knew would happen is happening. It's a police state that functions only to keep the elite separate from the consequences of its policies. They are out of money, and they are out of excuses for their people. All they have left are scapegoats. It's going to get very, very ugly, very, very soon."

"It is. And I don't want to be caught in the middle of it when it all goes to hell."

"My daughter Amanda is over there, Mr. Turnbull. In the middle of a coming chaos we can barely imagine."

"How did that happen?"

"She defected."

"She did not defect!" interrupted the young man. "She's just confused."

"Mr. Turnbull, this is my son George Junior. His twin sister is Amanda. They were close. George chose to do his military service after college. Amanda went to UT in Austin then stayed for grad school. Unfortunately, not all of the progressives picked-up and headed to a coast after the Split. Some stayed here, especially at universities, and they are like a cancer. They spread their lies and some people, like Amanda, get taken in. She decided that all this, all this prosperity and freedom, is immoral. She believed the People's Republic was some kind of paradise. So she left. As you know, we don't keep anyone in. We keep them out. She and some friends crossed over a year ago and we had no idea what happened to her until my sources started telling me she was appearing in PR propaganda."

"Got a picture?"

"What?"

"A picture of Amanda. I think I might have seen one of her billboards."

Ryan produced his smartphone and found a photo of a pretty blonde girl on a horse.

"Yeah, that's her. Must have been a real coup for them, having the daughter of a guy like you willing to shit on her own country. I didn't hear about it here."

28

"I'm not proud of her, I assure you, Mr. Turnbull. Since there's no real direct communication between the two halves of the country any more, it was fairly easy to use my influence to make sure this did not get out into the media. But, regardless, she is still my daughter and I love her and I want you to go in and get her and bring her back home to me."

"Well, how do you know she even wants to come back?"

"I don't, not for sure."

"She wants to come home. *I* know it," George Junior said, impatient. "She got confused. I just need to talk to her. She'll see the light, and I'll get her to come back with us."

"Wait one, who exactly is this 'us' he's talking about? I work alone. The 'by myself' brand of 'alone.' Remember the loner part that's no doubt part of the psych profile Clay there must have given you? That's me. A loner. Ergo, alone."

"You need to take George Junior with you. Like I said, he's close to Amanda. He can talk sense into her. He can get her to come home. If you try it by yourself, there's no way she would cooperate. She might even hurt you."

"She seems scary. But I don't need to carry an amateur. My ruck's full enough."

"George knows how to handle himself. He's a Blood Citizen."

"Congratulations on getting yourself shot, kid. Helluva way to earn the right to vote. Now, before we continue, let's not get ahead of ourselves here, because we seem to be operating under the unspoken premise that I am willing to go back in a week after I came out, while they're looking for me, and go extract a defector who probably doesn't even want to be extracted. And that is a *false* premise."

"There's no one else who can do this. I need you, Mr. Turnbull."

"I appreciate that, Mr. Ryan, but I need me too, preferably not swinging from some rope off a crane as a spy."

"Money is not an issue, Mr. Turnbull."

"Well, it is for me. What kind of money are we talking about?"

"Five hundred thousand."

"Not enough."

"A million."

"Still not enough."

"Mr. Turnbull, I've talked to some of your previous employers. You've never gotten more than $500,000 for an extraction."

"I've also never been asked to do a job by a billionaire. Mr. Ryan, I'm a capitalist and if I was doing this job – *if* – I would charge what the market would bear. And I think it would bear, say, $5 million."

"Would you do it for $5 million?"

"I would sure *think* about doing it for $5 million. See, that would pretty much set me up to retire and I could stop going back and risking my ass to solve other people's problems."

"Mr. Turnbull, I'll pay you $5 million to do it."

"One in advance."

"Agreed. But there are conditions. You will take George Junior with you. And if you do not recover her relatively intact, you forfeit the remaining four million."

"'Relatively intact.' Okay. But I have conditions too. First, I take Junior here to the range tomorrow and decide whether I'm willing to have him tag along. If I do, Junior understands that the chain of command is me, then him. He does what I say, when I say it, how I say it gets done."

"Agreed."

"I want to hear Junior say it. Junior, do you understand?"

"Yeah, I understand chain of command. I was a lieutenant."

"Oh good, a lieutenant. That's reassuring. I guess I'll be handling the map and compass. And speaking of equipment, I'm going to have a shopping list and some of the stuff Clay here is going to have to provide. Which brings me to another thing that's been gnawing at me. Why is there a spook here?"

"I'm just here to assist. This is a private transaction. The government is not involved, of course."

"Oh, of course not."

"We'll chat after you and Mr. Ryan are finished."

"Uh huh. Naturally."

Ryan sat down across from Turnbull.

"You'll do it?"

"If you meet my conditions, and if your spy friend here can get me what I need. And if what he tells me doesn't lead me to think that *I'm* not coming back relatively intact."

"Thank you, Mr. Turnbull. I'll have my people start making the arrangements."

"Okay. And Junior – tomorrow, my ranch, nine a.m."

George Junior nodded. His father rose out of the chair and George Junior followed him to the door.

"Bring my daughter back to me safe, Mr. Turnbull. Please."

"I'll do my best."

They went out the door, leaving Turnbull and Clay at the table alone.

"Why are you involved in this, Clay?"

"Well, let's say that Mr. Ryan has a lot of friends in high places and those friends have my phone number. You should be happy. You can retire after this one."

"There's a big empty space I gotta fill between the agreeing to do it part and enjoying the money part."

"Just a bit of one. So, what the hell happened in Los Angeles? You've always been a shoot first then shoot again kind of guy, but four blue cops?"

"I deny all knowledge of any violence," said Turnbull. "But PSF aren't cops. They're glorified muscle. All the real cops picked up and left with the rest of the working people after they saw how things were going to go. So you got a few rich people, a lot of poor people, and an army of thugs keeping them apart."

"Do you think they made you?"

"I think it started as a shakedown, but what was weird was that they were *mad*, Clay. Usually when they shake you down or rip off your stuff it's just business, but these guys were angry. They saw I had a car and a pretty high privilege level and they got pissed. Everyone's pissed. It's falling apart over there."

"That's how we assess it. We always knew the blue model would fail. It was just a matter of time. We kept the farms and the fuel, and they kept the mouths to feed in the big coastal cities. They won't exploit their resources – they still buy most of their energy and food from foreigners, and they are running out of credit. They picked on the people who did the hard work, and those people came here. We told people here that if you don't work, you don't eat and the

31

ones who wanted handouts picked up and went blue. I think we got the better part of that deal."

"Yeah, the People's Republic is what happens when you let movie stars and college professors pick the government. Okay, we all know it sucks and it can't last. So why me? You have your own network inside the PR. Where do I come in?"

"Well, for one thing you aren't in any network, meaning you are hard to compromise. Those socialist bastards may suck at most everything, but they are good at the oppressive arts. Our people keep getting swept up. We aren't sure who to trust. But there's not much chance they know you."

"Wait, you said they are looking for me."

"They are looking for some blurry bourgeois terrorist who capped some local heroes. But they are focused inward – it's part of a factional power play. The players in the government are trying to use the incident against each other for leverage. They aren't looking for you to come back and bring something out for us."

"Is this girl that important?"

"No, she's just a stupid girl who went to college and got stupider. Oldest story in the world. No, there's something over there we really want and we need you to walk it out."

"Can you tell me what this mystery McGuffin is?"

"Data on a hard drive some of our friends on the other side liberated."

"What kind of data?"

"Classified."

"I still have my clearance. You know I'm still in the Reserves like every other citizen who's too young for a walker."

"We got a source inside the PBI HQ and the source tore out a hard drive. It's got the files on their informers. It's gold – every narc, weasel and snitch on the West Coast on one little hard drive. If we get it out, we can figure out who they've turned and who they haven't and rebuild our networks."

"Okay, but why walk it out? You can plug it in, go online and transmit it to some foreign country, then back here to get around the e-blockade."

"Too risky. All of Silicon Valley didn't pick up and move. It might have protection that would let them detect and block or alter the transmission. Or it might report who we are interested in. Regardless, we need to decrypt it here, on an air-gapped system."

"Carrying it out by hand is safer? You thought that through?"

"Marginally safer. I can trust you'd have sense enough to ditch it if the heat comes around the corner. So, basically, I'll square you away to go in and all you do is make a quick stop with a contact in LA on your way home, pick up my hard drive and bring it out along with the girl and you get your millions and I get my data and everyone's happy."

"It sounds so simple and easy. So why are there hairs standing up on the back of my neck?"

"Because you're not a fool. If it falls apart while you are over there, you could get caught up in the reckoning. Plus, as soon as it goes bad in the blue we're sealing the borders. Now, you'll have a primary and supplemental re-entry point and we'll be waiting for you, but if a couple million blue staters start marching our way determined to leave the nest they shit in to come here and shit in ours, all bets are off."

"Well, let's just hope that they can hold their shit together for a week or two so I can get paid."

Clay sat back and smiled. "Try not to get killed, Kelly. You're extremely useful."

"Useful, huh? Carve that on my tombstone."

3.

Kelly Turnbull's ranch was about 500 acres in the dry hills some 90 miles southwest of Dallas, far away from annoyance and inconveniences like cities and highways and other people. To call it a ranch would be a misnomer; there were old stables, but he had no horses or livestock. They were too much trouble, and he was often away regardless. The only occupied structure was the white one-story house, small but sturdy, and he had done much of the renovations himself. He liked working with his hands, finding it relaxing. He could set his mind on auto-pilot and simply build; when he was on the job, every second he was on edge, planning and evaluating, thinking through scenarios, preparing for threats.

Best of all, he liked not having to check behind him.

He sat on the porch, drinking coffee, his stupid dog curled up beside him. It was nearly useless, that dog, a light brown mix who had no real purpose except to mooch food and demand attention. It had followed him home one day and he had never bothered to chase it away. Maybe his time in cities had made him soft, he reflected. A real rancher would have gotten rid of it long ago. The damn thing couldn't even be bothered to kill rats.

His smartphone pinged; a vehicle had entered the property and was coming down the driveway. The time was 0845 hours. A good sign. Somewhere along the line, some NCO had taught Lieutenant Ryan that if you weren't fifteen minutes early you were already late.

Junior pulled up in a tan late-model BMW 6-series. Pricey. You had to get it from Cuba, because of the EU boycott of the racist, imperialist, and insufficiently Islamacist-subservient United States. Cuba, having finally tossed out its communist government (with just a little bit of help from the United States – Turnbull savored the memory of the rum), was now growing rich selling to the Americans what the Europeans refused to sell them directly. The Caribbean island was the world's second largest buyer of German cars, right after Germany itself.

The dog looked over, bored, and then put his head back down. Not a bark, not even a growl. Sheesh, sighed Turnbull.

Junior wore tan combat boots, khaki tactical slacks with a checked shirt, and he looked remarkably crisp in the wilting 90 degree heat. He carried an HK-style USP in .45 – perhaps likewise bought through Cuba, but more likely built at one of the weapons plants dotting the Southern states. The few gun makers left in blue states at the start of the Crisis had been among the first to depart after the Split.

"So, I'm here."

"Let's go shoot. Follow me." The dog watched them go; there was no way he was leaving the shade.

Turnbull had set up a range behind his house. A table held a pair of modified M4 carbines; they were accessorized with close quarter battle sights, fore grip handles and suppressors.

The table also held a pair of Glocks, plus eye and ear protection. There were dozens of boxes of ammo and a stack of empty magazines that they proceeded to fill.

"The Glocks are simple, reliable, and shoot 9 mm, probably the easiest round to find on the black market over there. Clay used his intel connections to get us a couple modified ones from the special ops guy's secret stash, sixth generation, special handgrips, improved slide. We'll each take ten mags plus one in the gun. They aren't flashy on the outside, and some cops still carry them, so it's a good relatively inconspicuous choice. The M4s are an improved version of a time-tested weapon. You guys on active duty still use them. Full auto, of course. Clay dropped them off yesterday afternoon. They're clean – they can't be traced to the US. Neither can the Glocks."

"So why are we using the M4 platform? There are a lot of others we could choose from."

"Familiarity. We both used it in the service. The bad guys sometimes use AK series rifles bought from China or wherever whenever they can, but there are enough M4s still over there that they won't draw special attention in and of themselves. Plus, the four provides good firepower – these are full auto. The suppressors won't make them silent, but will quiet them down a little. Think of these carbines as a last resort – they only come out to rock and roll if we have to."

"Like you did in Los Angeles last week."

"I never admit anything. But yeah."

"You took on four armed PSF officers all alone. That seems a little crazy."

"I wasn't alone. I had two powerful allies, surprise and aggression. The People's Security Force are really just security guards with a license to kill. Don't think of them as cops; cops are professionals and have a code. These guys have greed and an attitude; they don't help people, they only help themselves. They aren't picked because they're smart and they aren't trained to do much more than bully people who can't fight back. Our edge is that they think they've broken the populace, that no one will resist. When someone does, there are a critical few moments when they are mentally resetting into a combat mindset. You need to take advantage of it. That's where the aggression comes in. They expect you to run away. Instead, you charge. They aren't trained to fight even odds or without the initiative. So when you attack, it throws them off balance. At Ft. Benning, what did they train you to do in an ambush?"

"Turn and attack into it."

"Right. See, we think like soldiers, not sheep. These guys aren't used to soldiers. They assume we're sheep. So when we battle instead of baa, we have an edge," he said. Then, "So how did you get wounded?"

"I was in the 36th Division along the border in Kentucky. My platoon was running a security op in the DMZ with Ohio and we ran into some traffickers. We got six of them. I took a round in the thigh. They had AKs."

"The proudly gun-free Peoples Republic. Yeah, the PR hates armed citizens, but if you're a criminal you're good to go. Or if you're one of their PBI stormtroopers. Or guarding the rich folks. Then guns are great."

"What's that one?" Junior asked, pointing to a pistol on the table that looked like a high-tech Luger.

"That's a present from Clay, too. It's a Ruger 22/45 .22 semi-auto pistol, and it comes with this suppressor. I'm going to use subsonic, frangible rounds. Silent but deadly on an unarmored target. They won't penetrate for shit, except through a skull."

"How silent?"

"Well, let's find out." Turnbull loaded a 10 round magazine and screwed the silencer onto the end of the barrel. Inserting the mag, he cocked it and quickly brought it up to his dominant right eye and squeezed off six rapid rounds, two each at three metal targets. The dings of the hits echoed across the range, but that was it – the action made a little noise, but other than that, the only sound was a dull *thuft*.

"Okay, that's useful," said Turnbull. "Now, I want you to forget everything they taught you about shooting in Army school. Pick up your four and follow me."

They shot all day, going through various engagement scenarios with the pistols and the carbines until Turnbull was satisfied that he had broken at least the worst of Junior's shooting habits. The Glocks and the M4s were just as Clay had promised – top of the line. Except you could take the best weapon and turn it into a brick by putting it in an untrained shooter's paws. Luckily, the kid learned fast, took correction, and he generally kept his mouth shut and listened. That was a good sign too.

"You ever been on the other side?" Turnbull asked as they cleaned the weapons on the porch. Bottles of Shiner Bock sat beside them, glistening with moisture in the hot, thick air. The dog came over and demanded attention from Junior, who petted him.

"Hey, don't encourage that mutt," said Turnbull as he wiped grime out of the lower receiver. "He's useless. He's a welfare cheat and I'm Uncle Sucker."

Junior scratched the terrier's head anyway. "When I was a kid we went to California and New York a few times before they seceded. I don't remember much. Of course, I wasn't of age when the Split happened so I had to earn my citizenship."

"How about after the Split, but before they blockaded us?"

"No. Dad was really busy as part of the transition, setting up the government here after the Split. It was a weird time."

"You're telling me."

"You fought in it, right?" Junior asked. The dog, bored of the attention, turned and walked to the corner of the porch and plopped himself down.

"There actually wasn't that much real fighting before the Split, but when there was I always seemed to draw the short straw and end up right in the middle."

"Like getting sent into Indian Country? How bad was Indiana?"

"Pretty bad. No war is vicious like a civil war. Southern Indiana should have split off with us from the start. The blues wanted to make an example of it, show the rubes who was boss. We helped them resist. And they sure as hell resisted."

"They taught us some of you guys' tactics at Ft. Benning. That must have been a hard mission."

"It was," Turnbull said. "I don't much like blues. You kill them or they kill you. I learned that in Indian Country."

"And before the Split, what were you thinking when she ordered you guys into the streets? What did you think when she sent you against your own people?"

"Well, I was thinking I'm not going to die for her or her bullshit politics. If she wants to confiscate all the guns, she can suit her sickly ass up in Kevlar and go do it because I'm not going to make war on my own people just because she hates anyone who doesn't live in a coastal city. That's pretty much verbatim what I was thinking."

"I like to think I'd stand up and say 'No' if I got that kind of order too."

"Well, we don't elect people like her here. Her generals were ready to do it. A lot of the colonels too. Careerist cowards. But the rest of us? You know the Army runs on sergeants, and when the sergeants aren't with you, nothing happens. It was kind of like they had a war and nobody came. Then Texas told her to go to hell and suddenly we had something to rally around. Some bad stuff happened because some folks didn't walk back from the brink, but the politicians talked it out and we split. They were so happy to see us gone too. We were the hicks, the religious gun nuts, the flyover people, and they didn't need us or our Constitution. They were going to start all over without us, show us how much smarter they were than those stupid Founders. And you're about to see how that turned out."

4.

The SUV ride to Utah took about 18 hours. The roads were good – it was simply far away. The driver, supplied by Ryan, said almost nothing as he drove, and both Turnbull and Junior tried to sleep as much as they could. Otherwise, they simply watched the scenery pass – the oil rigs in Texas, the ranches and farms in Colorado, then the crimson desert of southern Utah.

St. George was a remarkably green and manicured town in a valley surrounded by red rock cliff faces. Straddling the old I-15, which was blocked at the DMZ down in the northwest corner of Arizona and no longer ran southwest to Las Vegas, the town was notable for the white spire of the Latter Day Saints chapel – the first in Utah – and for the sprawling Army camp to the east erected after the Split. As they drove into town, Turnbull noted the many American flags everywhere, albeit with far fewer stars than he remembered from his childhood.

The driver left them at a Best Western near the edge of town, where they checked into their rooms and slept as they waited for a call on the land line. It came at about 10 a.m. Turnbull hung up and called Junior's room.

"Pack. They pick us up in 10 minutes."

Elijah Meachum was at least 220 pounds and bearded, and he would have still looked ferocious even if he wasn't wearing a battle rig over his camos and carrying an M4. He nodded at Turnbull and opened the rear door of one of the two dusty brown SUVs idling in the parking lot. Both were marked "USDF – Brigham Young Brigade." A "Utah Self Defense Force" tape was velcroed across the breast of Meachum's battle rig, and underneath the black oak leaf of a lieutenant colonel, along with the red star of a citizen.

"Good to see you, Elijah," Turnbull said as he tossed his gear into the back. "These all your sons?" Meacham was accompanied by five tough, handsome and similarly equipped men, aged probably 16 to 25 or so. They each wore USDF enlisted rank, while some of the older ones had their red citizenship star showing they had already completed their US Army service.

"Some of them. They're all good local boys. Know how to handle themselves. Who's this, Kelly?"

"A passenger. You can call him Fred. Hear that, Fred?" Turnbull replied, and Meachum nodded, understanding it was none of his concern who Junior was, only that he got where he was supposed to go. Junior said nothing, and made a mental note to answer if he heard someone say "Fred."

They got in the backseats of the first SUV, with Elijah sitting in the front passenger seat beside the driver. The late-model Chevy moved out of the lot and into traffic, going west. "We'll head to my ranch and spend the day there, then cross tonight. How far in do you want us to take you?"

"Well Elijah, you know you boys aren't supposed to be crossing the border."

"Uh huh. So how far do you want us to take you in?"

"To the link up with your cousin, if you can."

The vehicles slowed at the DMZ checkpoint on the edge of town, manned by regular military. The troops waved the USDF vehicles through. Under the Treaty of St. Louis, as mere paramilitaries, they were authorized inside the 10 mile wide demilitarized zone to perform routine security duties.

The DMZ was not empty. Many people, like the Meachum family, still had ranches and farms inside. The local residents took the lead on security for the border near their homes. Most were Mormon hereabouts, hence the nickname of the local brigade. They went to church together, they worked together and, when necessary, they fought together.

"Any raiders lately?" asked Turnbull.

"More than in a while. My cousin about 20 miles up ambushed a half-dozen last week that had hit a couple out for a picnic. Raped the woman, killed them both."

"I take it those raiders did not get back over the border."

"No sir, they most certainly did not."

The People's Republic barely watched the borders out in the wilderness. They probably figured their internal movement controls would keep most people from getting out there, and that no one would be crazy enough to try to sneak *into* their failing country, so there was little point. As a result, the borders on the PR side often tended to devolve into a more savage version of the Wild West. If some of the violence and anarchy spilled over into the US, well, that was pure gravy.

The Meachum ranch was large and modern and readily defensible. Brush was cut back 300 meters so an enemy would have to approach over open terrain. Turnbull's trained eye noted the loopholes running across each face of the house so the family could defend the redoubt while reinforcements were being called via the antennae on the roof.

Meachum's wife met them on the porch with lemonade and no questions – she knew that when visitors came to this remote part of the border something was going on that was none of her business. The house was modern and comfortable. A huge big screen monitor, tuned to a correspondent speaking from Fox News's Dallas headquarters, hung on one wall. On the next wall was a rack of at least a dozen M4s and other weapons, plus piles of neatly stacked loaded magazines. A second monitor displayed a map of the local border sector, with icons over the locals' homes and key infil/exfil routes displayed.

After lunch, they inspected their old Army surplus packs again. Both were worn and stained. Sewn up inside the lower back pad of Turnbull's ruck were 20 one-ounce gold coins. There was some basic gear, like binoculars and wire cutters. There was a roll of OD green hundred mile an hour tape and a couple hundred feet of 550 parachute cord. And then there were the weapons. The M4s were broken down inside too, out of view. In the top pocket were worn clothes from the other side – they would walk over in USDF camo and change at the handover point. The goal was to look like another pair of homeless men wandering the byways of the People's Republic.

Turnbull handed over Junior's documents – ID card, ration cards, and various receipts and papers that made up a typical resident's pocket litter. Clay had come through for them. There was cash too, lots of it, new series bills with extra zeros on the denominations the government printed to try and catch up with the hyperinflation. Clay had come through with that too. They stuffed as much as they could into old, cheap wallets and the rest they rolled up and stuff down into their packs.

There were other things too, blue state toiletries like sour toothpaste, flimsy razors and runny shave cream. Turnbull carried a

PR pain reliever bottle, but the pills inside were high quality Motrin made in Louisiana. Hidden at the bottom of the pack, where a cop would have to really dig to find it, was a medical kit, complete with forceps, syringes and vials of morphine and antibiotics.

And then there was toilet paper – Turnbull handed over one of the rolls.

"Charmin?" asked Junior, puzzled.

"I'm telling you, that's gold when you need it. And you will. The water quality is bad and the food is worse. Take your Cipro today and every day. Don't forget. The only worse thing than being over there is being over there with the runs."

"They can't even operate a water system? "The kind of people who actually run things mostly left; the good ones that stayed got replaced. Too much privilege, so someone else had to get those jobs. And, shockingly, when the place your great-great-great-grandfather was born is your key criteria, competence is rarely your end product."

"Well, if you make everyone sick because you aren't doing your job, don't you get, you know, fired?"

Turnbull laughed. "What's the fun of accountability when it means admitting you hired incompetents? No, it's better to blame greedy wreckers and saboteurs and, of course, the US. Because all their misfortunes are our fault. Just remember that. Make it your default when talking to people. If someone complains about something, mutter about how the United States is to blame and you'll be fine."

They ate a big dinner with the large Meachum family that evening. A whole bunch more children and relatives appeared and, after grace, they set upon the spread of roast beef, mashed potatoes, gravy, bread and vegetables.

"Enjoy," Turnbull told Junior. "It's the last decent grub you're going to get for a while."

They set out at sunset with Elijah and a half-dozen boys. Everyone carried a long weapon, including Turnbull and Junior, who had reassembled their carbines from inside their rucksacks. They looked like what they were supposed to look like – a regular USDF patrol. The moon was up enough that no one needed night vision. At the edge of the farm, they dispersed in a 360 position and took a knee for ten minutes to let their eyes and ears adjust to the night.

Elijah's radio man called in that they were crossing the line of departure and the small column moved west, trudging up the hills quietly, not needing GPS to know where they were. The Meachums had been here for more than a century, and they and their neighbors were intimately familiar with every rise, bluff, wash, and boulder within 20 miles.

Turnbull and Junior walked in the middle with Elijah, following a trail they would not have seen if their guide had not taken them along it. One of the older boys, a citizen, was at point. Another son was trail. The radio man monitored comms via his earpiece. No one had to say a word; in the few instances Elijah needed to give an instruction, he did it with hand signals that his team instantly understood and obeyed.

After an hour, Elijah stopped and whispered in Turnbull's ear, "We've crossed."

Turnbull nodded, and they kept moving.

About ten minutes later, the radioman suddenly turned and nodded to the leader. Elijah made the sign to rally off the trail, and the team silently formed a 360 degree circle facing outwards, Elijah and Turnbull in the middle, each of the six other men taking security over a 60 degree piece of the pie.

"Our motion detectors picked up multiple contacts forward–looks like about a klick ahead–coming this way," Elijah whispered.

"Our people?" asked Turnbull.

"No, not yet. We don't know who they are. But they might be raiders."

If they were just refugees – unlikely out here – then the USDF would evaluate them. If they looked useful, like they might contribute to the US, they would lead them back for processing. If not, they would just turn them around. But if they were raiders, then they were coming to steal and probably worse. They couldn't be allowed past.

"Okay, where do we take them?" asked Turnbull. Elijah was visibly relieved that detouring from the insertion was not going to be an issue with his charge. If these were bad guys, the people they were coming to hurt were his people, and that simply was not going to happen.

"There's a stretch over the next rise, very tight. We can do a good L-shaped ambush if they're raiders."

"Let's do it."

Elijah knew how to pick his kill zone, and how to distribute his men. The trail ran along the side of a hill and up for about 50 meters in a straight line. Elijah put one son with an M14 at the top, his field of fire straight down the path. The rifle's .308 rounds would be able to cover the length of the kill zone. He placed himself and the rest of the team on a low, brushy ridge perpendicular to the trail segment, his son at the far end charged with locking down the kill zone and ensuring no one else entered or exited from the west.

Turnbull and Junior took their place on the line, lying on their bellies facing the kill zone. Each of their M4s held a 30 round magazine of the 5.56 mm ammo the USDF troopers carried; they did not want to waste their untraceable, sterilized rounds.

They waited.

The night was warm and very still. Turnbull's eyes, already acclimated, grew clearer in the moonlight. He heard everything, right down to Elijah's calm breathing to his immediate left. Slowly and deliberately, he put rubber plugs in both ears.

Even with the plugs, he heard their voices. They were laughing, and swearing too, like they were on a hike to some remote party spot to smoke some dope and drink some beers.

"How fucking far is it?" one complained from down the trail in the darkness.

"Few miles. Are we over the line yet?"

"Yeah, I think so," replied another near the tail of the column, peering down at a GPS screen. It was bright enough it might as well have been a searchlight. Amateurs.

The first of them came into view, a ghostly apparition in the dark. Then another, and another, until there were six walking up the trail.

Each male, each relatively young.

Each carrying an AK.

On his left, a faint *click*. Elijah would initiate with a burst. Using his thumb, Turnbull flipped the selector on his carbine from safe to automatic, and placed the third in line in the center of his sight.

Slow your breathing.
Relax.

Then Elijah fired a stream of bullets, the roar of the M4 slicing through the ear protection. Turnbull reacted as if on autopilot; he squeezed the trigger and the flash swallowed up his target. All along the line, the troopers were unloading into the kill zone. The night was ablaze with muzzle flashes.

The rate of fire dropped off, and the glare subsided as the targets came back into view. There were fewer standing, maybe two or three. Then one jolted to the side once, and again, as the heavy thud of the M14 rounds from the trailhead echoed over the desert. Turnbull pivoted to another target; he was vaguely aware of Junior firing to his right. The raider in his sight had his AK up; there was a flash from the AK's muzzle. The crack in the air above his head told Turnbull his target was panic firing high.

Sight picture.

Center mass.

Exhale.

Squeeze and hold and release.

The target stumbled back under the impact of three bullets to his sternum, dropping his rifle and falling flat back against the hill.

"Cease fire, cease fire!" It was Elijah yelling. Turnbull swung his weapon from black lump to black lump, gauging them for movement. None.

"Let's go!" Elijah was rising to his feet and Turnbull followed, as did the other troopers not engaged in securing an end. They moved forward quickly, but carefully, weapons up at their shoulders and on the potential targets. At Benning, they called this "assaulting the kill zone."

Five of the raiders were clearly dead. Another lay groaning, gut shot and a forearm hanging by a thread.

"You need him?" asked Turnbull. A prisoner might have some good info. But then there were other considerations, like the logistics of carrying him and the fact he was ambushed in his own country.

"No," said Elijah. Turnbull nodded and shot him twice in the head. The sound echoed over the desert.

"Jesus," said Junior. In the Army, they took prisoners.

"Them or us," said Turnbull. "Reload."

A search of the bodies came up with some interesting information. The dead men were all young and lean, and all

45

appeared to Turnbull, though not an expert, to have gang tattoos. They all carried nearly identical rifles. The similar serial numbers indicated the weapons all came from the same lot, meaning it was likely someone armed these guys all at once. And the only entity in the People's Republic moving that many weapons was the People's Republic itself. The conclusion that they had been sent here was reinforced by the fact each had a valid travel pass from Sacramento to this zone.

"It looks like they're shipping scumbags out here to mess with you guys, Elijah."

"We've started to see this a lot," Elijah replied. "The local PSF and military know not to mess with us. You know, until the Split we never even noticed the Utah-Nevada border. All the locals, the ranchers–they're all relatives and they're all LDS. You mess with one and you mess with all of us on both sides of the line. So anyone from here or even stationed here for a while knows not to poke our little beehive."

Turnbull smiled. Early on, the PR's officials had tried to pick on the local ranchers on their side of the divide the way they had other industrious, religious folks elsewhere. Believers, particularly ones who lived traditional lives, were a perpetual scapegoat for blue state failures all over the PR. But those officials kept ending up dead out here, often with a .30-06 bullet through the forehead. Guys like Elijah saw the Old Testament as an instruction manual, and "an eye for an eye" wasn't just a cliché in the desert. Eventually, the local poohbahs figured out that messing with the Mormons was a helluva a lot less fun than messing with other, less feisty Christians. So to live, they let live. And they left the dying to the clowns the government shipped out of the inner cities to make trouble.

Each of Elijah's men took an AK – you didn't leave perfectly good rifles lying around – and they moved out to the west. After another fifteen minutes of marching, they observed three quick light flashes from a dry wash up ahead. With a nod, Elijah sent two of his boys to make the link up. After another five minutes, one returned to guide them all up to the wash. There were three men in civilian clothes waiting, one a ringer for Elijah minus the beard: clearly Elijah's cousin, Matt Hansen, and a couple of his boys. While Elijah and Matt talked – Turnbull caught a few fragments about the ambush earlier that night – Turnbull and Junior packed up their M4s and changed into the civilian clothes they had brought. One of Elijah's sons would pack out their fatigues.

"Kelly, Matt here is going to take you as far as a truck stop on the old 15. You can catch a ride into Vegas from there."

"Thanks, Elijah. I owe you."

"Yeah, again. You boys be safe. Come visit sometime when you don't need to cross."

Turnbull shook hands with the big man. It would be a while before they might see each other again – Turnbull never came back out the way he came in.

Matt was not much of a talker, nor were his boys. Together, they waited in the wash until the last of Elijah's squad disappeared back toward the east – they took a different route home than the one they had come west on. Matt gave it a few more minutes, then stood up and motioned Turnbull and Junior to follow. By now there was a chill in the air and the moon was low. It took a great deal of effort to keep their footing, and a turned ankle out here could be a disaster. They walked for about an hour, covering only two miles, until they came to a battered Ford pick-up truck parked in a wash off a dirt road running north-south. The travelers hopped in the back with their gear and one of the Hansen boys, who was about as chatty as his father. Bundling up in his threadbare leather jacket, Turnbull tried to keep warm as they headed south.

It was another hour or so before they came to a bluff overlooking the long ribbon of freeway that was I-15. To the northeast, about 20 miles up, it ran into the DMZ and the border at Arizona. The town of Mesquite, on the Nevada side, had been a prosperous vacation spot before the Split. There were resorts and golf courses kept green by piped in water. Those were gone, the grass a memory and the hotels deserted except for squatters, addicts, and "voluntary labor" draft dodgers. Other than them and some PR security forces, it was pretty much abandoned now; Turnbull had passed through there once on his way out and ended up in running into a couple of overly inquisitive PR military at a checkpoint. Their commander probably listed them as deserters since one night they just seemed to have vanished off the face of the earth.

Junior got out of the pick-up first and Turnbull handed him their packs and hopped out on the ground beside him. One vehicle, some kind of truck, was heading west. Other than that, nothing was moving down there.

Hansen stepped around to them and pointed out to the southwest, finally speaking.

"Over that rise is a truck stop. Probably five miles. You can buy a ride into Las Vegas from there. They may or may not have fuel. Usually don't, but the drivers will stop to eat at the diner anyway, so you might not have to wait that long."

Turnbull nodded. "Thanks."

"Yeah, you're welcome. Now, take care in there. That's the only place for 20 miles either way and it attracts a bad crowd. Mind your business and you should be fine."

"Can I give you some cash?"

"Don't worry about us. You just forget us if you get caught."

"Forget who?" Hansen's leathery face broke into something like a smile, then he got back into the pickup.

Turnbull's watch told him it was almost 6:00 a.m., just after dawn, when they reached the truck stop. But it was less a truck stop than a ramshackle old gas station next to a diner that had seen better days. Its whitewash was now a dull brown, and one of the front windows had been replaced by a sheet of plywood some time ago. Through the other windows, they could spot a little movement inside. The hum of a generator explained where the diner got its power; the two hours of morning electricity did not usually start until 8:00 a.m.

The big gas sign that had lured in customers from the freeway years ago was rusting and hanging at an off angle. It hadn't worked for years and seemed on the verge of falling to the ground. Turnbull could not make out the brand – some of the plastic was a faded blue so he suspected it was a Chevron. The shape was right, as he remembered. It had been replaced by a smaller painted wooden sign reading simply "FUEL FOOD" held up by two wooden posts pounded into the ground at the foot of the old sign. Brand logos and such were consumerist and frowned upon; genericism was in fashion in the People's Republic.

The big parking lot had been designed with tractor trailer rigs in mind; the fading asphalt spread over a couple hundred square yards. At the fringes, which never saw any traffic anymore, the desert plants were breaking through and slowly reclaiming it. There were two rigs there this morning. One looked like it was always going to be there; the remaining tires were flat and it seemed like someone was living in the cab. The other truck was beat up and dirty, with the legend "Chasen's Trucking" on the side of the dinged-up trailer, except the word "Chasen's" had been allowed to fade such that it was now really just the generic "Trucking." There were four or five other cars or pick-ups in the lot, all close to the diner.

No one was at the pumps; as Turnbull approached he could see they were all padlocked. No self-service anymore. Fuel was too valuable not to be dispensed very carefully.

Only the aimless server in a yellow uniform and a couple sour-looking locals at the counter looked up when the two scraggly desert rats walked in and took a booth near the back. The others were just passing through; time wasted on considering the newcomers would mean that much more time they had to spend there. They ate like prisoners, hunched over their plates and shoveling food into their mouths and swallowing it in rapid, joyless gulps.

The tabletop seemed to be made out of some form of linoleum; the seat cushion where Turnbull sat had been slashed.

"Vato Loco 69," Junior read quietly. It was carved into the linoleum.

"Just stay cool. Remember, we're typical lowlifes. Don't draw attention."

The server stepped over, clearly irritated to have been called away from her idleness by the appearance of these two. She had a tattoo of some kind of dog on her forearm and the left side of her head was shaved.

"I guess you're our waitress," Junior said, smiling. "Can we get menus?"

Oh shit, thought Turnbull.

"Fucking 'waitress'? Are you kidding me, asshole? What kind of sexist asshole are you? I'm a facilitator, asshole! And menus? You think you're funny?"

"Yeah, don't be such an asshole, asshole," barked Turnbull to his stricken companion. He turned to the facilitator. "He's been, you know." Turnbull pantomimed smoking a joint. The facilitator scowled. "What do you want?"

"Coffees?" Turnbull said, smiling hopefully while kicking Junior under the table. Junior took the hint and was silent. The scene having calmed, the rest of the patrons went back to their own business.

The facilitator scowled down on them again. "We have responsible coffee."

"Great. And to eat?"

"Egg and toast. You got rat cards?" She asked suspiciously.

"Sure, right here." Turnbull pulled a couple of burnt orange ration cards out of his pocket; he had pre-crumpled them earlier. The waitress grunted, then turned on her heel and retreated to the kitchen, but not before shooting some more hate Junior's way.

Turnbull leaned in. "Are you fucking kidding me?" "What is her problem?"

"What is *your* problem?"

"I just tried to order breakfast."

"Okay, first, there are no waiters and waitresses here anymore. It's oppressive or some shit. And –ess is sexist. You basically told her she was your servant."

"That's ridiculous!"

"Yeah, it's ridiculous. Welcome to the PR. Everything is racist, everything is sexist. And you're terrible. Why do you think they have privilege levels on their ID cards? At home, it's about the individual. Here, unless you're elite, you're not an individual. You're just your skin tone, how you pee, who you pray to, and who you want to fuck. That's it. That's the PR." Turnbull glanced over to make sure the facilitator wasn't coming back yet, and when he saw she wasn't he continued.

"Okay, if you want to survive you have to understand one thing. These people are crazy. What they do makes no sense. None. Except when they are hunting you down – they manage to do that pretty damn well. They were rich, they had resources, they had freedom, and they threw it all away for a bunch of bullshit notions about social justice. And every time things get worse for them, instead of going back to what worked, they double down on what screwed everything up. Do you get it?"

"Yeah, I get it."

"And asking for a menu? Are you serious? This is not Dallas or Houston or Omaha. These people have no food, or at least no choice about their food. Get your head in the game. And don't complain about the coffee."

50

The facilitator appeared, plopped two chipped coffee cups full of light brown liquid on the table and left without a word. Junior suppressed his urge to ask for cream and sugar; Turnbull had been almost imperceptibly shaking his head and mouthing "No."

Cautiously, Junior picked up his cup and took a sip.

"Okay," he said quietly. "What is that?"

"That is responsible coffee. Drink up."

"It's terrible. It's dirty water."

"Of course it is. It's *responsible*."

"Why do they call it 'responsible'?"

"Because reusing the grounds until there's nothing left saves the environment by not having to import so much coffee or truck around so much coffee or something. Apparently every cup of coffee causes the Earth to warm or cool or whatever."

The facilitator appeared again, this time with two forks and two plates, which she slammed down before walking off again. The toast was small and dry as dust, and probably was well before it was toasted. The artist in back had somehow rendered both of their eggs into small piles of a rubbery, vaguely green, scrambled matter. Junior looked at his food, then looked at Turnbull, who was already digging himself a fork full.

"No, no salt, no pepper. Now eat."

Junior sighed and picked up his utensil.

"You wanted to come," Turnbull reminded him.

Junior ate slowly, not because he wasn't hungry but because he dreaded every mouthful. He stopped eating when he noticed Turnbull pausing. A customer in a blue work shirt wearing a red ball cap had gotten up and was headed to the toilet. As he passed the table, Junior saw what was written on it – "Chasen's Trucking." Turnbull rose without a word and followed the driver into the head.

They were in there for about ten minutes. Junior was getting uncomfortable on several levels, and he was relieved when the trucker came out. Turnbull came out a minute later and sat back down. The facilitator had left the bill - $278.65 and two Series A rat cards. Turnbull fished around for his cash.

"Do we tip?" Junior asked.

"Oh hell no. It's racist or something. Let's get out of here and wander over to the truck. Don't be conspicuous, or at least don't be more conspicuous than you can help. We've got our ride to Vegas."

51

5.

The trucker didn't say a thing as they got in the back of the cab. Turnbull handed him a wad of bills, and he started up the rig and off they went to the west.

They did not see much huddled in the back of the tractor's cab. Occasionally, in the distance a cloud or the top of a bluff would pass by, but during the long drive that was about it. The truck rarely got over 45 miles per hour – too many bumps and it wasted too much gas to go any faster.

They were stopped at one check point, but only for a moment. The People's Security Force officer did not even bother climbing up to the cab's window. He yelled something from the ground that the passengers could not make out, and the trucker replied "Coming back empty. Want to see my manifest?"

Apparently he didn't. The cop said something and the truck rolled forward back down the highway. Turnbull and Junior put away their weapons and went back to resting as comfortably as they could on top of their packs.

The trucker let them out at the eastern edge of Las Vegas, on a side street in a residential area that looked like a minor tornado had ripped through it. Turnbull handed the driver the other half of his pay for delivering them and off he drove without another word; the empty backhaul would now not be a total loss.

The street was lined with cars, and the cars themselves were almost uniformly dirty, many with broken windows, and most with desert detritus built up against their cracking tires. Occasionally an operable one would pass by on the street. Mostly, at least in this part of Vegas, people walked, either all the way or to bus stops. It was already 90 degrees.

The high rise casinos of the Strip in the distance poked up over the rooftops. They walked that way with their packs, and they drew little notice from passers-by. Just more transients coming through. A couple thuggish young men with tattoos and morning beers sat on a porch and briefly considered the pair, then thought better of it and turned up the hip hop on the old battery operated radio beside them. There was no point in plugging it in; the power would not come back on until five.

There was not a house in the neighborhood with a living lawn. Instead, their yards were all long ago baked dry. Most of the houses could have used a coat of paint; the ones that were still occupied – maybe a third – had bars on the windows. From somewhere, there was a string of obscenities in a woman's voice, and then she went silent.

After a few blocks, they came to what looked like a church. At least, it had the shape of a church, including a spire, but what looked like it had been the cross on top was sawed off, leaving a lonely foot-long stump. A sign hanging over the door read "People's Shelter." A couple bums lounged on the front steps in front of the open door, laughing and drinking something out of a paper bag.

"After they got rid of the tax exemptions for churches, most couldn't pay and the government took them to pay the tax bills," Turnbull explained. "Let's go in."

"Why?"

"Because no one ever asks who you are in a homeless shelter."

The manager was a sweaty, balding man in a t-shirt that read "HUMAN SERVICES." He sized up the pair as they approached, clearly displeased.

"Can we get a couple racks? Nice ones. Maybe kind of private?"

The manager scowled a little, but then saw that Turnbull had produced a $50 bill. That was an hour of work at the minimum wage. "Yeah, there's an office you two can have. Just keep it quiet. Don't wake anyone up doing your thing." He leered a little.

"We aren't –," Junior began, but Turnbull cut him off.

"We'll take it."

"I don't want to see any hard shit. Booze and pot are fine. No hard shit. Do what you want, but I don't want to see it or I'm calling the cops."

"Sure," Turnbull said, passing him the bill, which the manager stuffed into his dirty cargo shorts.

Any reminder that this had once been a house of worship had been deliberately stripped away. Even the pews were gone, replaced with a mosaic of cots and tattered lean-tos occupied by a cast of

53

wretches who either shot them suspicious glances or chose not to notice them at all. On the walls were a variety of posters, some extolling the prosperity of the People's Republic, some soliciting reports on the activities of its internal enemies.

They went through what had been the sanctuary and up a flight of steps someone had mistaken for a urinal to the second floor. On one side was the manager's office; it was secured with a padlock. On the other was their room, bare except for a couple of cots.

"You better leave the windows open. It's going to get hot and the last guy in there didn't like to go downstairs to piss at night," the manager said. "Don't piss in my room, understand?" he added. Turnbull nodded.

The manager left, and Turnbull shut and bolted the door. Almost immediately, the smell rose into their nostrils. The room was pungent with the tang of ex-beer.

"Ah, shit," Junior said, scrunching up his nose. He went to the west-facing window and forced it up and open. The hot air rushing in helped, but only a little. From the second floor, he had a better view of the Strip, glittering and shiny even at mid-day. Evidently, the casinos did not have brownouts. And in the sky beyond them, there was a stream of small planes flying into and out of Harry Reid International Airport. The elite loved their Vegas adventures.

Turnbull's voice brought Junior back. "Let's get some sleep. Tonight we need to find a way to LA."

When they woke up it was dark outside; the oddly-shaped bare bulb hanging from the ceiling was giving off a weak, pale light.

"What the hell is wrong with the light?" Junior asked.

"It's a florescent bulb. Supposed to save the world from global warning. If it was incandescent like ours back home, someone would have stolen it by now – they go for a lot here."

"I can't even see," Junior replied, then his eyes were drawn to the window. There was no such problem seeing the Strip. The casinos were awash in light, their glow illuminating the night sky. Red, blue, yellow – a glittering jewel in a field of coal.

"Brings in the foreigners. Chinese, Japanese, Euros. And they bring their cash. They call this Sin City and that's Sin Central."

Outside there was a shrill whistle, then a crash like a cymbal, then shouts. Junior went to the window. Down the street there was a crowd marching up the road, shouting and chanting, blowing whistles and smashing cymbals.

"It's a parade!" he said.

Turnbull joined him at the window and stared for a moment. "No, it's a protest."

There were about fifty of them. The marchers were generally young, with a few fossils thrown in – probably from the University of Las Vegas. The long white banner the front rank held before it said "PEOPLE DEMAND AN END TO CLASSISM AND RACISM NOW!" in bright red letters. Others held signs: "PEOPLE'S CONGRESS FOR JUSTICE," "ACTION FOR SOCIAL JUSTICE" and "UNITED TO DEFEAT ZIONISM!" The transients occupying the former church who were milling about in the front yard smoking pot barely looked up as the protestors chanted:

You can't run
You can't hide
Racism takes
Human life!

"That doesn't even rhyme," observed Junior.

The marchers passed the former church and continued off into the residential neighborhood, clanging, blowing and shouting all the way. "Why are they protesting here? Why not out on the Strip? That's where the people who run things probably are. They sure aren't here."

"They'd never get close to the Strip. Security's too tight. This used to be a nice, middle class neighborhood. What do they call it – bourgeois? That's who they're protesting. Not the people in charge."

"Didn't most of the bourgeois people leave the blues after the Split?"

"I guess these dipshits can't stop themselves from beating up on the ones who are left since they aren't allowed to mess with the people who really run things. Now let's get our stuff and get going."

They left their packs in the room; Turnbull used a padlock to secure it from the outside. They took their Glocks and Turnbull also took the silenced .22 – just in case.

It was hot on the street, and angry. Most of the people out were young and a bit feral; others were clearly between homes. The normal people, assuming there were any, must have been off the

55

streets and behind their barred windows. Many of the windows in the houses they passed flickered with the soft light of television sets.

They were headed toward the Strip, the lights on the horizon their beacon. The residential neighborhood gave way to a zone made up primarily of small businesses. About half the storefronts were boarded up. There were lots of do-it-yourself laundries; they were packed mostly with women and a few kids. As the appliances from before the Split wore out, more and more people found themselves using the pay washes when they found they were unable to replace their old washers and dryers.

"Can we get something to drink, like a Coke?" asked Junior as they passed what appeared to be a liquor store. Turnbull nodded and they both went in. The greasy clerk barely looked up from his television; it was some sort of reality show that seemed to consist of women screaming "Bitch" at each other. He found it endlessly amusing.

The store was cramped and dingy, and the shelves were intermittently stocked. There were some chips for sale, and some unappetizing snack cakes, and quite a lot of soda pop. The reason was pretty obvious – cans of Coke were $112 each, including the "health tax" on sugared food.

There was plenty of liquor, but only one or two brands of each kind. Junior didn't recognize any of them. And pot – there was a wall of marijuana. Junior took a can of Coke and a small bag of chips and went to the counter. The TV was now showing an ad; the announcer was telling the audience, "Only you can prevent racism, denialism, and homophobia. Report social criminals to the PBI. Free speech does not include hate." Some sort of male cartoon mouse was on the screen hugging another male cartoon mouse. The clerk looked up, bored.

"Series C."

"What?"

"Your rat card. Series C, for the chips. Your ration card?"

"Yeah, I got it," Junior dug into his pocket, remembering what Turnbull had taught him about how to buy food in the Blue.

"Extra ten, we can forget the rat card. I'll write it off as lifted."

"No, I got it." Junior handed over one of the burnt orange stamps and the clerk seemed disappointed. The cartoon mice finished hugging and the next ad came on, this one explaining why brownouts were necessary to save the Earth from global warming.

Outside, Junior popped the top on the Coke and tasted it. It was warm, and it was like no other Coca-Cola he had ever tasted. Whoever made it had stinted on both the sugar and the cola. He left the rest of the most expensive soda pop he had ever purchased sitting on the sidewalk.

They walked on, Turnbull's eyes darting about as he walked while his face was usually angled downward, or sunk inside his jacket.

"Why do you walk like that?"

"Habit. I don't like cameras, though I doubt the PBI bothers with any out here. I like making it difficult for them."

"Hmm," Junior grunted, then he angled his own face downward.

Finally approaching the Strip, until they came to the security fence that surrounded it. Above the wall, the casino lights flashed and danced; one sign announced the 20th anniversary of Britney Spears's residence in its theater. A group of bored guards protected the entrance gate, and a surly line of people waited for them to check their employee IDs and allow them through to cook, clean, and generally serve their elite masters.

Just outside the gate were a collection of seedy bars and manifestly déclassé small time casinos. This was where the locals came to drink and gamble, and where the out-of-towners who wanted to slum came to play beyond the lights and surveillance cameras of the Strip. And there were women – lots of them, mostly older, mostly trying too hard – the women the Strip had used up. This is where they plied their trade now.

"Wanna get blown?" offered one middle aged crone in a tight white dress that hid nothing, including what should have been hidden.

"Uh, no thanks," Junior replied. The woman hissed, and then her attention shifted.

"Those assholes," she said, looking past Junior.

Across the street, four People's Security Force were none too gently throwing a drunk against the wall. Their cruiser idled at the curb. A small crowd gathered, cursing and yelling insults and threats.

"Get the fuck back, get the fuck back!" shouted one of the blues, hand on his piece. More people started converging on the incident. He looked panicked, and said something over his shoulder Turnbull couldn't make out. His buddies threw the man to the ground and one gave him a vicious kick in the gut, but they did not try to take him with them. The quartet piled into the cruiser and drove off. A beer can flew from the crowd and splashed foam over the trunk. The cruiser didn't stop; it just went on down the road.

"Do they always back off, Kelly?"

"No, when people get uppity they usually call their buddies and set an example. They were scared." The crowd was still growing, and the obscenities were not decreasing even as the police car's lights faded away down the street.

"Let's make this fast."

After another minute of walking, Turnbull turned into a bar called Clancy's. There were no windows, only a metal door that was propped open. You could not see much inside, but there was loud K-pop spilling out. The doorman, who looked like he should either be riding a motorcycle or bench pressing one, barred their way, then motioned to Turnbull to halt and be patted down. Turnbull stopped, but held up his palm.

"Nope. I need to see Ricky. He here tonight?"

"Who are you?"

"I'm the guy who's here to see Ricky. Go get him."

"He's busy."

"Not too busy to see me. You tell him his pal from Oregon is here. You need to do it now."

The bouncer looked them over, the cogs in his brain rotating slowly. They came to the correct answer. "Stay here." He disappeared inside.

"You're from Oregon, Kelly?"

"Hell no. What am I going to say? Hey, I'm from Dallas? He's helped me before. He'll know who I am."

The bouncer returned to his position and yanked his right thumb back over his shoulder. They went inside, unsearched, and were greeted with a large "NO SMOKING" sign right inside the doorway. It was stained with years of vile tobacco and pungent pot smoke. The place was much bigger than it looked from the street; there were at least 100 people inside, mostly lowlifes with the

58

occasional cluster of rich punks making memories about that time they visited a seedy dive bar. They didn't realize they were safer there than anywhere in Vegas – there was exactly zero chance Ricky would invite the scrutiny that would come with some assemblyperson's son catching a knife between the ribs. That was for locals only; no one really cared, and if some cop pretended to care, a few bucks or a tryst in the back room with one of his girls would end that inquiry real quick.

No one was dancing even though the Asian dance music was pounding; a skeletal dancer in a silvery latex bikini and a prominent caesarian scar gyrated listlessly and unwatched in a corner.

Turnbull knew where he was going, to the office at the back. Biker bouncer's twin stood outside, glaring. He kept glaring as Turnbull and Junior ignored him and went through the door into Ricky's office.

Ricky sat behind his desk, which was piled high with papers and an old IBM PC. He wore a bad tan suit with a yellow tie. He seemed sweaty even though there was an A/C unit in the high window; the place had its own generator to power it.

There were a couple wooden chairs in front of the desk, and Ricky motioned for them to sit even as biker bouncer's brother pushed the door closed behind them. The terrible music was mercifully baffled.

"I'm seeing a lot of you lately, friend," Ricky said. He motioned to Junior. "Who's he?"

"He's okay. You know what I need, right?"

"Don't say LA."

"LA."

"I told you not to say 'LA.' I can't do it. Not for you. Not now."

"You can't get me just under 300 miles on a straight shot southwest?"

"No, I can't. Not for a while. Maybe a week."

"I don't have a week. I need to go tonight."

"Can't do it. 15 is sealed tight. You'd have four, five checkpoints, and you look like the guy they're looking for."

Junior looked over at Turnbull, who did not break his lock on Ricky's eyes.

"They looking for someone?"

59

"At least one. The alert just went out tonight. Somebody capped some guys on the border. The PBI thinks we might have infiltrators. Of course, you're from Oregon."

"Portland all the way. Do they have a picture?"

"No, but you sure looked like someone the TV was saying smoked some cops in LA last week, you know, three days after I got you transported there. Probably just a coincidence, right?"

"Totally. We need to get to LA, Ricky. Fast."

"Yeah, well, fast kinda stopped when the damn country fell apart and they started making laws about driving and making you get movement authorizations and all. So it's not like you can just jump in your car and drive from here to there anymore."

"Maybe we could catch a plane," Junior said, annoyed.

"Yeah, sure. You a movie star? Politician? Rich guy? You think I can get you the carbon credits to fly?"

"There's gotta be a way," said Turnbull.

Ricky sighed. "Maybe. You want to go the long way?"

"How long?"

"By bus, up to Reno, over the mountains, then down south to LA. I haven't heard anything about any new checkpoints going up that way. Might take a day or two."

"Can you hook us up?"

"I can get you travel passes in a couple hours. I'll say you're visiting your sick mom."

"Yeah, she hasn't been feeling her best. So, what's with the cops? I just saw four blues get run off by a crowd out front."

"People are pissed, man. They cut the food rats again, not that the stores have anything anyway. If you aren't working, you're standing in line."

"You seem to be doing okay."

"Hey, they don't ration booze or dope, at least not yet. You want to see a freaking revolution, tell people they can't drink or smoke."

"Where's all the food gone?" asked Junior.

"Hey, do I look like a farmer? Ricky said, looking at Turnbull and smiling. "The TV says it's the USA doing it, it's their fault. Not sure how that works. How is it over there?" "He wouldn't know," Turnbull answered. "He's from Portland too."

"All I know is that if you got money and know the right people you can buy what you want and you don't need a ration card. I remember before the Split there was plenty, maybe too much. And now there isn't any."

"Here are the names for the travel docs," Turnbull said, passing over their People's Republic IDs. "We're staying at that People's Shelter in the old church a klick or so from here."

"Jeff?" said Ricky, looking at Turnbull's. "You don't look like a Jeff. And Privilege Level 7. Nice. You got some sweet reparations going? They cost me enough, until I got myself a grandmother from Ecuador put on my records. That cut my reparations tax in half."

"How long?"

"Three hours," Ricky said. "I have wheels. I'll drop them off to you at the bus station. Buses go out all night. Just be there when I roll up – I don't like that class of people."

"You can pull travel docs after hours with no problem?"

Ricky seemed annoyed. "I can do anything…Jeff. Just need the cash. Fifty grand."

"Done. Half now, half on delivery."

"See you at midnight."

As they stood, the music went off and the door flew open; one of the biker bouncers poked his head in.

"Boss, they're sweeping the streets. A whole bunch of cops."

"Crap. Okay, you two out the back. Don't be late."

"You got this?" asked Turnbull.

"Yeah, I got this. Go."

They slipped through the empty kitchen – the club didn't serve food anymore – and out the back into the hot air of the alley. Over the top of the building, they could hear some sort of commotion – shouts, the occasional siren, and bullhorns demanding people disperse. This last demand cranked up the obscenities.

Whatever was happening, they wanted no part of it. They headed the other way and worked their way back to the former church. A few people lounged out front or inside on their beds, smoking and drinking. The pair attracted more attention this time, as if the observers were watching them to see what they would do next. Turnbull stepped up the pace, crossing the desanctified sanctuary and taking the stairs up to the second floor.

61

"Fuck me," he said. Junior saw why. The padlock that secured their room was still there, but the entire mechanism had been jimmied off the door. It stood slightly ajar, the room inside dark.

Turnbull put his finger to his lips and drew the silenced .22 and a small flashlight. Junior covered his back down the stairs with his Glock. Slowly, Turnbull approached the door, then kicked it open and turned on the flashlight, which he held parallel to the pistol.

Nothing.

He cleared the room and the closet in a matter of seconds and came out.

"They got our shit."

"Who?"

"Some of these damn lowlifes. Now we need to figure out who they are and where they went before they start digging through it." Turnbull put away the gun and walked across the hall to the manager's room. He pounded on it.

"Fuck off," replied the occupant.

There was a peephole; a bit of light flickered in it.

"Fucking open it or I'm coming in. You have three seconds. Two...."

There was a click and a clatter and the door opened a half-inch, secured by a chain. Turnbull threw his weight on it and it smashed the manger in the face, the chain anchor that had been ripped out of the jamb swinging wildly. The manager stumbled back, grasping at his bleeding nose, hitting the rickety table by his cot that held his bong. It fell over on the floor, the noxious bong water spreading across the wood floor.

"Damn it!" he moaned. Turnbull and Junior moved inside. Junior shut the door behind them while Turnbull grabbed the collar of the manager's scruffy "HUMAN SERVICES" t-shirt. Scrunched up, in Turnbull's fist, it read "HUM VICES."

"Who stole our shit, asshole?"

"I don't...."

"Hey dipshit, I saw the peephole. Don't tell me you didn't look when you heard them breaking in. Who stole our shit?"

"It was dark –" Turnbull smacked the top of his head with the butt of the flashlight. It made a loud "THWACK."

"Owwww!"

"Listen, stupid. Now, my shit's missing and I fucking want it back. You tell me who has it and where to find them or your fucking head is going missing. You read me?"

"Yeah," Junior added. "He's not kidding. He will cut your head off. And add it to his collection."

"Okay, fuck," said the manager, rubbing his skull. Turnbull let him loose. He looked around for a moment, trying to evaluate his options. Turnbull stepped forward and raised the flashlight again. The manager's evaluation settled on the least painful course of action over the short term.

"Okay, there's these two guys, Whitey and Blackie."

"Let me guess. One's white, the other's black."

The manager nodded. "Yeah, but Whitey's African-American and Blackie is…"

"White?" suggested Junior.

"Well, he's really more Latinx." Junior and Turnbull stared. "You know, Hispanic. He also kind of identifies as trans –"

"Okay, I got it. Where the fuck are they?"

"I'm not –"

"You better shit me a location, asshole." Up went the flashlight again.

"They go smoke out in one of the houses three doors down, this side of the street, all right? Fuck. That's all I know."

"What, they don't smoke here?" said Junior. "Everybody's smoking dope around here."

"Not pot. Meth, man. They're meth heads. No hard stuff here. I have fucking standards."

"Uh huh," Turnbull said, calm and reasonable. "We are leaving now. We won't be back." The manager wisely suppressed the urge to reply "Good."

Turnbull continued. "You need to forget we were ever here. Do you get that?"

"Yeah."

"No, I mean blot it from your memory. Can I rely on you to do that because you understand that I will absolutely come back here and beat you to death in this shitty little room with this flashlight if you even whisper one word to anyone about us? Is that absolutely clear?" The manager nodded; his mouth was too dry to talk.

63

Turnbull pulled open the door. Junior smiled and said, "Hey, great meeting you. Later." Then he followed his partner out the door and downstairs. They walked through the old sanctuary with a purpose, not looking at anyone but neither looking away. The spectators had been curious to see how it would go; the cold seriousness of the strangers was a lot less fun than the screaming and shouting tantrum they had been hoping for to break the night's monotony. Perhaps it would be best to simply mind their own business. These guys were Whitey and Blackie's problem; no one else felt like making them their own problem.

None of the houses on the street were still occupied by their actual owners. Many had left for the red when they found middle class folks were the designated bad guys in the People's Republic's mythology. Others finally got overwhelmed with the various reparations assessments for crimes that occurred a couple centuries before and lost their homes. When the church became a People's Shelter, there went the neighborhood and that was the last straw.

Turnbull and Junior went through the back yards, avoiding the street. It was easy enough – the fences between yards had long been battered through. The houses they had surrounded were wrecked too. The first one's windows were gone, along with the gutters and spigots, scavenged of their metal. You could smell from across its yard that some of the locals used it as an improvised latrine.

The second house was burned out. There was a rusting dishwasher in the backyard, sitting there in the middle of the desiccated lawn. There was an unstable-looking garden shed too – they could hear snoring coming from inside.

They entered the backyard of the third house by scrambling over a portion of the grey wood-slat fence someone had kicked over. There were lights inside the house they could see from the back, flickering and dancing – probably candles. Down the side, there was another window. Turnbull pointed to it, then to his eyes. Junior nodded and drew his Glock – Turnbull shook his head and covered an ear. No noise. Junior nodded and he put the gun back in his belt, then quietly moved to the side of the window. Carefully, he peered inside for a moment before dropping back down and facing Turnbull.

64

He held up two fingers. Turnbull drew his .22 and tightened the silencer. Then he took it off safe.

The rear patio was piled with garbage; the sliding glass door's glass had long ago been a casualty of the mindless stumbling of an oblivious meth head. Someone had nailed the edge of an old wool Army blanket to the wall above it to act as at least something like a door; Turnbull carefully moved it aside, leading with his weapon.

It was some kind of living room. There was candle light flickering out of a doorway up the hall. And voices, laughing.

"Holy shit, man, we got a gun!"

"It's all in pieces."

"We can sell it –"

Turnbull entered the first room, and then crossed it slowly, the pistol up and locked on the doorway with a two-hand grip.

At the edge of the doorway he paused, then exhaled, relaxed, and spun into the room. They were sitting on the floor; one pack was open and Whitey held the two halves of a broken down M4. They looked up, surprised. The front sight swung to Whitey's forehead first. Turnbull squeezed the trigger and the gun kicked ever so slightly, the report a mere *fwoop*, and a soft click as the action cycled. The pieces of the carbine dropped into his lap, and he fell awkwardly to his left, eyes and mouth open. Turnbull swung the gun to Blackie.

"Do. Not. Move." Blackie sat still, eyes wide, mouth slack. Junior came up from behind.

"Check the pack." Turnbull entered and moved left so his partner would not cross his line of fire.

"I think it's all here."

"You sure?" asked Turnbull.

"Yeah, it's all here."

"Good." Turnbull shot Blackie about an inch above the bridge of his nose. The addict fell back, against the wall, and slumped over onto his face.

"Repack it, and let's go."

6.

The bus sucked.

Junior had half expected a nice coach, with wi-fi, a bathroom, and reclining seats. Instead, the bench seats, covered in green vinyl, were stained and sometimes slashed. Wisps of white filler poured out where it had not been worn down to the yellow foam. It smelled like unwashed bodies and diesel.

The bus hit another pothole; the jolt seemed to wake some of the passengers for a moment, but then their heads flopped back against the windows or against the jackets they wadded up as makeshift pillows and they returned to half-sleep for however long until the next bump in the road. Sitting in an aisle seat, Junior could see out the front window, past the bored driver whose crappy music was leaking out of his earphones as a tinny hiss punctuated by too much bass. The lights – the left one was noticeably stronger – illuminated the road maybe 100 yards out. After that, it was just formless blackness. The yellow line running to the left disappeared then returned, then disappeared again because no one had bothered to repaint it. It reminded Junior of Morse Code. Dot-dash-dash-dot-dot.

They were probably five hours from Reno; it was nearly four a.m. and he could not sleep.

They had gotten to the bus station on time despite their deadly detour. Ricky met them as planned and Turnbull handed over the rest of the money. The travel docs worked; a bored security guard scanned them and they were a go. He waved them past and down to the buses. They loaded on time but left an hour late. A long hose had broken in the cooling system and the bus driver had to wrap it a dozen times with duct tape. There were already two other taped up holes in the same hose.

The passengers were in no mood to talk; this was a purely utilitarian exercise – you left Vegas at night and got to Reno in the morning with minimal hassle. Most people tried to catch some shut eye; the only noise was the loud clacking of the engine and the music leaking from the driver's earbuds.

66

Junior had thought a lot about what happened in the house, how he would not have killed the thieves if it had been up to him. He had told Turnbull that, and Turnbull replied, "No, you probably wouldn't have. That's your problem." And Turnbull had not said anything more, packing a jacket in a tight ball next to a window pillar and bracing it with his head before shutting his eyes.

When they got pulled over at a checkpoint, Junior saw Turnbull's eyes crack just a bit, his hand disappear under his shirt. The PSF officer was well-aware of the essential shittiness of holding down the graveyard shift out on People's Route 95. He half-heartedly swung his flashlight from face to face, alighting for a moment on Turnbull, who did not react, and shining it in Junior's eyes – Junior held up his hand and blinked. Nothing. Just another batch of surly, stinky people in a crappy bus in the middle of nowhere. The thug turned and walked off the bus without a word. The driver closed the door, reinserted his ear buds, and started back up the highway.

They transferred buses in Reno, taking care to stand apart during the long wait – the bus to Los Angeles was two hours late – just in case the PSF was looking for two men traveling together. The bus finally rolled out wheezing and belching black smoke.

Reno had never been a showplace city, but it was barely a city at all any more. The high rise casinos were closed. Many of the businesses were boarded up. The people on the street seemed listless and without direction – they did not seem to be going anywhere. Junior looked for one, but never saw a single smile.

They turned south on old US 99, now the Prosperity Freeway. The bumps and jolts from the ruts in the road shook their teeth and made sleeping impossible. They stared out the window.

The Central Valley's legendary farms were gone. Once, settlers had merely poured the Sierra Nevada's bountiful water on the earth and the crops had practically sprung up overnight. But the water was gone. The run-off of the snowpack that California's intricate system of dams, reservoirs and canals used to catch and store now ran out to the sea through the Delta unhindered. After the Split, free from the constraints of the federal government, the new government had decided to fix what it saw as the mistakes of the past and had decided to restore the California that existed before any of its 40 million inhabitants' grandfathers had been born. They started tearing down the dams. Not all of them, to be sure. The Hetch Hetchy dam, which fed the Crystal Springs reservoirs hundreds of miles to the west on the San Francisco Peninsula that slaked the thirst of the coastal elite, stayed intact. Those were deemed necessary. But the others, the ones that stored water for farmers and for people in less exalted places like Modesto and Stockton, came crashing down to widespread self-congratulation. Turnbull and Junior watched the result pass by outside their windows – miles and miles of burnt brown former farmland now reclaimed by the desert, and towns abandoned and empty.

Every few hundred yards they passed a derelict vehicle, sometimes a car, sometimes a bus or a tractor trailer rig. They had run out of gas and lay where they had stopped. Their owners never bothered to come back for them. Most had been pillaged, their hoods propped up and all the parts that could be carried away long gone, taken by the scavengers who wandered the empty landscape of what had been the breadbasket of the west.

The billboards, though, were all new, replaced every few weeks, but rarely before some graffitist marked them with his tags. "PRESIDENT DE BLASIO LOVES CHILDREN" one said, the picture showing the grinning, elderly President surrounded by eager, uniformed kids. The graffitist – who knows where he got the purple spray paint, since such items were so hard to find in the government stores – had added an engorged appendage to the aging President's photo that unwholesomely changed the nature of the love for children the text referenced.

Another billboard warned, "THE PEOPLE'S REPUBLIC STANDS AGAINST RACISM, SEXISM, DENIALISM, TRANSPHOBIA, AND ISLAMOPHOBIA!" The photo depicted a diverse group of angry young people, fists up, implicitly promising to unleash their wrath upon those who failed to meet their exacting standards. The artist had hit this sign too – in purple, capital letters he had written "WHERE IS OUR FOOD?"

A third billboard quoted the President: "WE WILL NOT TOLERATE WRECKERS AND HATERS FROM THE UNITED STATES ATTEMPTING TO STOP OUR REVOLUTION!" In the background was the latest flag of the People's Republic. The artist had not got to this one yet. Maybe he had been deterred by the pile of stinking garbage strewn around the base of the sign.

The billboards were all posted on wooden frames; metal would have been taken by scavengers for scrap within a matter of hours.

The bus was making good time, despite the desperate condition of the freeway, largely because the road was nearly empty other than a few buses and some trucks. The air conditioning was out, so the bus's windows were cracked as far as they could be. It was stifling. An old man sitting in the row in front of Turnbull was sweating profusely, and had finally reached his limit.

"These buses used to be comfortable!" he shouted. "They used to work! Everything used to work!"

"Shut up," said a bitter woman across the aisle who, under other circumstances, probably would have been fat.

"I won't!" the old man cried. "I remember how it used to be before! It was good before. The stores had food! We had cars!"

"You old racist fucker, shut up!" the woman screamed.

Shamed, the old man looked down. "It was better before," he mumbled.

"I'm calling the police!" the woman spit. The old man just looked down at his knees.

There was a rest stop at fifty kilometers south of Stockton. Dust and litter blew across it before being carried off into the distance. The old cyclone fence that had divided it from what had been the surrounding farmland was gone, the metal poles had been cut off a few inches above their cement footings and the metal dragged away for scrap years ago. The bathrooms were shut tight; those so inclined could walk to a stinking ditch and do their business behind a rude screen of plywood nailed to shallowly-planted beams. Feral cats wandered about, wary of humans, gorging on the rodents.

Some Mexican food entrepreneurs had set up crude stands on the grass; Junior caught the smell of cooking meat and realized he was hungry. Turnbull was more concerned with the two black uniformed People's Security Force thugs lounging beside their SUV at the south end of the lot, their AKs hanging off their shoulders. No doubt they were collecting a cut of these unauthorized capitalists' business.

"You want some food?" Junior asked.

Turnbull satisfied himself that the thugs were not giving even a second thought to the bus and its disgorged passengers then replied.

"Yeah, but not here."

"It smells good. Anything wrong with me getting a taco?"

"What kind of meat is it?'

"What kind?"

"Yeah, what kind? You see a lot of cows around here? I do see lots of kitty cats."

"I'm not that hungry." Junior took off toward the improvised latrine.

By the time Junior returned, the angry lady from the bus had found her way to the far end of the lot, and was animatedly describing the old man's heresy to the thugs. They seemed bored, yet they followed her back to the bus. It was hot, but apparently not too hot for some fun. They confronted the old man, who sheepishly tried to explain that he was just so tired that he didn't know what he was saying.

"You some kind of racist?"

"No, I'm just tired!" he protested.

Junior seemed on the verge of opening his mouth, but Turnbull subtly grabbed his arm.

One thug swung the butt of his AK into the old man's gut. He crumpled to the ground, then rolled around moaning. The other passengers watched, indifferent. Then the thugs turned away to return to the SUV; they made their point and there was no sense hauling him in. The bitter woman smiled as the old man struggled to his feet and stumbled back to the bus.

They rode south for several long hours, the bus shaking and clattering nonstop as the driver seemed incapable of missing even a single bump or pothole. The old man clutched his abdomen and moaned every once in a while. The passengers tried to sleep or just stared out the dirty windows.

A few miles south of Tulare, which was nearly deserted, there was a sign for the Corcoran State Prison and Social Rehabilitation Center. Most of the traditional criminal convicts had long since been released as victims of the racist prison-industrial complex. The prison, and the camp built beside it, was now devoted to social criminals in need of reeducation. The bus grew quiet as it passed by the sprawling penal colony.

They covered still more miles. Bakersfield was never a particularly pretty place even before the country split apart, but now it seemed to be barely a city at all. There was almost no activity to be seen from the freeway – the factories and warehouses and grain silos were silent. Parking lots were empty except for abandoned cars and the occasional bum pushing a shopping cart. The fast food places that had once lured travelers were simply abandoned. Before, when a particular restaurant had to close, the company would swoop in and remove all the signs, logos and trade dress. It would not do to have a closed down McDonald's just sitting there. But here in Bakersfield, no one had bothered. McDonald's, Carl's, Jr., Wendy's – at some point the companies had just walked away.

When the country split, there had been promises of free trade, that nothing would be different as far as commerce, that it was simply a matter of social laws and lifestyle and that the two nations would be like brothers, just living in separate houses. The blue coasts would live their way, and the red interior its way, but nothing would get in the way of business. That lasted about a year, and within five years the blues had closed themselves off from the red states completely. Many companies just walked away from their investments in the blue states – they left everything. And now the corpses of those thriving businesses simply decayed, anything salvageable long-ago pillaged by the scavengers.

The bus wheezed and chugged as it began the long climb up old Interstate 5 – now the Barack Obama Freeway – to the Grapevine, the pass through the mountains north of the Los Angeles basin. The road rose on a miles-long ramp from the floor of the Central Valley through a crack in the hills heading south. At the base lay abandoned what had been a massive truck stop and rest area – the faded signs promised Starbuck's and Chevron and a host of other forgotten brands. It was a transient camp now, made possible by the government water tanker parked in the middle of the parking lot. Junior estimated the line of people waiting in the sun to fill their jugs and bowls was 200 meters long.

Another billboard came into view: "DEATH TO THOSE WHO SUBVERT THE PEOPLE'S RULE!" It depicted a bunch of smiling kids gathered around a gallows. The former blue states had

71

largely gotten rid of the death penalty for actual crimes well-before the Split. Once independent, their new leaders wasted no time in resurrecting it for crimes that involved challenging their rule.

As the freeway continued south, it worsened. The bus slowed considerably, which at least buffered the jolts and shaking from the deteriorating road bed. Without air conditioning, the atmosphere inside the coach was stifling. Turnbull felt the sweaty skin of his arms stick to the vinyl seat back, peeling off slowly whenever he moved.

The bus entered into the main cut of the pass, the grade steep enough to slow the bus to a crawl. There was a shudder, unlike the usual ones from the potholes, and then a stream of obscenities from the driver. The engine now sounded like it was grinding metal upon metal, and from under the front window rose a cloud of steam condensed on the glass. The driver, with effort, turned the slowing bus to the right and pulled off to the side against a sheer cliff face of grey shale.

"What's wrong?" yelled a bald man sitting behind Turnbull and Junior.

"Shut the fuck up!" the driver shouted, opening the door and stepping out. A tractor trailer rig passed by and made its way slowly upwards.

"This could suck less," said Turnbull.

"What do we do?"

"What they always do here. Sit here, wait to see what happens, and hope it doesn't get any worse."

The driver managed to get the cowling up, and the steam dissipated. But he just stared at the engine as if doing so would somehow change the circumstances. It was clear he had no idea how the bus he operated worked. So he just stood there.

"What's going on? What are you doing?" the same man shouted. This time the driver ignored him.

"This is bullshit!" swore another passenger.

The hateful woman who had narced on the old man turned around in full scold mode. "You shut up! You should be grateful we even have a bus! You think they have buses like this in the racist states?"

Junior raised an eyebrow. They certainly had no such public transportation in the red.

"Fuck you, bitch," the bald man responded. "There aren't any cops here and I will fuck you up!"

"Racist –"

"Bitch, you better shut the fuck up!"

Outside, another bus pulled to the shoulder in response to the driver's desperate waving of arms.

"Time to go," said Turnbull, standing up and making his way forward past the angry woman. She stared at him, as if she were demanding his intervention, but Turnbull ignored her.

The driver ran to the door of the rescue bus. It opened and he disappeared inside just as Turnbull and Junior exited their own.

"Get our gear," Turnbull said as the other bus's door slammed shut and its engine roared.

"You're shitting me," he said as the other bus pulled back onto the freeway and began to climb the Grapevine again.

Junior re-appeared with their packs from the storage bin underneath. "No way."

"Way." He took his pack and stepped around to the roadway. From inside the bus, they could hear the passengers screaming and shouting at each other. There was a crash of glass – someone had kicked out a window.

Down the road was a pick-up truck slowly grinding its way up the grade. Turnbull dropped his pack and stepped out into the freeway waving his arms. In his hands, he held a stack of bills.

More people were coming off the bus now; inside, it sounded like they were tearing out the seats.

The blue Ford pick-up, probably from the early 2000s, slowed and stopped. The driver was in his fifties, with a dirty denim shirt and greasy hair.

"You want a ride, huh?"

"LA. We got a hundred."

"Four hundred. Each."

Turnbull did not hesitate. "Okay. Four hundred each."

"Well, if you'll pay four hundred, you'll pay five hundred," he said.

Turnbull threw his pack in the back and nodded for Junior to join him. Then he opened the door to the cab and leaned in to the leering driver.

"How about four hundred each and I don't rip your throat out and take your piece of shit truck?" he said pleasantly. The driver took the eight hundred total, and Turnbull hopped into the back. They shared the space with an old transmission and about twenty feet of rusty chain.

"Keep down," the driver said through the cracked rear window. "It they see you riding back there I'll get pulled over."

There was a *whoosh* from the bus, and inside a flickering orange light. Someone had set it on fire. Now the passengers were pelting it with shale rocks from the cliff face.

The pick-up began to inch forward slowly, but then the frightened face of the angry woman appeared over the side, her hands gripping the edge.

"Let me in!" she howled, trotting along with the accelerating truck. "I'm Privilege Level 6!"

As if that mattered out there in the middle of nowhere – your privilege level was useful for leveraging jobs, schools and getting a residence inside a secured sector, but not so much when the government was not watching.

Privilege levels were sold as similar to reparations. They were to be a way to remediate historical oppression and discrimination by creating a new hierarchy of the favored to replace an alleged hierarchy of oppression that had largely faded away decades before. The high would be brought low, and the low raised high, or something like that. But that had only inspired more jockeying for oppression pole position. Did someone whose great-great-great-great-great grandfather might have been a slave outweigh the oppression of someone whose great-great-great-great-great grandfather might have been shot by Custer? What if your cousin had been a transsexual in the 1970s – that had to be worth something, right? Soon, everyone named O'Connor or O'Malley was claiming their ancestors had been brought here as indentured servants, and that this ancient injustice had to be worth a point or two on their privilege levels.

Not surprising, as always, those with the greatest privilege prior to the introduction of privilege levels miraculously dominated the highest privilege levels afterwards. Rich people, movie stars, government workers in the Westside Sector – they were the eights, nines and even tens. In Compton and Inglewood, you *might* find a four, but he was probably only there to score drugs.

Turnbull sat up, smiled gently, and offered his hand to Ms. Privilege Level 6 as she trotted behind the pick-up. She took his hand gratefully.

He twisted, hard, and she shrieked in pain as he forced her off her feet and left her sprawling on the asphalt. As she receded in the distance, Turnbull could see the old man coming up behind her, something dark and heavy in his hands, something he raised above his head and threw down on her as she lay there. Payback was as much of a bitch as she was.

Turnbull reclined on the pick-up's dirty floor. Over the edge, a thin reed of smoke was rising from where the bus sat burning on the shoulder.

"They're torching their own bus. It's going to get cold tonight and they burned their only shelter," Junior said, incredulous. "What the hell is wrong with these people?"

"These people aren't much for thinking things through," Turnbull said. "If they were, they wouldn't have split off from the part of the country that fed and powered them. Plus, I think they just don't care anymore."

The drive that would have taken 90 minutes a decade before took four hours. Their driver knew the area well enough to pull off and take backroads past the northern Los Angeles checkpoint. This meant a detour through some mostly empty mountain towns; the forest seemed to be reconquering much of it.

"Where are the people?" Junior asked.

"A lot of the kind of people who lived out here crossed over after the Split. It was pretty clear they weren't beloved by the blue state types. Too independent. Too traditional. And since there's no work out here anymore – no tourists, no water to farm – most of the ones that stayed had no choice but to move into the cities where they could get enough to eat. The rest, I guess, went off the grid. We won't see them. That's how they live, below the radar and out of sight."

"So, basically, the countryside is depopulated."

"Yeah, the People's Republic figured out that it is a lot easier to control the people if they are packed into cities – especially when you control the food."

"So, ration cards and government stores?"

"Right. No obedience, no dinner. Country people didn't need the government before. They could grow their own food, or buy it from each other. And the People's Republic can't tolerate that."

"I thought they liked diversity."

"They do – they like a diverse variety of people who all agree with them and obey their commands."

The old I-5 corridor through Valencia and Castaic was largely empty. Most of the restaurants, and nearly all of the gas stations, were closed. Magic Mountain amusement park was still there, but it did not seem to be operating. It was called "People's Park" now – the government had liberated it from the Six Flags Corporation after the Split as an "essential industry."

Coming south into the San Fernando Valley, there were considerably more private cars – though derelict vehicles still lined the freeway in even greater numbers. There were more billboards too – several offered the maniacally grinning and massively retouched visage of the elderly Hillary Clinton, who had presided over the Split, overlaid by the quote "WE WILL NOT TOLERATE THE SUPPRESSION OF WOMEN BY ANTI-PROGRESSIVE FORCES!"

The Valley was smoggy and hot and teeming with people. Yet it looked broken and worn, as if no one had bothered to maintain or repair anything in the last decade. Much of it was boarded up – there were massive auto dealerships that had closed and their lots were now filled with tents and lean-tos. "Abandoned" property could be taken by "the People" for housing, Turnbull explained. And by "the People," they meant squatters. And by "Abandoned," they meant "any property the squatters felt like taking – assuming the owner was not someone the PSF would actually care about pleasing. So in the Valley, full of regular citizens, there was plenty of squatting. In the Hollywood Hills, in Brentwood and Pacific Palisades, where the elite lived behind a wall of security and had people with guns to do their bidding, there was zero.

Their driver leaned back and cocked his head around, shouting through the cracked rear window.

"Where you want me to drop you? South Central, Koreatown, Shariatown? Hollywood?"

"Hollywood," replied Turnbull, getting close to be heard. "You know that restaurant on Sunset and Gower – they called it the 'Rock 'N' Roll restaurant'?"

"The old Denny's?" the driver asked, shouting over the wind. "Not a Denny's anymore."

"Take us there." Turnbull sat against the cab, watching the I-5 recede behind him. The pick-up slid right into the exit to the old 170, which a sign announced was now the "LGBTQ!MCX*" Freeway. It did not provide a legend to help them decipher the acronym.

Most of the vehicles were buses, old and dirty, spewing black exhaust. There were more private cars on the road than they had seen so far, but not enough for the kind of traffic jams that used to gridlock the Southland's roads. Some of the cars were quite new – many of them shot by in the "Privilege Lane" where the old carpool lane had been. It was hard to tell what constituted privilege, other than having a late model BMW or Mercedes.

Occasionally, a small convoy of three or four black SUVs would speed by, the other vehicles clearing a path.

"Who are they?" Junior asked.

"Officials. Movie stars. People with juice," Turnbull replied. "Shit."

"What?"

"Look," Turnbull said, pointing back. There were many billboards with many messages, but Junior immediately saw the one Turnbull meant. There was a young woman, blonde, smiling. It read "VICTORY OVER THE RACIST HATE STATES! REPORT SPIES, DENIERS AND HATE CRIMINALS TO THE PBI! DIAL 911!"

"That's Amanda," Junior said.

"Looks like she's found herself a gig over here."

"They're making her do that. She'd never do it by choice."

"Uh huh. When we find her, you just better be very, very persuasive when you tell her she's going home."

"She'll come. I know her."

"Did you know she was defecting?"

"No, I was doing my service."

"Yeah, well people change and not always for the better. Just be ready, because you have no idea who she is anymore. Or what they have done to her."

7.

It took another 30 minutes to cover the ten miles. A car had caught fire in the number one lane after the old 101 interchange – the 101 was now the Barbara Boxer Freeway – and blocked traffic after its owner abandoned it. There seemed to be a lot of fires today; Junior counted a half-dozen tendrils of black soot rising over the Valley as they drove through.

They got off at Sunset and headed west. The streets were full of people milling about, many evidently transient. Many of the storefronts were shuttered; about half the stores in the mini-malls that lined Sunset along that stretch were closed. Junior noticed immediately the lack of advertising and logos. There just were not very many. The signs were mostly generic – "Convenience Store," "Shoe Store" and the like. He remembered learning in school that in the blue, they saw having many different brands as economically "inefficient." And, of course, all the food stores were nationalized. Each one they passed had a long queue of sullen people waiting to be allowed inside, except for one where the line was dispersing; a banner reading "NO FOOD TODAY" hung across the door, and bored workers stood around inside.

The pick-up pulled into the parking lot of what had been the Denny's. It was now called simply "Café," but you could see underneath the surface and the peeling white and red paint job its origins as the popular chain restaurant. They still existed back home – a few weeks ago he had gotten himself a grand slam breakfast. This one had been notable for the rock stars who would convene there in the wee small hours of the morning after their gigs and their post-gig partying.

"Right on time," Turnbull said without elaborating. He leapt out and pulled on his pack.

Along the perimeter of the parking lot, which was largely empty, there were crude tents and shelters. The denizens looked over the pick-up truck sullenly; the driver did not wait for good-byes before accelerating out and away. Wearing their packs, the pair walked around the lot and over to the front entrance. A dead palm tree dominated the dry landscaping of the street side facing; it smelled like it was a popular field expedient latrine.

There was no hostess. You just found a seat yourself and sat down. A crudely drawn sign made of cardboard warned "If you don't have your rat card, don't bother." The place was hardly full, even at the dinner hour. A couple of waitresses, one with a Mohawk and the other a blonde who looked like she'd seen far too much use stopped gossiping long enough to check them out.

"You got cards?" snapped the one with worse hair.

"Yeah," said Turnbull, walking past toward a booth in the back. They set down their packs and Junior picked up the dirty plates and glasses left behind by the last customers, depositing them on a nearby table. They sat. The noise from the TV was distracting; it was reporting on the prevalence of sexism at the Port of Los Angeles and concluded by reading a statement from the mayor promising to crush all forms of hate.

"Remember," Turnbull said. "No menus. They'll tell you what they have."

"Facilitators," said Junior.

The facilitators took their time, apparently not imagining that anyone would actually want to get the slop they served any sooner than absolutely necessary. Turnbull took the opportunity to examine the clientele. Some Hollywood weirdoes, some regular working folks, plus some musicians, judging by their instrument cases, which they tied to the table post in case someone decided to try and snag them. And an older man, maybe 50, in a brown suit coat that had been carefully patched in several places. He held a paperback book, open about half-way, and was nibbling a piece of bread as he read.

The TV went to a logo reading "SPECIAL REPORT" and a young Hispanic announcer began reading a prepared text. "Because of the success of our agricultural plans while still fighting the threat of climate change, the People's Assembly has announced that the minimum wage has been increased to $55 per hour effective today. Workers' representatives and union leaders have been unanimous in their praise for this major step toward fairness and equality. By contrast, in the Racist States the rich continue to prosper while the poor and the working class fall further behind."

The old man betrayed no expression. He looked back down to his book. No one seemed to pay much attention at all.

"Guess a raise doesn't mean much if there's nothing to buy," Turnbull said.

"They call us the Racist States?"

"Among other things. They never call us the USA. They couldn't wait to change their own name, but they are steamed we kept it. I think they picked People's Republic because they knew it would piss off all the normal people who were still here, and us too. It was kind of a way for them to show us who was boss by rubbing our noses in it."

"Sure looks like it worked out great," Junior said. "I'm hitting the head."

"Take some toilet paper. Trust me." Junior pulled a roll out of his pack and went to the restroom. No one seemed to find that odd.

The used up server eventually wandered over.

"You got coffee?"

"Responsible or real?"

"Irresponsible. Gimme two. Any food?"

"Meat. And potatoes."

"What kind of meat?"

"*Meat* meat. You want it or not?"

"Yeah. Two meats, well done."

"You got rat cards for meat?"

Turnbull produced a pair of Series As, which she took and pocketed.

"That's well done," he reminded her.

She turned and left. There was a commotion out in the street. A group of maybe a half-dozen men was at an intersection on Sunset trying to pull the driver out of a food delivery van. He hit the gas, sending several flying off and bouncing across the asphalt as he shot through on the red light. One man shrieked, holding his foot, which had likely been run over. He limped over to the sidewalk by himself, his associates paying no attention to his cries.

"It's getting ugly." The old man was sitting in Junior's seat, the book on the table underneath his folded hands.

"It's been ugly for a while."

"Not like this, though. Can you feel it? People are hungry, hopeless."

"You can get arrested talking like that, Mister."

81

"Not if you talk to friends."

"Friends are in short supply these days," replied Turnbull.

"I'm a friend of Abraham."

"Which one?"

"More than one, as it happens. But Abe Lincoln is certainly one of them."

"Well, you look like your picture and you said the magic words. What now?"

"I suppose you can eat your dinner."

"We're having meat," said Turnbull. "You want to join us?"

"No, the bread here was pushing it. The meat would be well over the line. But you can enjoy it and I'll wait."

"Somehow I don't see us enjoying it. We'll roll."

Junior returned, puzzled, the toilet paper roll in his left hand.

"Ah, he's learning," the older man said.

"Who's this?" Junior asked.

"A good friend. His name is…what's your name?"

"You can call me David."

"Get your stuff, Junior. We're leaving now."

"What, no food?"

"For all practical purposes, food wasn't going to happen anyway. Let's go."

The worn out hostess watched them step out, holding a cup in each hand. "You don't want your coffee?"

"Crisis of conscience," Turnbull replied. "I can't drink coffee while the polar bears are melting."

They headed west on Sunset, trying not to make eye contact with any of the locals, faces down by habit. There were occasional cameras; the men all knew not to face them.

They moved at a quick pace, but not so fast that it would draw attention. It was still light out, so they had some time left to get off the streets.

"How far? " Turnbull asked. David shrugged.

"Not too far." They turned north on a side street lined with old apartment buildings.

"Interesting juxtaposition," Turnbull observed, looking at a poster stuck on a teetering wooden fence. It featured the Star of David on fire and the words "Smash Zionism!" And across it someone had spray painted "G-D Rules."

82

"Somebody has a little fight left in them," Junior said.

"Yes, a little," David said. A shape rushed out of the bushes and tackled him onto the dry patch of dirt between the sidewalk and street. Three, maybe four shapes followed, preparing to face Turnbull and Junior, but they were too late. Turnbull's pack was already falling to the ground thanks to the quick release on the shoulder strap even as he was accelerating into a run.

They were in their late teens, maybe early twenties, wearing denim or leather jackets, thin and tatted up on their necks and arms. The sight of Turnbull charging them simply did not compute – people were supposed to run away or beg for mercy – and the second of indecision as they tried to figure out how to respond cost them dearly.

Turnbull punched the closet one in the throat, the force multiplied by his 200 pounds moving at sprint. The thug went down, gripping his throat, gasping.

Turnbull rushed past him toward the next one, connecting the thin punk's chest with his right shoulder and taking him down to the sidewalk flat on his back. Turnbull was past the other two, who simply stood gaping. Turnbull stopped, turned on his heel, and charged back; they broke and ran.

The punk who tackled David did not notice any of this; he was too fixated on his victim. "Hey fucker, where's you rat-"

Junior grabbed a hunk of greasy hair and yanked backwards, pulling the punk off to the rear and laying him out flat on his back. The punk looked up in terror as Junior's boot came down heel first on his gonads. He screamed like a little girl, a harbinger of things to come considering the damage Junior did to his testosterone farm.

In the meantime, Turnbull dispensed with the one he tackled with a kick to the face that shattered his jaw, spewing blood and teeth across the concrete. Walking back to his companions, he paused to viciously bring his heel down on the groin of the one whose throat he had punched. The punk uttered a silent scream of agony. Satisfied the enemy was gone or incapacitated, he extended his hand and pulled David to his feet.

"You okay?"

"I'll be okay. Them, maybe not so much."

"They're lucky they're not dead," Junior said. "Believe me. This guy is a one man mortality rate."

"We need to go," said Turnbull, and they left the three rolling, groaning thugs behind.

8.

There was a metal sign at the corner that read "Neighborhood Watch In Effect." Someone had used a black marker to announce, in oddly elaborate gothic script, that "VAG '14" had marked his territory. Underneath, in the same color marker but less gothic, was a crudely rendered male member spraying the word "Watch" with some unspecified but readily identifiable fluid.

The neighborhood watch concept had changed significantly since the Split. Before, it involved neighbors reporting to the police on suspicious criminal behavior by outsiders. Now, designated residents reported to the PBI on the activities of other neighbors. Racism, sexism and deviant behaviors like religious activity were of particular interest.

They crossed the street to a weathered, multi-story apartment complex. The outside revealed nothing of the interior; all the facing windows had blinds drawn. Flickering lights indicated candles. This particular city grid was in brownout.

A high, wrought iron fence with sharp spikes lining the top barred the way into a corridor that led inside. They waited for David to find his key, which he did after a few moments. From the second floor, Turnbull could see the corner of a blind drop back into place. They were being watched.

The gate creaked open – it could have used a spritz of WD-40, if that had been available to regular people anymore – and they hustled inside and down the corridor. The gate clanked and locked behind them. Turnbull seemed relaxed, which relaxed Junior a little, though he kept his hand on the Glock under his shirt.

The corridor led through the width of the building to a central courtyard which was entirely enclosed on all four sides. There were trees and grass, though most of the interior was taken up with a garden, where kids played, laughing and running, out of sight and safe. There were adults too, eyeing the newcomers. The men wore kippahs.

"Welcome to our home," David said, pulling a skullcap from his pocket and fitting it on his head.

"We're Jewish," he said helpfully.

"I didn't think any of you were left," Turnbull replied. A boy of about 14 ran up and hugged David, then looked at the strangers.

"My son, Abraham."

"I think we're already friends," Turnbull said, extending his hand. The boy took it cautiously, and shook firmly. Then he did the same with Junior.

"We should go inside," David said. "Come."

The apartment was up three flights of stairs – Junior had been in the blue long enough not to bother asking about the elevator. It was modest in size, but comfortable and warm – the first such place they had experienced since Utah.

And there was food, rice with some chicken and boiled water – no one drank straight from the tap. The visitors ate it gratefully; both understood how, as guests, they were certainly eating better than their hosts.

"Just curious, but how do you keep kosher?" Turnbull asked. The kosher butchers and grocers had been targets early on of the anti-Zionist protests. At least, the government called them protests; "pogroms" was more accurate.

"We do what we can," David replied. "This is nothing new. In fact, what it was before in America, *that* was something new for us. We could live openly, our own way, not bothered, not frightened. This is how our ancestors lived, so we can't complain."

"Why didn't you leave?"

"This was our home. We thought it would pass. Some of us even welcomed the Split. They thought it would make for a fairer, more just society. After all, you red people were supposed to be anti-Semites, and anti-black, and anti-everything else."

"A lot of Jews came over early on. They seem to be happy in the USA."

"We waited too long and got stuck. That's not unprecedented. We try and keep to ourselves, live our lives as He wishes. When they ended the religious tax exemptions, we lost our temple to the state. Most of the Christian churches were foreclosed too. Only a few are left, the ones they wouldn't dare not give exemptions too. Black churches, some Catholic churches in the Latinx areas. But the ones in the suburbs? All closed down. There's still one temple left in Beverly Hills, so we couldn't get there even if we wanted to. The Jews who declared themselves non-believers still go and play at Judaism on the High Holidays. No prayers, no Torah, no Lord. Less a temple than a social club. The rabbi would probably eat bacon cheeseburgers if there were bacon cheeseburgers anymore."

They continued eating. Abraham came in and sat by his father. Turnbull looked quizzically at his host.

"He's a man now, at least since last week," David said. "We had his bar mitzvah on Sunday. We were very quiet. Anyway, he should know what we do since someday he will be helping us do it."

"And what do you do?" asked Junior.

"Whatever we need to do to survive: buy, sell, trade. Perform tasks for our friends on the other side."

"Do you know what we need?" asked Turnbull.

"Help. What kind they did not see fit to let me know. And then there's something I have to give you to take back."

"The hard drive."

"The hard drive. It was very hard to get to."

"And the PBI is looking for it."

"Certainly. Which is why it is not here. It's too dangerous to have here."

"We can get it on the way out. But we need to find our target first."

"And who is he?"

"She. His sister, in fact. You might have seen her. She's a defector. Blonde. On billboards. Maybe on TV."

David shrugged. "We're not much on television here. Too much talking about how things are wonderful and we and everyone else they hate are terrible. What's her name?"

"Amanda Ryan."

"Do you have any information on where she might be?"

"We think Los Angeles. Where, we don't know."

"Can I see a picture?" David asked. Junior handed him one he kept in his pocket. David examined it and handed it back.

"She's pretty. Pretty girls, they...powerful men like pretty girls, if you see what I'm saying."

Junior glared. "She's not a whore."

"I didn't mean that. It's just that we all use whatever we have to survive. If she is on billboards and television, then perhaps she is

87

running with the crowd in the Secured Zone. The rich people. The powerful ones. It can be hard to get in there."

"We need to find out where she is first," said Turnbull.

"We have a man, Jacob, who works in the PBI center downtown. He can find out."

"Isn't he a little conspicuous?"

"He doesn't wear his kippah and eats whatever they put in front of him. He passes. It's a sacrifice, but we all do what we have to."

"And we'll need transport."

"Sure, a car. Gasoline. You have money for the car? It's not free."

"We have money. Now, what do we need to pay you?"

"Pay us?" David was confused.

"Yes, you're taking a risk. How much money do you need?"

"No, you don't understand. We have an arrangement. You're a small part of it. But after we help out here for a while, your people over there will get us all out." He patted Abraham on the head. The kid had not been able to live a normal life since he was a toddler.

"All of you? How many are you?" asked Turnbull.

"Twenty-seven. And a half – we have a pregnant lady. That's our deal. We help your people here, they get us all over there."

"That's a hell of a price." Turnbull's mind began running through the logistics of getting 27 ½ people over the border; it was daunting. And, to his relief, it was not his problem.

"We do a hell of a job helping people like you. Now, you need to rest."

Turnbull nodded, and they followed young Abraham to an empty apartment where they quickly collapsed into sleep.

9.

They slept until almost noon the next day, then spent several hours cleaning their weapons and double checking their gear. Their hosts left them largely alone. Life went on inside the complex; the children were quiet most of the day inside the empty room the community used as a classroom. The curriculum was English reading and writing, math, and history, as well as Hebrew and Torah. If they had gone to one of the grim schools within a few blocks away, all half empty thanks to the plummeting birthrate (but fully staffed because no unionized government worker could ever be let go), the curriculum would have been much different. They would take "Language and Writing" instead of "English" – English was no longer privileged over other, equally valid languages. Mathematics had been scrubbed to remove the sexist and culturally-biased concepts of the past. It consisted of, essentially, group work that amounted to exercises that involved counting. The science classes spent much of their time on global warming, though the global temperature averages had not increased since the late 1990s. And People's History focused on the wicked legacy of oppression of the red states, and the new dawn of freedom in the People's Republic since visionary President Hillary Clinton had cast away the backward red states that were holding back the forces of social justice.

The children also learned how the United States had broken the Treaty of St. Louis, forcing the People's Republic to cut off all relations with the poor, backward red states. And it promised that someday the People's Republic would liberate the oppressed masses trapped between the two blue masses on the West Coast and the Northeast that made up the People's Republic. How it would do that with only the shell of a traditional military was never explained; while it spent generously on internal security to stamp out dissenters, the PRNA Army had withered into almost nothing. The People's Republic chose to spend its money on other things, knowing its boasts about liberating the red were lies and secure in the knowledge that the United States would never bother trying to recover its lost territory.

At six o'clock, Abraham retrieved them and brought them to David's apartment. Another man was there, nervous and quiet.

"This is Jacob," David said. "He works for the PBI as a civilian. He has the information you need."

Jacob offered a weak handshake.

"I assume you got the hard drive out?" Turnbull said. "How did you do that?"

"It was difficult," Jacob replied, uneasy.

"He found your Amanda Ryan for you," David said. "You may find this more complicated than you imagined."

"Why is that?" Junior asked.

"She is a minor celebrity, like you thought," David replied. "She is also a partner with the senior People's Bureau of Investigation official in Los Angeles. A man named Martin Rios-Parkinson. A very bad man."

"She's a PBI agent?" Turnbull asked, mentally preparing to pull the plug on the whole thing.

"No, not that kind of partner. A domestic partner. A girlfriend."

"That can't be," Junior said.

"It is," Jacob said. "Her name was blocked on the system. I had to use a special authorization to access it. She lives with him."

There was a rumble outside the complex, yelling and then honking. Something made a crashing sound. The men in the apartment kept perfectly still for a moment, listening. A siren sounded. It was some distance away.

"These things are happening more often," David said.

"Yes, things are getting worse," said Jacob. "More violence. Looting. The news won't say it but the police in San Francisco had to open fire on looters yesterday. They killed many of them. We expect it to get worse when they announce a food rations cut tomorrow."

"So how do we get to her?" asked Turnbull.

"She takes graduate classes at UCLA during the day at the Department of Social Justice. I printed her class schedule," Jacob said, handing them a sheet of paper.

"What about her home address?"

"I couldn't get that. I'm sure the Director's address was flagged on our system, and that if I had enquired it would have alerted the Internal Security Division." Jacob said sheepishly, looking down.

"I need to go, David." David nodded, and Jacob rose, then made his way to the door.

"Be careful," David said, then Jacob left them.

"He seems edgy," Turnbull said.

David shrugged. "The pressure he's under every day is very hard on him. But he's helped us tremendously. He got you your hard drive. There is a great deal of suspicion within the PBI. When they discovered it was gone, he was suspected and interrogated, along with dozens of others."

"Seems like he got through it. When do I get the hard drive?"

"On your way out of town. It's too dangerous for you to carry it around more than necessary. You stop by here after you get Amanda and we will go get it and give it to you. It's nearby, but only Abraham knows exactly where. Not even I know. Not even Jacob knows. It's more secure that way."

"Come back here? I don't like going out the way I came in. It's dangerous."

"As I said, carrying it with you around is dangerous. You get caught, it's gone. Come back here and we'll give it to you after you get the girl. Assuming she wants to be gotten."

"She does," said Junior.

"Maybe," said Turnbull.

"She's not his girlfriend or his whore. He's making her do it," said Junior.

David looked at Turnbull, who rolled his eyes out of Junior's eye-line.

"Of course she's not," David replied patiently.

"UCLA is in the Westside Sector. How do we get in there?"

Somewhere outside, blocks away, there was another crashing noise, more yelling, and what sounded like gunshots. It subsided.

"What are the privilege levels on your identification papers?"

"Sevens," replied Turnbull.

"I would not chance it. You'll need passes."

"From you?"

"I know someone. He'll have your car too. I have to send a runner – we have no cell phones here for obvious reasons – but this man is very efficient. He's full service for people like you."

"When?"

"Tomorrow. Thursday. Then Friday you do what you have to do."

"We'll be coming back here on the Sabbath then. You can help us on the Sabbath?"

"We can. After all, the Lord understands that sometimes we must be a little flexible."

David and Abraham saw them off at the gate to the complex, hanging back for the little group was out of sight of prying eyes along the street. They had their instructions to the three kilometer walk west to their next rendezvous; Turnbull and Junior had ensured that they looked derelict enough to be mistaken for just two more transients wandering through the unfashionable part of Los Angeles.

"Thank you," said Turnbull.

"Our pleasure," said David. "And be sure to forget us if you happen to end up meeting our friends from the PBI."

"I have no intention of getting caught," Turnbull said. "At least not while I have a bullet left."

"I think you'll appreciate Mr. Jackson," David said. "He and his group seem to feel much the same way. He'll have your car and be able to outfit you with papers for Friday. But he will want his money. He's very business-focused."

"If you can't make some money while you're having a revolution, then what's the point?"

David smiled.

"Now, the hard drive," Turnbull said. "How do we get it?"

"You are right about not coming back here," David said.

"We might be followed. We might be in a hurry. A big hurry."

"Abraham will have it, but you won't rendezvous here. About a half kilometer west is an old, empty fast food restaurant. I believe it was a Del Taco – obviously I was not a customer, but I remember it was very popular before. He will be there starting at five o'clock Friday evening until dawn waiting for you. He will have it."

"Sorry about spoiling your Sabbath, kid." Abraham smiled.

"Good luck to you. And when you get home, please make sure our mutual friends remember their commitment to bring us out.

92

This is no place for our children to grow up." He tousled his son's hair beneath the kippah.

"I'll make sure they remember. Thank you."

Junior led the way through the gate and onto the street. They took a right, walking north on the cracking sidewalk past abandoned cars, dying trees, and boarded-up homes.

There was a low stucco retaining wall holding up a patch of dead grass. Someone sprayed "FUCK USA" on it in black, and someone else crossed out the "SA" in red.

No one was walking on the street, though a few blocks south they could see buses passing east-west on Sunset. A 20-year old Ford sedan passed them heading north. What was probably a Toyota headed east a block ahead.

"I always feel like I'm being watched here," Junior whispered as they turned west and drove on. He glanced around. No cameras here, at least none he could see.

"Maybe you *are* being watched," Turnbull said, eyes darting around the street. Still empty, except there was one old lady walking aimlessly a couple blocks ahead. They kept going. "Do you notice the total lack of assholes?"

"Yeah," replied Junior.

"There's usually a higher shithead per block ratio around here. Or maybe they're all still sleeping off last night. Let's go."

After some walking, the old Del Taco came into view – you could still read in less-faded paint where the neon words had been pried off the side of the building. None of the glass had survived, and the inside was pillaged. Even from outside, you could see that, ironically, someone had tried to set fire to a fryer. A red picnic table sat empty out front, the benches broken. There was a parking lot around back and an empty cinderblock enclosure where the long-lost dumpster would have been kept. Both warily surveyed the empty husk of the fast food restaurant as they passed it by, but not too obviously – it would not pay to show too much interest in their rally point if they were being surveilled.

Two more blocks and they came to an alley running north toward the hills. Turnbull grabbed Junior and pulled him in.

"Run," he said, and sprinted north as fast as his pack would let him. Junior followed.

They took the next left, pumping their arms and legs past a long wooden fence line that was bedecked with tattered posters lauding revolutionary heroes for having turned in all manner of spies, denialists, racists, transphobes, and whatever "cispigs" were. The fence gave way to a three story red brick building, or rather, the empty shell of one. A street side door was off its hinge and Turnbull darted in. They plowed down a long hallway, past mostly empty but sometimes occupied rooms, breathing in great lungfuls of the fetid, urine-tinged air. The few inhabitants they passed simply stared at them dumbly for a moment, then returned to their sordid business.

They burst out the other side through another broken door, moving south toward Sunset through a narrow alley. Junior glanced behind them – nothing, no one.

Turnbull led him on several more zigs and zags, until they were along Sunset at the edge of a large parking lot anchored by an old Ralphs supermarket that was now a "People's Food Center." The lot was bereft of cars, but full of people. They were gathering around the front entrance not in the usual sullen yet orderly queue, but in a milling, seething semi-circle.

"Come on," Turnbull said, leading junior toward the crowd.

A thin, reedy voice rose above the angry murmur. "The rations have changed. Series B is half of what it was yesterday. That's how it is. It isn't my decision!"

"Fuck you, man. I want my rice!" someone yelled. Turnbull and Junior wended their way into the crowd; they could feel the unrest.

"It's the rules!" shouted the sweaty manager at the semi-circle of angry people that was closing in on him. "To get in, you need to show me your Series B rat cards! You need twenty points to buy. Twenty!"

"That's bullshit," screamed a dark haired woman of maybe thirty, holding a crying kid of maybe four.

"You even have food in there today?" shouted someone else.

"Yes, but you need twenty Series B points to even come in!"

A large gentleman in a blue work shirt stepped forward. The perspiring manager stopped and looked up, just as the large gentleman grabbed his collar and threw him to the side. The manager crashed into a cardboard cutout of a smiling family carrying overflowing grocery bags beneath the words "THE PEOPLE'S REPUBLIC PRACTICES FOOD JUSTICE."

"We're getting us some motherfucking food, motherfucker," he said, striding into the store, followed by the crowd.

"Come on," Turnbull said, looking back behind him but not seeing anything. They entered the store. It was oddly hot – it had never occurred to Junior that it would not be like the air conditioned markets at home. It was also dim – the brownout was in effect and the sputtering portable generator echoing through the cavernous interior only powered the refrigerators.

The workers, all in white aprons, saw the mass of humanity flooding in and quickly made the calculation that if one can't beat them, one should join them. They turned and rushed down the aisles to gather what they could for themselves.

What jarred Junior most was not the mass of agitated humanity streaming through the door toward the aisles. It was the store itself – the lack of any kind of color or advertising or even endcap displays. A good portion of the shelves were empty, and the rest were piled with a few dozen muted cans or packages. Back home, at an HEB or Kroger's, besides having cool air circulating and bright lights, there would be displays, colorful ads, and brand signage. Here, none of that – there was so little, there was no need to advertise at all.

They rushed with the crowd, finding themselves in the personal care products aisle. A hundred or so eight-inch boxes of what appeared to be toothpaste sat on a middle shelf; the brand was in Chinese, but there was a smiling Asian woman showing gleaming white teeth that revealed the nature of the product to those not fluent in Mandarin. But there seemed to be no toothbrushes in stock.

Further down, there was a good deal of "Worker's Friend" deodorant – just one brand, with lots of empty shelf space around it. One of the People's Republic's basic premises was that its residents should not be forced to make difficult choices, not between body odor reduction preparations, and not between leaders.

"Did you see someone following us?" Junior asked, catching his breath. More were piling in through the front doors as passersby saw that it was open season on the food center. They stood against the shelves and people passed by them as well as the unwanted toothpaste and deodorant. It was clear the score was the food; now there was yelling and fighting echoing up from the parallel aisles. A white puff of dust – flour? – arose one aisle over, followed by a stream of vicious obscenities screamed by what sounded like an elderly woman.

"I don't know," Turnbull said. "But it felt wrong to me. You know how in bad movies they say it's too quiet? It felt like that. Anyway, we can slip out the back, lose anyone following us."

"What's in those packs, man?" asked a leering little guy in his twenties standing in the middle of the aisle. Behind him, three friends, two of them tall, but all of them thin, like most blue staters. One of the tall guys had a daisy tattooed on his left check – either he lost a bet or had jumped into Los Angeles's least threatening gang.

"Just move on," Junior said, annoyed.

"I asked you what's in the bag, bitch," the little guy said.

"One of my guns," Turnbull said. The little guy looked puzzled.

"Here's my other one." Turnbull's Glock 19 was out and pointed at the little guy's forehead. "If you even think – not that you're big thinkers – that I won't splatter your fucking brains all over this place, you are dumber than you look. And I seriously doubt that's possible. So you and the rest of the human centipede need to about face and get the fuck out of here, or I will drop all four of you, and no one will give your twitching bodies a second look while I piss on them."

The little guy's jaw started to quiver, like he was about to say something.

"Nope, don't talk. Turn around, and run. Three."

The little guy looked puzzled.

"Two."

He stood there, confused.

"Dipshit, when I get to zero, I'm shooting you. One."

The four stepped backwards, then turned and ran out of the aisle and off to the left somewhere.

"I thought we were a second from a clean-up on aisle five," Junior observed.

"Let's go out the back and –"

Sirens. The PSF was entering the parking lot in force. Turnbull stepped up to the head of the aisle to get a better view. There were at least a half-dozen cruisers piling in, stopping around an unmarked Ford that was already parked there. Two men in plainclothes were standing by it.

"They're going to need riot cops," Junior said.

"I've seen that Ford before. They're not here for the riot," Turnbull said as he was hit from the side by the Daisy-faced punk and sent sprawling.

Junior pivoted as the other tall one rushed him, grabbing the punk's filthy t-shirt and swinging him around so that his body weight carried him past and into the shelves.

The little one charged Junior, a silver flash of steel in his hand. The knife sliced into Junior's left arm, sending a jolt of fire up the nerves. Junior struck the little guy's jaw hard with a right cross, and felt the teeth underneath give way and shift from the blow.

"Get the gun, his gun!" the fourth shouted at Daisy-Face and he grappled on the ground with Turnbull. The guy was tall but light; Turnbull was tall and heavy with muscle mass. Still on his back, he grabbed the punk's collar with his left hand then reached across the tatted up face with his right, grabbing a hunk of hair and an ear on the right side of Daisy-Face's head and pulling it hard across into the floor. Turnbull threw pulled the quivering thug off him and sat up. The cheerleader looked on slack-jawed as Turnbull reached under his shirt to produce the Glock.

"Zero," he said, then he shot the cheerleader in the face. The thug's head jolted backwards under a fine pink mist; on the ceiling, the round kicked up a bit of dust where it hit. The thug fell, and only at that moment the looters seemed to notice what was happening. There was a momentary pause, and then the frenzy the store was already in kicked up exponentially.

Junior slammed the stunned little guy's head into an empty shelf; he fell to his knees. The other big one hit Junior from behind. There was a loud blast – a gunshot – and the big guy paused for a moment, confused. Junior drew his Glock and shoved it against the punk's abdomen.

"Wait!" the punk screamed. Junior pulled the trigger. Adios, liver. The punk crumpled.

Turnbull was on his feet. The store was utter chaos, and outside the cops were taking cover. He briefly considered taking some shots at them to suppress them, but he realized that would invite a massacre when they returned fire. To his right he noticed

Daisy-Face trying to stand and casually shot him through the back of the head. His nose came apart as the round exited and splattered against a poster sternly warning that "RATION CARD CHEATS ARE FOOD CRIMINALS!"

Junior was breathing hard. The little one was on his knees in the aisle, drooling blood.

"Kill that piece of shit and let's go," Turnbull said, sprinting down the aisle.

Junior shot the little one in the face and followed, dodging the looters, and heading toward the warehouse in back.

They got out through the loading dock, blending in with the mass of humanity carrying off whatever they could hold. A woman juggled a half dozen cartons of milk, dropping one, two, three of them before she got to the edge of the parking lot. Another tripped, sending a dozen cans of beans scattering across the pavement. For some reason, an elderly man was making off with the mop and a bucket the food center used to clean up spills.

They made their way out of the lot before the PSF surrounded the place. Even as they kept going they could hear shouts and gunfire from behind them. They kept to alleys and passed through abandoned buildings and yards as best they could, avoiding the main streets. They saw cruisers pass, but managed to take cover; no one bothered them and no one caught Turnbull's eye. Exploiting his counter-surveillance training, he doubled-back, periodically rushed ahead, and generally zig-zagged his way west. The half-hour walk instead took them four hours to get to "TRISTAR FOREIGN AND DOMESTIC AUTO CARE" located on a side street off La Brea. There was one car out front, a Fiat from the 1970s, and it was on blocks.

They did not go right up to it. Turnbull positioned Junior to observe the front as he walked around a one block perimeter. Finding a good location on a porch of an abandoned townhouse, he sat and watched the rear of the building for about an hour. There was a fair amount of foot traffic into the convenience mart next door, but nothing into the repair shop. Yet it was obviously occupied; he could see vague movements through the filthy windows.

After surveying the surrounding area, Turnbull was fairly satisfied that the repair shop was not under surveillance. He could still be wrong, in which case he would be dead meat, but he was reasonably certain and that was the best he would get. He went back to where Junior waited and gave him his pack to watch. Then he headed over to the repair shop, knocked on the front door, and disappeared inside.

Junior waited for ten minutes, becoming more and more restless. His arm hurt where the punk cut him. He was almost ready to investigate when Turnbull appeared at the doorway and waved him over. He came as quickly as he could carrying the two packs.

The repair shop was dark, and a generator whirred somewhere out where the lifts were. The front door opened into a kind of waiting area with ancient vinyl bench seats. An office was to the left, piled with papers. To the right was a surprisingly compact work area; a yellow Volkswagen Jetta from the early 2000s was hoisted up, its transmission on the cement floor below. A black Lexus from the 2010s was on the floor at the far end. Its windows were slightly tinted, not so much to be noticeable, but enough to obscure the view of the curious.

Turnbull stood with a black-bearded man in a silvery-blue jumpsuit. The name tag said "Jackson" – evidently this was their host.

"You need better clothes," Jackson said. "I can do that too. I've got a nice selection."

"Where?" asked Junior, puzzled.

"Downstairs."

The stairway down was hidden by a large, wheeled Snap-On Tools cabinet. Jackson pushed it aside and they descended. The basement area was about as large as the work space upstairs, but was divided with wood walls. There were racks of clothing in one space, a work table with lights and a computer set up in another – the forgery area. A third held sheet metal presses, lathes and drills.

"You make your own auto parts?" asked Junior.

"Sometimes," said Jackson. "Mostly, we make guns. We can do a couple of STEN submachine guns a day. Real simple. That's how the British designed them, so they could sub-contract the work out to local metal shops during World War Two."

"How about bullets?" asked Turnbull.

"Harder, now that Mexico built the wall to secure the border. We also get some from the reds. But mostly, we make our own." He pointed to a reloader. "Getting the propellant and primers is pretty easy. If you have connections you can get most anything. We get the brass from PSF training ranges. They make their people collect the shells at the training ranges, turn it in, account for it, and then we buy it through the back door."

"So," said Turnbull. "Will we be good to go by tomorrow?"

"Yeah, if you have the money."

"I have the money."

"Well, I got a guy coming in tonight. He'll do your papers up, get them entered in the PSF system. You should be able to cross into the Secured Zone no problem."

"You got us wheels?"

"See that Lexus upstairs? Sweet. And no trackers. I reprogrammed the GPS myself so it can't send."

"Gas?"

"Full tank."

"Sounds like we're good to go," said Turnbull. "Any loose ends?"

"My arm," Junior said.

"Yeah, we need a place we can fix him up and where we can crash."

"Got those too. I got anything you need, as long as you got the money."

"Shit," cried Junior, pulling back his arm. Turnbull locked it down to the table and pushed the needle through his skin again, then through the outer side of the wound and pulled the suture tight.

"Next time, don't get cut."

"Oh, okay. Sounds like a plan," Junior replied, annoyed. Turnbull handed him the rubbing alcohol.

"Since you're such a baby, you can pour it on yourself." Turnbull got up and lay down in his cot. A stylish grey suit hung on the wall next to him, selected from Jackson's inventory.

Junior continued cleaning up the knife wound. It was one of the power hours, so the TV was on. On the news, they were announcing the widespread public joy at the new and improved ration allocations – apparently the populace was thrilled to be getting less. Turnbull changed the channel to *People's Court*. But this was not the old *People's Court* where quarter wits argued over who committed what petty tort against whom. Here, some poor, pale, middle-aged schlub was dragged before a jeering audience of mouth-frothing community college students and accused by a shrieking, teary-eyed creature of "microaggressing me as a trans person of color by invoking his male gaze." Seated in a chair center stage and flanked by two PSF thugs, the terrified protagonist stared in horror as his accuser fell to her knees wailing "You are eye-raping me!"

After ten minutes of this, the crowd declared him guilty by acclamation – he never said a word – and the announcer appeared on camera to announce that "Justice was done and always will be done to hate criminals, deniers, racists and economic criminals! Long live the battle against rape culture!"

"I don't get it," Junior said, dabbing his wound with an alcohol-infused cotton ball. "Why it's still a rape culture if they've been in charge of their own country for a decade? Doesn't that say something about the People's Republic?"

"You're applying facts and evidence and logic to it," Turnbull said, turning off the tube. "None of that matters. Nothing matters. It's all a lie. It's all about power. That whole kangaroo court thing, that wasn't about who was guilty or innocent of what, but about who gets to use the power. Now, those college students are going to leave there and go back to their shitty, cold dorms and be back to having no power again. But for a little while, there in that studio, the people who really have power lent them some power for a little while. And they took it out on that poor guy. He's probably off in some rehabilitation camp learning how everything bad that ever happened to anyone was his fault."

"This place is crazy."

"No," Turnbull said. "It's not crazy. It's the opposite. There may not *seem* to be any rhyme or reason for what's happening, but there is. Like I said, it's all about power. Pay off this group, let that group have some latitude, then balance it against another group. It's a balancing act. The problem is sometimes, in a balancing act, you can lose your balance and it all comes crashing down."

"You think we'll find her tomorrow when we go to UCLA?"

"I don't know. I'm still wondering how they picked up our scent and followed us to the food center."

"Do you think they know why we're here?"

Turnbull lay back on his pillow. "I don't know. But if they do, then tomorrow they'll be waiting for us."

101

10.

Martin Rios-Parkinson stood in front of his mirror and scrutinized his haircut as he listened to the report over his cell phone. The corner of his mouth trembled, half fury, half fear.

"We would not be in this situation if you had ensured the loyalty of your people," he said. "I do not need to remind you that we must recover the hard drive. And if we do not, it is on you."

"I understand," replied the reedy voice on the other end. An incompetent, but one department had to have a gender non-binary head and xe was the best one available. That was the problem – there were always considerations beyond competence.

"Find them," Rios-Parkinson said, now calmly. "But we need to be ready to execute the alternate plan in case you can't. We know where they are going regardless. We can reacquire them up there and they'll take us to it. Do you understand?"

"Yes, Director."

"Then do it. And do it right. Because if you do not, you will be accountable." But, of course, so would Rios-Parkinson, and this disaster could mean the end of everything he had worked for. Unless, of course, he recovered what had been stolen. And if he could capture the spies who had probably been the ones who shot their way in from Utah while doing so, he could turn this fiasco into a coup.

He hung up and considered his hair. It was perfect, projecting the image of efficiency, yet projecting an edge of nonconformity that would fit in well in the circles he navigated. It was a far cry from the white boy dreadlocks he had sported as an undergrad at UCLA twenty years ago.

And now there were flecks of gray, but that was understandable. He now had responsibilities beyond the minimal requirements of getting up and getting to class as a student. And beyond getting up and getting to class to teach as a graduate student teaching assistant, and then as an assistant professor of political science.

Yes, as the Director of the People's Bureau of Investigation in the California region, he had many responsibilities.

And perks. He heard his latest one stirring in the bedroom. Rios-Parkinson stepped out of the spacious bathroom into the master bedroom. The south wall was a window looking out over Los Angeles from high in the hills. There was downtown on the left, Century City on the right and beyond that, the ocean. In the distance, hazy and dark, beyond the Palos Verdes Peninsula, was Catalina Island. And, in the bed, a blonde, rising to her elbows.

"You need to get ready," he said.

"I don't want to go," she moaned.

"Education is important," he replied. "In your case, reeducation to correct the red lies that still infect you. Now get out of bed."

Rios-Parkinson was not his birth name. Born in Huntington Beach to a housewife mother and an aerospace engineer father, Martin chafed at the unfairness of his position in the social hierarchy of his Orange County public schools. He was no surfer, and no soccer or football player. He was not blonde, and not conventionally handsome. And he was not rich; his parents drove a Ford, not a BMW or even a Volvo like everyone else's parents.

What he *was* was clever; his grades were always good right from the beginning, and repeating back what the teachers wanted to hear came easy to him. It occurred to him as early as middle school that it was therefore cruelly unfair that those who were clearly his mental inferiors dominated his little society, and that he was nothing.

And the anger grew inside him, the gnawing resentment that the power and respect due him was instead invested in the dull and the frivolous-living Orange County stereotypes that surrounded him. He should be the one walking the halls that everyone greeted. He should be the one they should respect, and fear. He should be the one with the power. But instead, he was nothing, just another kid who wasn't handsome or athletic who no one noticed and no one ever thought about.

But then, he found his path. In ninth grade, his social studies teacher's casual leftism offended the default conservatism of his classmates. He was someone who stuck his finger in the eye of everything everyone held dear. He told them their comfy Orange County lifestyle was born from the exploitation of others. He told them that they were pawns of corporations and shadowy rich power brokers who manipulated the system for their benefit. He told them that maybe America was not the greatest country on Earth.

Rios-Parkinson – back then simply "Parkinson" – was fascinated as the former hippie dropped new and powerful words he had never heard before, words that seemed to have the power to knock the other kids back on their heels. Racism. Sexism. Homophobia.

He had never thought much about minorities growing up – there were some around, but no one really seemed to care. Yet Rios-Parkinson found that when he spoke about other's crimes against race or gender or the like, the tenor of the conversation changed. The assured and the powerful became uncertain and weak, and suddenly he was in control. They were reacting and responding to him for once. And he savored it.

He had never been particularly patriotic, or unpatriotic, but when he was a junior and saw an opportunity, he ran a Mexican flag up the school flag pole, and in the ensuring uproar a television news crew came and put a camera on him and he said, "I reject the racism that the American flag represents." All hell broke loose – his parents were beside themselves – and suddenly Martin Parkinson was no longer some brain on the fringes of the Huntington Beach High Class of 2009, but the school's most famous student.

After he went on Fox News and argued with Bill O'Reilly, a cheerleader led him behind the bleachers and demonstrated to him an unexpected fringe benefit of his notoriety. "I always wanted to do that for someone famous," she said, wiping her mouth. He was too stunned by the whole experience to respond to her, but not to learn the lesson. This was his path.

Before applying to college, he took the name Rios-Parkinson to honor the Hispanic heritage represented by his great-great-grandmother, whose stepfather had been named Rios and adopted her. He was inspired by some of the news anchors on television. A blonde would be "Susan Wilson" one day on Channel 7, then show up on Channel 5 the next day with a tan calling herself "Susana Wilson-Suarez." He understood the game.

That he had not a drop of actual Hispanic blood was beyond the point. He only knew that checking the "Hispanic" box on his application would up his chances for acceptance exponentially.

At UCLA he insinuated himself into the network of leftist organizations and groups, learning to navigate their intricate power structures and becoming fluent in the language of progressivism. He certainly believed the views he embraced, but he never fetishized them as some around him did. He simply believed them because to be a leftist meant he had to believe them. The language of Marxism and critical studies were merely his tools, like the hammer and saw of a carpenter, and he used them to build his career. He earned his PhD and was accepted as a political science professor; his thesis was titled "Genuflection and Reflections: Centralizing Core Paradigms of Racism and Sexist Power Structures for Progressive Empowerment."

For years he was in the forefront of organizing to subvert and disrupt the stable, prosperous society that he had inherited. During the waning months of the Obama presidency, he helped blow up any incident where a cop was forced to shoot a criminal into a fresh cause. Facts, he found, were beside the point. Truth, he learned, was simply an abstract concept that served only to distract from the all-important narrative. Who cares if the victim was a thug, if he had pulled a gun? That was mere objective truth, the weakest and least important kind. Instead, Rios-Parkinson learned to offer a new truth – that the victim's hands were up, that he was slaughtered by a laughing cop with KKK ties while he walked from the school where he was an honor roll student on his way to the local church to help feed the homeless. Narrative truth—that was the only truth that mattered.

And when radical racist leftists declared war on police officers and murdered them in deliberate ambushes, he smiled. It was action, striking a blow, and it was working. Between the threats to their lives and the threat to their livelihoods and even their freedom if they were caught on camera using force against some criminal, the police withdrew. Crime rose, but Rios-Parkinson and his cohort savored the instability. Unburdened by any affection or affinity to norms, traditions, or the rule of law, they would not merely survive but prosper in the coming chaos.

And when the Crisis erupted, Rios-Parkinson was ready. Certainly, the sickly Hillary Clinton had been nothing like the president he and his fellow travelers truly wanted – she gave a pittance to the progressives, just enough to keep them with her, while lavishing her largesse on her Wall Street and corporate cronies. But when about half the country simply refused to obey her executive orders regarding gun confiscation from law-abiding citizens, illegal alien legalization, and the destruction of their carbon energy industries, Rios-Parkinson and his allies saw their chance.

Rios-Parkinson instinctively knew what he needed to do – organize and turn out as many people as they could find into the streets demanding she act to suppress the rebellion. And so, the same man who a month before had burned the American flag, calling it the "Swastika of rape culture," was now clutching it and holding it close, demanding that the President defend it against some enemies – not foreign (he tended to side with those), just domestic. Destroy the red traitors once and for all!

He saw another chance when the military sat on its collective hands, refusing to budge – not that it could do much budging, considering the massive desertions and the sheer number of sergeants who simply shrugged when reporting to the few remaining Clinton-loyal officers that their units' vehicles just wouldn't seem to run for some reason. Rios-Parkinson began to organize a People's Militia – militias had suddenly become *in vogue* again – to take action in support of the President. The media, slavishly loyal to the ruling elite on the coasts, eagerly covered this "spontaneous" and "patriotic" movement.

In reality, the leftist militias that sprang up in blue cities around the country were gigantic clusterfucks composed of bored students, convicts, whiny social justice warriors, and the occasional radicalized veteran. Naturally, it was always the one guy who had served as a latrine orderly in Baghdad and was now a sophomore who got interviewed on the news while being identified as an "Army Combat Vet." The 300-pound, tattooed, genderqueered feminist who cried and screamed about patriarchy after tripping and scrapping her bloated cankle while trying to learn to march never appeared on screen.

For most Americans, the Crisis was a terrifying time of uncertainty and fear. For Rios-Parkinson, it was liberating. He abandoned his teaching to assume command of the Patrice Lumumba Battalion based in Westwood. When his paycheck stopped coming, he sent 20 of his "troops" over to the provost's office. The checks started arriving again.

106

He called himself a "colonel" – he looked at Wikipedia to learn the military ranks. Every day at noon, the ragged five hundred or so (the number varied as bored enlistees dropped out and others joined) marched down to Wilshire Boulevard and the federal building, carrying a wide selection of mismatched firearms and stopping traffic. Eventually, they "liberated" the Veterans' Administration complex west across the 405, evicting the elderly residents and setting up their own little realm. No one challenged them, so they pushed harder.

The LAPD was well aware of the sympathy of the mayor and the governor for this movement – Governor Newsom actually appeared with them and, standing beside Rios-Parkinson, who had taken to wearing a black beret he had found in an Aardvark's recycled clothing shop, called the mob "patriots and heroes." Ordered to stand down, law enforcement did nothing

Not when the militia marched in the streets, with guns, in violation of the anti-open carry laws passed to harass decent citizens by the same politicians who were now applauding.

Not when the militia decided to "liberate" goods and merchandise from the local stores.

Not when the militia began threatening and then attacking their critics.

And Rios-Parkinson soon found himself taking calls from the power brokers in the city who would never have taken his call just months before.

Commanding the militia – actually, the militia theoretically ran on consensus, with frequent meetings where the participants wiggled their fingers to show approval because clapping traumatized some violence survivors – came naturally to him. But he soon found the more doctrinaire members growing tiresome. They preferred endless debate and ideological purity, while Rios-Parkinson was learning the cruel, relentless logic of action and force. Guns were bad yesterday because people he hated had them; today they were good because his people were the only ones who had them.

He found this new freedom from ideology liberating. He found he loved, and understood, force. Because only from force came real power.

But some of the practical matters he did not understand. He was given a .38 revolver and, in his condo, he accidentally shot off the tip of his little toe and had to hobble in pain for a month. A number of his "soldiers" ended up accidentally killing themselves with firearms. These tragedies, of course, never made the news. Rios-Parkinson early on made it a point to deploy a team of People's Observers to each of the local television stations every morning to ensure that coverage was "fair" and "honest." After several producers were beaten, and the police never came, the stations capitulated. Rios-Parkinson found himself in control of the local media. Much of each broadcast was devoted to the perfidy of the red state traitors, and soon it became clear that the negotiations that would lead to the Treaty of St. Louis were going to result in the country breaking in two, to the promises of a bright future free of the knuckle-dragging racists who infested the vast wasteland between the coasts.

And Rios-Parkinson learned about people. He learned that the students and the activists he had spent years with talking about revolution and action were prepared for neither. They were soft, sometimes even sentimental. He ushered them out of the Patrice Lumumba Battalion, preferring instead the homeless kids he found on the streets and gave food and shelter, and the petty (sometimes, not so petty) criminals who joined up. Of course, they were not really criminals – the true criminals were the people who had cast them into the dungeons of the prison-industrial complex. So they had stolen, so they had robbed, so they had done – allegedly – worse things? Rios-Parkinson found they had the edge the soft, suburban social justice warriors lacked. They could give and take a punch. And they were very, very useful.

Soon, Rios-Parkinson was commanding an army of 2,000 of them within the heart of Los Angeles. And the police were powerless to stop him. In fact, once the Treaty was signed and the borders were set, most of the cops simply stopped showing up for work. They were among the first to see where this was heading, and therefore they headed east from Los Angeles to the red states to start over.

In the wake of the Split, the presidential election was cancelled due to the "emergency" and was thereafter never uncancelled. In the blue states, the liberal elite that was left in complete control suddenly found itself without any constraints whatsoever. It wrote a new Constitution, a better one (they promised), one not infected with the virus of racism and oppression

108

inherent in the one it replaced, written as it was by a bunch of dead white males a zillion years before. There was a right to free speech, but not to racism or hate crimes or a variety of other exceptions— exceptions inserted by design to swallow the rule. The same with the freedom of the press and assembly. You could print what you wanted and protest what you wanted, assuming what you wanted was what the ruling elite wanted.

And Rios-Parkinson was now part of that ruling elite, as his militia was folded into the new police force and he was installed as the police chief. The past police chief was by then retired to Norman, Oklahoma, having decided that Los Angeles deserved whatever miseries it decided to inflict upon itself. So when the new People's Constitution was signed– the new government had begun using the modifier "People's" to rub the new reality in the faces of the reactionaries who remained in the blue states – Rios-Parkinson was on the VIP reviewing stand for the parade. Except no one called them VIPs – they were just fellow citizens, citizens who merely happened to have power. And despite having 218 amendments in the New Bill of Rights – which included the rights to a job, a home, to "climate justice" and "to be free of cisnormative bias," those were the only people with any power at all.

And now Rios-Parkinson was where he had always known he belonged – wielding power. He left the police department (which was soon nationalized, along with all other law enforcement organizations) to take over the California branch of the People's Bureau of Investigations, which also provided oversight of the People's Security Force. In doing so, he found himself among the handful of California's most powerful men and women and non-binary persons (the current mayor of Los Angeles was named simply "Chris" and refused to accept any specific gender identity; "xe" was Chris's preferred pronoun).

And as a member of the elite, he had claimed Amanda Ryan.

"Get up," he said again. She did, but slowly, and it grated on him. It did not occur to him at any conscious level that she looked quite like one of the affluent Orange County blondes who had ignored him through most of his youth; that weirdness was submerged deep in his roiling psyche. But he understood that he derived a great deal of satisfaction from the fact that she belonged to him, both physically and emotionally.

And though he never gave it any specific thought, he understood that his satisfaction would increase exponentially when he had fully broken her to his will.

"Why do I have to go? I'm sick of school. All they do is talk," she said.

"You are contaminated with red state bullshit, Amanda. And you need to be decontaminated." He went over to the bureau where she kept her things and picked up her purse, reaching in to pull out a wallet of photographs that Amanda often flipped through.

"Put that down," she hissed.

"You can't seem to give up your old life, can you, Amanda?" he said, smiling a reptilian grin. "These people, these family and friends, they are all dead to you. Or, at least, they should be. You are lucky, you know. Most people who crossover end up in rehabilitation camps, like the friends you came with, and the camps are not quite as comfortable as this place."

Amanda moved toward him and took the wallet, replaced it in her purse, and put it back on the bureau top. Then she walked over to a credenza where she kept several bottles of imported whiskey and poured herself a tumbler full.

"It is eight in the morning," Rios-Parkinson sneered.

"Then it's ten o'clock back home," she replied, drinking a gulp and staring.

"Your problem is you still think of the US as your home. Sometimes I wonder if you really meant it when you told me you came here because you believed in what we are doing."

"I did. Then I got here." That was true. She had come believing the blue would be a Utopia. She had been thrilled when a valiant defender of the People's Republic had selected her as his own. And then she came to know both the People's Republic and Martin Rios-Parkinson.

"I have arrested people for less than that, Amanda. You should watch your mouth. Now put the glass down." Rios-Parkinson could not have her drunk. She was too important to his plan.

Amanda smiled and took another swig. "You're going to arrest me? That'd be pretty embarrassing for you, your own domestic partner, your defector girlfriend in a camp. That'd be the end of the famous, powerful Director Martin Rios-Parkinson."

That pushed him too far. He stepped forward and slapped her on the right side of her face – she tried to dodge the blow but drowsiness and the booze had slowed her enough so it connected. She dropped the tumbler onto the carpet.

He stood there for a moment, himself shaken. He had rarely done any violence himself. Though sometimes he liked to watch it done, he always had others to do it for him. But she had gotten under his skin, probed at the festering sore of resentment that would never quite heal.

She blinked for a moment, and then smiled, and then she began to laugh.

"You call that a slap, you fucking pussy? You hit girls, and you hit like a girl!" She continued laughing, a bitter but genuine laugh. "The big, bad Senior Director of the PB fucking I and he hits like a little girl!"

"You better shut up, bitch," he said quietly, and her expression changed and she fell silent. "I need you at UCLA today, and if you aren't in the car in ten minutes I will send Arthur and Sam up here to bring you to UCLA. Do you understand?"

She stared at him with hatred. Arthur and Sam were the two thugs who escorted him in to work each morning. They would smash her face in as soon as they would look at her.

"Do you understand?" he repeated.

"Yes," she hissed, and now Rios-Parkinson smiled as he watched her dress. He had broken her to his will. And now he would put her to use to turn this disaster into another triumph.

11.

The Lexus turned over and hummed; Jackson had tuned it up nicely. The tank was full; the range read as 456 miles. Their packs were in the trunk, along with two extra sets of People's Republic license plates. Junior held a thick, tattered paper map book Jackson had handed him. The cover read "Thomas Guide – 1995."

"You use the index in back to find the page with the map section for wherever you are going," Jackson had told them.

"My dad used to have one of these in his car, back before nav systems. Everyone did," Turnbull had replied.

"It's forty years old, but it's still pretty accurate," Jackson continued. "Obviously it doesn't show the new names of the streets they renamed for being offensive or for PRNA bigwigs. And it doesn't show the security sector walls or the gates, but other than that it's pretty good. Best of all no one can trace you online when you look something up."

They wore suits; Junior had selected a red power tie. Their new IDs were in order, with Level 8 privilege, a nice bonus. Getting that done, arranging for someone inside to make the changes in the national database, had cost plenty – all 20 gold coins.

"You ready for this?" Turnbull asked Junior, who sat in the passenger seat checking his Glock.

"I guess."

"You know what you'll say to her when you see her?"

"I'll tell her I'm bringing her home."

"And what if she doesn't want to come?"

"She'll want to come."

"Hope is not a plan. Think it through." Turnbull looked out the open window to Jackson, who stood wiping his hands. "Thanks,"

"Yeah, you're welcome. Now forget you ever met me."

Turnbull smiled. "Forget what?"

Jackson returned the grin. "Yeah, that's right. Good luck. Don't come back this way."

"Never go back the way you came," Turnbull replied. He put the sedan in reverse, backed out of the garage onto the street, and accelerated away.

They headed south to Wilshire and turned west. There was a little more activity in this area than in the others they had passed through. Some of the businesses were open and there were more cars the further west they went. Turnbull kept checking his rearview; nothing caught his eye.

Turnbull caught sight of a billboard featuring a beautiful blonde. It read, "I ESCAPED THE RACIST RED STATES. BE VIGILANT – THEY SEEK TO DESTROY THE SOCIAL AND ECONOMIC JUSTICE WE HAVE BUILT HERE!" Turnbull wanted to ask Junior if his sister spoke like a community agitator in real life – if so, they would need some of their hundred mile an hour duct tape. But he said nothing. Junior had obviously seen it and had descended into a silent funk.

The checkpoint was at Doheny. Three or four cars were lined up to cross into the Secured Zone. A cyclone fence ran north and south along the east side of the street. There was a sign reading "WARNING: AUTHORIZED ADMITTEES ONLY. 100% ID CHECK."

"Guess they gotta keep out the riff raff," Junior observed.

The gate was manned by the uniformed element of the PBI. The folks who lived in the Westside Sector could not be expected to put up with a bunch of barely trained thugs keeping order. The PBI were much better trained thugs.

Ahead, an officer was arguing with the occupant of an old Toyota. The officer waved her out of the line and she turned around, cursing that she would lose her housekeeping job as she pulled out of the queue and U turned around. The guards seemed more bored than excited; apparently this was nothing unusual. Lots of people wanted inside.

Turnbull put his hand out and Junior handed him his ID card, then rested his hand under his suit jacket. He counted five PBI officers, all armed with AKs. He would take the three on the passenger side and hope that Junior would be able to put down the two on his side should it all go bad.

It didn't. Turnbull handed over the cards without a word and the bored officer scanned it on his handset. He stared at the screen for a moment, then wordlessly handed the cards back and gestured for Turnbull to drive through. The Lexus smoothly accelerated and they entered the Westside Sector.

113

It was an entirely different world. The businesses were open and the streets were clean. People were well-dressed and there was none of the seething sullenness they had seen before. Cars – nice cars, many newer models – filled the roads. It was not the gridlock of before the Split, but it was substantially more traffic than they had seen elsewhere.

"It's almost like home here," Junior said, marveling. "Restaurants, coffee shops. People doing things."

"You need a privilege level of 6 or higher to live in here; if you don't live in here you need a pass to get in. Mostly they give them to worker bees. Everyone who can live in here does. And they do patrol the walls."

"How big is it?"

"It runs west to the ocean and north to just over the summit of the hills. Basically, anywhere that was a little fashionable. There are other ones too – the whole South Bay from LAX south, El Segundo, Manhattan Beach, Hermosa Beach, Redondo Beach and all of Palos Verdes are sealed off too. Things got bad and the folks running things decided the best way to solve the problem was to seal off the problem."

"Wait, I thought the privilege levels were supposed to compensate for systemic racism and inequality and all that."

"Yeah, well, in a stunning turn of events the same people who ran the blue states into the ground ended up with exceptions to the privilege level rules. So some poor Mexican kid from East LA gets a 3 and a Hollywood producer's girlfriend driving a Porsche gets a 9. They did the same thing with the reparations campaigns. They got exemptions while the working stiff in Rancho Cucamonga got hit for 20% of his assets every time some group got paid off with another reparations tax, and when he couldn't pay, they took his house. A lot of those guys showed up in the red with nothing after working for decades."

"Until I got inside here, I didn't see where all that money went," Junior said. "This is living large in here."

"Yeah, they pretty much stole the money and then flushed it. And now, I don't think there's much left outside of this sector to steal."

They made good time heading west, passing out of Beverly Hills and into Century City, with its high rises that were modern-looking over a half century before. Junior pointed eagerly.

"Nakatomi Plaza!"

"What?"

"There! You know, *Die Hard*!"

"The movie?"

"Yeah," Junior said, delighted. "That's a great movie. A great Christmas movie. Every Christmas we used to watch it. You know, so many old movies before were filmed in LA that I kind of expected LA to look like them instead of … this."

"Half of Hollywood followed the money and got out after the Split," Turnbull said. "Now all the movies look like Houston."

"I had an actor in my unit when I was doing my citizenship service. He'd been in commercials. Said he wanted to vote so he was doing his service. He was worried he might not get any work afterwards. A lot of the Hollywood people who crossed over are still pretty left wing and he says they're pissed that they can't become citizens without serving."

"Fuck 'em," Turnbull said. "The best thing we ever did in the red was not let the people coming in from the blue bring their shitty politics with them."

"Amen," Junior replied, looking around. "How long you think the People's Republic can hold up?"

"Shit, it could fall apart in a day or keep dragging on for a decade. I guess the bullshit stops when the people decide they've had enough of social justice and climate justice and economic justice and all the other kinds of justice except *justice* justice."

Century City shrank behind them. Now they were among high rise luxury apartment buildings. PBI were visibly standing watch.

"Rich people land," Turnbull said.

"You know, I haven't seen any more of the billboards since we crossed in here," Junior observed.

"Nope. They're pretty ugly, and it won't do to block these special snowflakes' views. Besides, I think these people in here are in on the scam. The signs aren't going to fool anyone in here. The propaganda is for the nobodies."

115

In Westwood, Turnbull turned right. Up ahead lay UCLA and their target.

12.

Rios-Parkinson sipped a sparkling water from the cooler in the rear of his black SUV. Arthur and Sam were up front, separated from him by a thick glass partition. He was able to review his morning briefing papers, delivered earlier by courier, in quiet as they headed down from the hills.

His continuing operation in Los Angeles could not take up all of his attention, as much as he wished it to. All over California – all over the two halves of the People's Republic, in fact – there was too much going on. Yesterday's bloody chaos at the food center was hardly unique. Besides San Francisco – 12 dead – there were other riots of varying intensity by hungry citizens in Seattle, Oakland, San Diego, Baltimore, Cincinnati, and two in Fontana. He was slightly surprised that desolate Fontana even had two food centers. He made a mental note to cut Fontana's food allocation as a lesson to them about power and its uses.

The security forces had quelled all of these disorders, but the trend was ominous. Moreover, Rios-Parkinson had already been briefed that the food projections were running just 62% of the levels called for in the Tri-annual Plan. That meant the recent ration cuts would not be the end of it – the rats would have to be cut again. He had been privy to some of the discussions of what to do about the chronic food and resource shortages over the last few months. No one at the table made any truly out-of-the-box suggestions, like deregulating the food production sector and returning control to the nominal owners of the farms, processing plants, and distribution companies. Instead, they agreed that the problem was likely saboteurs and wreckers whose selfishness was responsible for the nation's miserable output. New regulations would be drawn up, and Rios-Parkinson resolved to his comrades that he would prosecute and punish the offenders.

There was some talk of alleviating the shortages in the short term by stepping up purchases from foreign producers, but the huge commodity buys that were currently keeping the people from starving had had the effect of raising food prices world-wide, and the People's Republic was already short of cash. China and the EU,

117

though publicly supportive, were behind the scenes resisting the PRNA's demands for additional credit.

There was no discussion of ending the trade embargo with the United States. And there was not any discussion of how foreign nations were selling their own production to the People's Republic at inflated prices, then buying food for their own populace from the United States' prosperous, barely-regulated farmers.

Nor was there any discussion of ending the Special Rations program or closing the Restricted Shops for VIPs. Rios-Parkinson had no qualms when he had shared a pair of delicious filets with Amanda the evening before. After all, to provide his very best service to the People's Republic, he and those like him needed to be insulated from mundane concerns about material matters. Nor was there discussion of limiting the Security Force Special Rations that helped secure the loyalty of the people who wielded the guns.

Rios-Parkinson resolved that stronger measures were needed to control these outrageous betrayals by ungrateful social criminals. He would order that in the future, disorder at food centers in his region be always quelled by deadly force as the initial response. There would be zero tolerance for such disruptions from now on; he would set the example for the whole country in his area. And he expected his innovation would be rewarded.

The SUV did not bother stopping at checkpoints. The guards knew it and the ID transmitter alerted them moments before it even arrived. He was able to drive out of the security cordon around his neighborhood without even slowing down.

Once down from the hill, they made good time. Rios-Parkinson's focus was his reports – memos on operations, interrogation summaries, interesting transcripts from wiretaps and computer monitoring operations. The intercepts rarely identified traitors, and the people with the phones and the internet access his minions monitored were primarily connected members of the elite. What they provided him was information – who was sleeping with whom, who was stealing, that sort of thing. He rarely used any of it for prosecutions. He preferred to use it for leverage. It was remarkable how compliant people became when they found out they were compromised. He had learned that watching the Hillary Clinton email debacle of the mid-teens. If they have your communications, they have you, he noted, and he resolved to be the one who had them.

The Bernie Sanders Internal Security Complex occupied several skyscrapers in downtown Los Angeles. Most corporations departed for the US once the political and economic course of the newly split blue states became clear, leaving the huge buildings almost empty. The new government nationalized them, then proceeded to attempt to connect the buildings with a series of walkways and tunnels while simultaneously renovating them to meet the newly enacted green construction standards. This turned into an utter disaster; the bureaucrats knew nothing about managing massive building projects, and the people who did were long gone. By the time the only entity big enough to fill the towers – the internal security apparatus – moved in, the buildings were barely functional. They were unbearably hot in summer and frigid in the winter, and the elevators only worked intermittently. This is why Rios-Parkinson's massive office was on the second floor of the old Library Tower, rather than near the top.

The walls were of dark wood and covered with framed photographs of Rios-Parkinson with all manner of celebrities and legends. There was him with an ancient Hillary Clinton, another receiving a medal from President De Blasio, and another shaking the elderly Jesse Jackson's hand. Just after it was taken, the doddering Jackson asked if he was "One of them hymies," which Rios-Parkinson found extremely offensive. He hated that anyone might think him Jewish. It still galled him how the United States had remained Israel's staunch ally after the Split, ruining everything by cooperating to wipe out the Iranian nuclear program that could have ended the Zionist Entity forever. Hunting Israeli spies was second only to seeking out United States spies on his personal "To Do" list.

Jacob Wiseman was waiting in the outer office when Rios-Parkinson strode in, flanked by two beefy uniformed PBI tactical officers from his personal security detail.

"Bring him in," Rios-Parkinson had snapped as he walked past. Now the pair of goons marched Wiseman to the front of the massive oak desk. Rios-Parkinson sat in his black leather chair; Wiseman stood unsteadily.

"And?" the security chief began.

"They left yesterday," Wiseman said. "They were gone when I got back."

"I know that already. What else?"

"Nothing, Director."

"Nothing?" Rios-Parkinson replied, bored. He played with a pen on his desk. "No indication at all about where my hard drive might be?"

"No, only David knows. He won't say."

This displeased Rios-Parkinson. It meant he had to go forward with the more risky Plan B. But then, there was a fringe benefit – he would learn where Amanda really stood.

"You know, Jacob, I am very disappointed with you, and I simply do not trust you. You signed our dual loyalty disclaimer years ago and that clearly meant nothing to you. You still believed in your ridiculous superstitions and when you had the opportunity you betrayed your country."

"I'm sorry," Wiseman said miserably.

"And now that we caught you – did you really think we would not find out who took our hard drive? – you are about to betray your friends to save your own skin. So why should I believe anything you say?"

"I'm telling you the truth, everything I know! I'm cooperating!"

"We will see, will we not? And you have been in the building long enough to know what happens to enemies of the state who do not repent, correct? You do repent, right, Jacob?"

"Yes," Jacob replied softly. "Yes."

"And you have given up your silly religion too, right? Because the state can't allow dual loyalty. You are either obedient to your magical sky god or to the very real People's Republic of North America. You cannot be obedient to both."

"I will obey the People's Republic," Jacob said, lower lip quivering, tears in his eyes.

Rios-Parkinson smiles. "See, there you are. That was not so hard. You have a new god now. Can you feel its spirit?"

"Yes."

"Oh, good. Now get him out of here." The goons dragged Wiseman away.

Rios-Parkinson pushed the button on his intercom.

"Find Larsen and send him in." He leaned back in his chair and savored the feeling. The material rewards of his position were welcome after so many years of scraping by as an aspiring agitator and academic. The erotic rewards of Amanda and countless others before her were delightful, especially after his near-monastic first thirty years of life. But the power, the ability to take another human being and crush him, to force him through pure terror to renounce everything he loved, was the greatest reward of all.

And he could do that to nearly anyone he wanted at any time he wanted, with just a few exceptions. But someday, there would be no exceptions, no limit on his power. And all of the People's Republic would look to him and be afraid.

He sighed. *Soon.*

Larsen, his operations chief, entered the office after a sharp knock and a barked order to "Come."

"Any indication of internet transmission?" asked Rios-Parkinson.

"No, sir."

"We do not say 'sir' here in the People's Republic, Deputy. You know this. Your time in the patriarchal military of the former USA was long ago. I expect you to grow and adapt. Am I understood?"

"Of course, Director," Larsen said. "We're devoting all of our assets to monitoring for the alert software signal should they attach it to the internet. If they do, we will immediately remotely block it and locate its physical connection."

"Good. And?"

"Director, we have not reacquired them yet," he said, anticipating his boss's question.

"Then make sure you do when they try to approach Amanda," he replied, mildly annoyed.

"That's our plan. We have agents around the campus and in her classes. At 10:00 a.m. she has an institutional racism lecture. At 11:30 a.m. she has her self-criticism seminar. We'll cover her at lunch, but that might be difficult since she usually eats by the plaza, and there is a mandatory rape culture protest for all freshpeople, so we'll need to be close to her in case they try to use that to cover their approach."

"Do not let her see our surveillance."

"I've made that very clear to the agents. Most of them will appear to be students. I briefed them myself this morning – they smell very convincing."

"What about the afternoon?"

"She has her United States Crimes lecture then a People's Chemistry lab."

"Will you be able to cover her in the laboratory?"

Larsen shook his head. "It's a lecture class. They don't do actual chemistry experiments because hands-on work privileges…." Larsen paused, uncomfortable. "I'm not actually sure who it privileges, but someone, so in the lab class the professor talks about how science is intersectional with issues of gender, race and class."

"You just ensure that when they find her you are watching, and you do not lose them once you do. They are going to lead me to my hard drive."

Larsen nodded. "But sir," he said, unsure how to broach the issue. "What if she refuses to go with them?"

"Don't call me 'sir' again, Deputy."

"I apologize. It's hard to rid myself of my unconscious sexism," said Larsen. Rios-Parkinson raised an eye brow.

"And…racism too." Rios-Parkinson nodded, then went on.

"Well, obviously I expect her to refuse to go with them and to report them," Rios-Parkinson said. "When she does, you follow them. But she may feign cooperation to draw them deeper, so be ready to track them if she does. She is extremely loyal to the People."

"Of course," Larsen replied. "Of course she is."

"And when we take them after they obtain the disc, my own tactical team executes the assault. Everyone else mans – I mean *peoples* – the perimeter and stays back. Are we clear?"

Larsen was well-aware of the sensitivity of the lost hard drive, and equally well-aware of the precarious nature of his own position should the rising star to which he had hitched his career falter. "Very clear. I have a ten-man team ready. I mean ten-*person* team. Although all the persons are men."

13.

Westwood was thriving, with stores, restaurants and coffee shops hopping with student business from the campus of UCLA that lay just to the north. To the west was the former veteran's cemetery, recently built over with new apartments, then the 405 freeway. A wall along the east side of the elevated highway ensured one could not simply pull over to the shoulder and jump down into the sector. If you did not go through a gate past security's scrutiny, you were not coming in.

Those who came in every day, enduring the long lines and the grumbling guards, were easy to distinguish from the residents. Those living inside the sector were different than other people because they smiled; their apparel was fresh, their shoes not falling to pieces. Those who came in to work, to tend to and cater to their betters, were decked out in drab, worn clothing, at least for the short time that they were walking to their jobs – none of them could bring in cars, even if they had cars and could have found and afforded the gasoline.

A few years before, when the contrast between those from inside and outside of the various special sectors throughout the country became simply too embarrassing to ignore, the People's Republic imposed a new rule. Uniforms. Upon their arrival at work inside a security sector, the workers would change into a unisex costume of black work shoes, denim pants and light blue work shirts. On their chest, above their left shirt pocket, they would wear a name tag that identified their place of employment. In their pocket they would have, at all times and upon pain of arrest, their identification card showing that they had permission to be inside.

"Imagine being a blue shirt. You come in here every day, work like a dog, see all this, then stand in line for three hours to buy food before you go home to a house with no electricity," Turnbull said.

"Yay, socialism," Junior replied, watching a blue shirt step off into the wet gutter to get out of the path of a half-dozen smiling, laughing students.

Turnbull eased the Lexus through the crowded streets, looking for a place to park. Students, the children of the wealthy and connected, wandered along the sidewalks, oblivious to blue shirts manning the kiosks, fetching their lattes, sweeping up the litter the students casually dropped on the ground.

"They seem to have it pretty good in here," Junior observed.

"Some of them do," Turnbull said. He hit the brakes – traffic had suddenly come to a halt in front of him.

"What is it?" Junior asked.

The answer came not from Turnbull but in the form of shouts and yelling, clanging and whistles. Up ahead, at the next intersection, past the Mercedes-Benzes and BMWs, they could make out what appeared to be a parade heading east to west in the middle of the street. There were at least 100 people, some carrying signs, a few manipulating giant puppets that bore a passing resemblance to notable officials of the United States. And they were chanting:

"Racism, sexism, we say no! The USA has got to go!"

A middle aged man with a bullhorn and a man-bun walked along at the side of the column, adding his own input:

"Stop rape culture! Silence equals death! We demand liberation from corporate tyranny!"

To the right of the Lexus, in an Apple store, a trio of students took a moment to look up from their iPhone 16s and glance at the passing protesters. Then they looked back down and continued with their feverish pecking.

As the protestors trudged on, a few uniformed PBI officers looked over, disinterested. They made no move to clear the road.

"I think this is a scheduled protest," Turnbull said. "Every time I'm here, just like clockwork, there's a bunch of these idiots walking down that street with their signs and puppets."

"Planned spontaneity?"

"That's the best kind. Let the kids and the radicals blow off a little steam every day and maybe they don't try to actually upset the apple cart."

The passing parade had moved off to the west and traffic was moving again. There was a parking structure to their right and Turnbull pulled in. A sign proudly announced that there was no charge to park, parking fees being, apparently, racist and imperialist.

They found a racism and imperialism-free parking space on the second floor.

"Interesting how fighting racism and all the other -isms always seems to require measures that make things better for rich people," Turnbull said as he exited the Lexus, being careful to keep the driver's door from scratching the Tesla parked beside them. A power cord ran from the Tesla to the outlet on the wall, and the indicator indicated it was charging. There were no brownouts in the special sectors.

They headed out to the street, blending in with the served caste rather than the serving class, their faces down, both in dark glasses. They passed a pair of PBI thugs hassling a Latino man wearing a worker's uniform, demanding his papers; the conflict drew not even a glance from anyone else. Turnbull relaxed a bit after a few steps. His plan, had they been stopped, formed instantly and unconsciously. It was to punch the first one in the throat, draw, kill the other with two shots to the forehead, and then put two hollow points more into the face of the one struggling to breath.

The campus began where the shops and restaurants stopped – there was no signage demarcating the campus from the community. There was only a sign pointing toward the Hillary Clinton Medical Center – as a kid, Turnbull had gotten stitches there back when it was named after Ronald Reagan. Below the sign was a bank of newspaper racks. The *Los Angeles Times*, which cost seven dollars and was printed on 8.5" x 11" newsprint, had a headline which read "PEOPLE'S REPUBLIC SETS NEW RECORDS FOR PRODUCTIVITY AND SOCIAL JUSTICE." A second above-the-fold article was titled "GOVERNMENT RELUCTANTLY AGREES TO PEOPLE'S DEMAND FOR UNPOSITIVE RATION ADJUSTMENTS IN SOLIDARITY WITH OPPRESSED PERSONS."

In the next box was the UCLA student paper, *The Daily Entity*. It had been *The Daily Bruin* until a few years before when a student from Marin County, who claimed to be part Cherokee, demanded that the name be changed because bears were sacred to his people. The new symbol of UCLA was a circle; the original smiling bear had been changed to a stick figure human, but despite its lack of sex-specific characteristics it was deemed too "cispatriarchal," so the symbol morphed into what was essentially a

125

happy face. Then there were objections to that image by the visually impaired community, because it had eyes, and by protesters against "facial normativity" who passionately argued that the presence of a nose and mouth "disempowered and invalidated" the deformed. The present circle had its critics too; the student government was scheduled to discuss eliminating the mascot altogether. UCLA's new mascot was likely to be, literally, nothing.

The *Entity's* headline chronicled the latest defeat for the UCLA Entities basketball team; a photo showed the wheelchair-bound center forward going for the ball against her 380 pound gender indeterminate opponent. The headline read "ALL PEOPLE ARE VICTORIOUS WITH INCLUSIVE SPORTS!" Reading further down, one would find the final score was 6-9 in favor of the Stanford Reproductive Freedoms.

Perhaps fifty yards beyond inside the campus was a bronze statue of a smiling man, his right hand raised in greeting, with a plaque reading "People's Hero Barack Obama – 'No Justice, No Peace'." It was unclear whether this was honoring him for his presidency or his work as the United Nations Secretary General, which in some quarters was widely hailed as a smashing success despite the numerous acts of war and terrorism, economic disruption, and the Splitting apart of the United States that occurred during his tenure. Before fraternities were banned, one caused outrage by sticking a nine iron in his hand as a prank. Those not arrested for this hate crime were either expelled or forced into extensive reeducation to root out their manifest racism.

Past the statue in a small plaza was another protest, though "protest" might not be the correct word for the gathering of a couple dozen students and, clearly, nonstudents, in a drum circle. A tattered banner read "Drumming for Soldarity with the Peoples of Color of the People's Republic." There was no "i" in the word "Solidarity." If any of the students walking by during the banner's long lifetime had paid the protestors any mind at all, one might have noted the error.

Another speaker just a few steps beyond standing on a box outside an administration building, shouting demands that the government "stomp out the racists and deniers and the wreckers who refuse to support the People's Republic!"

"Aren't protestors supposed to actually protest *against* the status quo?" whispered Junior. That's how it had worked at college back home.

"I don't think the authorities would take real well to actual protests. They prefer a festival of acclimation. Oh, wait, *there's* some actual protesting," Turnbull said. "Look over there. The shaved headed women with piercings."

"Which ones?" asked Junior, confused. "The ones in overalls?"

"No, the other ones, the ones in old timey bathing suits. See their signs? They're protesting the rape culture here at UCLA. I assume that's allowed by the authorities to make sure the university stays in line. Can't let alternate power centers develop."

"Okay, I'm already sick of this place. So how do we find my sister? Let's get her and get out of here."

"According to Jacob's schedule, she's in class right now about halfway across campus," Turnbull replied, looking at his watch. "We can get her as she leaves. Assuming she doesn't freak out when she sees you."

"She won't."

"No, maybe she won't. But I'd feel better if she knew we were coming," Turnbull said, and then stopped and looked at Junior. "Do you *think* she knows we are coming?"

"What? We haven't even tried to contact her."

"I know. That would have been too dangerous. They could have intercepted the message. Then we could have been made by the PBI. Except, we *were* made by the PBI."

"You sure they were after us and not trying to quell the riot?"

"I don't know. But I felt like we were being watched the minute we left David's, and then the bad guys show up at the food center. But since then, nothing."

"You think we're being followed now?"

"I don't feel it, but…come on, in here," Turnbull said, pulling Junior with him into a classroom building.

The central hallway was light and airy – blue-clad janitors were sweeping up while oblivious students passed them as if the workers were invisible. To the right were three doors, each opening into a large lecture hall. The nearest one was wide open. From inside, a high, bored voice intoned, "In people's math, we ignore the racial and privileged freight that comes with so-called numbers, and reach for a deeper narrative of class, gender, and girth issues that it gives rise to. Two plus two is *not* four. It's *oppression*."

There was a muffled question, then the first voice responded: "Yes, that will be on the final. Which is open book, open notes, and a collective effort."

Turnbull and Junior huddled under a stairwell, away from the passing students, next to a garbage can and six differently denominated recycling containers. A hand scrawled poster on the wall next to them from something called the "Ear Justice Conspiracy" warned that "Speaking Is Hearist!"

"Think about it," Turnbull said. "They follow us from David's but they don't grab us. Why?"

"I don't know."

"They want something else more than they want us."

"The hard drive?"

"Has to be."

"They must know we don't have it."

"They must know we don't have it *yet*."

"If they know about the damn hard drive and about us then they know what we're after here. It's gotta be somebody in David's group."

"That Jacob guy."

"Yeah, the guy who told us where to find Amanda."

"Oh shit," said Junior. "We gotta warn David."

"No, they'll be listening for that. We try to call him and they'll know their plan is blown. They'll bust right in, grab David and try to beat out of him where the hard drive is."

"So what do we do here? They gotta be watching Amanda for when we show up to get her."

"Yeah," said Turnbull. "That's how they reacquire us. They watch her until we come and get her, and then we lead them to the hard drive."

"And then they take us."

"Yeah," said Turnbull. "But that leaves a question about Amanda unanswered. Now, they have to know that we can't really drag her kicking and screaming out of a crowded campus if she doesn't want to come. So either she knows what's up and *pretends* to go with us willingly, or they haven't told her shit because they *think* she'll go with us willingly."

"Told you she would come with us," said Junior proudly.

"Yeah, unless she's setting us up."

"That wouldn't happen."

"She *is* the head gestapo guy's girlfriend. You need to be ready for the possibility she'll sell you out as quickly as she would me."

"Not her."

"I hope you're right. But it's pretty clear we can't approach her here."

"So what do we do?"

"We get her somewhere else."

"Where?"

"Somewhere where there aren't 30,000 people around. Come on, let's head back to that administration building we passed."

They made their way back the way they came, which rubbed Turnbull the wrong way. He dealt with it, and surreptitiously scanned in front of them, behind them, and to their sides trying to spot surveillance, keeping his head down just enough not to draw suspicion but to frustrate any cameras peering at them.

Nothing.

The guy on the box was gone. His space was taken by three salty looking women with a sign calling themselves "Shriek Your Abortion!" Which was precisely what they were doing, loudly, shrilly, and in great, graphic detail. Apparently, abortion being legal and subsidized was not enough – everyone also had to hear all about it. But as loud as they were, not a student paused as they passed; the women were simply more human wallpaper, the background noise of the blue America university experience.

The administrative building's main entrance led to a waiting room with no exit, just a bank of mostly unoccupied service windows and long lines in front of the two that were open. They scooted around the perimeter looking for another way in. On the north side, out of sight of the main walkway, they stumbled upon a blue shirt walking out of an "AUTHORIZED PERSONS ONLY" door. Turnbull caught it as it shut. The worker stared blankly for a moment at the suit-clad man before her, shrugged, and walked away. Not her problem. Turnbull and Junior slipped inside.

It was quiet in the building. They moved down the hallway, trying to radiate the impression that they belonged there. Most of the personnel were blue shirts; none dared question the suited men. Some senior administrators passed by, and they too declined to engage.

The first floor contained no likely offices, so they went up the stairs to the second floor. More blue shirts hustled by pushing carts full of papers – apparently it was not a paperless office, something that struck Junior as exceedingly odd. You barely saw paper back home.

"DATA SERVICES" read a sign on a door, and they went in. The room was rather large, with a dozen cubicles each manned by a blue-shirted worker typing away on a desktop computer. They walked to the very last cubicle, where a young blue shirt sat alone pecking at his keyboard. Looking over his shoulder at the screen, Turnbull satisfied himself that he could figure it out.

Sensing them looming above him and seeing their unsmiling faces, he stopped, clearly concerned. Turnbull knelt down.

"Yes?" the worker asked, his voice unsteady.

"Hi," Turnbull said. "You have access to student records?"

The young man nodded. Turnbull read his name tag.

"Obviously, you're logged in, right Leon?"

Another nod.

"Okay, you need to take a piss."

The young man appeared puzzled but said nothing.

"Leon, you are going to stand up in a moment and go take a piss. When you come back, we'll be gone – forever – and you'll completely forget about us. Plus there'll be a thousand dollars under the keyboard. Okay?"

The man sat still; Turnbull could see on his face that he was working this unexpected development through in his mind.

"Now, it can go that way, in which you end up with a thousand dollars, or it can end up in another way which you don't even want to think about. So," asked Turnbull. "Do you need to take a piss or not, Leon?"

Leon swallowed, but after a moment's hesitation, the blue shirt stood up and wordlessly walked off toward the door. Turnbull nodded at Junior, who followed and planted himself outside the door as security in case Leon decided to narc them out.

Turnbull planted himself on Leon's seat and went to the student personal information menu. When the query window came up, he typed in "Ryan, Amanda," and hit return.

With time to kill, they decided to eat. Their walk off campus back into Westwood Village was uneventful. Turnbull amused himself by figuring out where he would place ambushes to bushwhack the numerous uniformed PBI patrols that ensured this island of prosperity was well-insulated from the turmoil outside the walls.

They chose to eat at what had been a Mexican place and was now denominated "Respectful Latinx Cuisine." Turnbull vaguely remembered the name had been "Pedro's," but that name was long gone. Instead, it was now simply "Restaurant," as were most of the other eating places around town.

The place was bustling, and there were actually menus, menus that even provided choices. The prices were high – a plate of tacos was $520 – but Turnbull noted that there was no reference to ration cards. Apparently that was yet another rule that did not apply inside the sector.

They waited a few minutes to be seated. Besides businessmen and women, there were a good number of students, half looking freshly pressed and the other half looking fresh from the hamper. Many wore light blue and yellow UCLA sweatshirts or hoodies, all with the circle mascot. Blue shirts hustled between tables, carrying trays, taking orders.

They were seated at a two-top by a street front window near a table of sour-looking male and female students, one of whom wore a "Class of '34" t-shirt. The students were complaining about their classes and the oppression of homework. Turnbull tuned them out and looked at the menu.

"Tacos," he said.

"You think they'll be any good?" asked Junior.

"Mexican food in California went downhill fast when the Mexicans quit coming," Turnbull replied quietly. "I assume if Mexico hadn't built the wall with the reparations money the PR gave them, Mexico might have some good American food by now, thanks to our emigrants."

"Okay, tacos. Hey, it even says 'beef.' Lucky I took my antibiotics this morning."

"I'm sure the food will be good to go. Can't be food poisoning the future leaders of the People's Republic."

"This is bullshit," hissed the girl in the "Class of '34" sweatshirt. A young, Hispanic blue shirt man stood at her table, his notepad out, his face blank.

"I know what I want and I want it!" she said. "Are you stupid? What the fuck is wrong with you?"

The blue shirt mumbled an apology, but '34 girl was having none of it.

"You better stop disrespecting me or I'll fucking tell your boss to throw you the fuck out of here."

"I didn't…"

"You think he's going to listen to you or to me?"

"I'll check in the back and see if they have it," the blue shirt said, remarkably evenly.

"You better," the girl said. The server left and she turned to her friends. "After all we do for them, they treat us like shit."

"You ought to complain and get him fired," another told her. "Otherwise, they'll think they can do whatever they want."

Turnbull was casually covering the side of his face with his palm, seeming to shrink into the chair. Attention to his general area was always unwelcome, and everyone had been looking over at the ruckus – mostly with approval for the student putting the uppity worker in his place.

"I hate it here," Junior said.

"Not long now. We get her tonight, we rendezvous with the hard drive, and we head home. Easy."

"Easy," Junior replied, but uncertainly.

The blue shirt returned, but he came to Turnbull and Junior's table instead, notepad out.

"Can I take your order…" he began, but he was cut off.

"Hey shithead, what are you doing with them? What the fuck is wrong with you?" It was '34.

Turnbull saw it in the man's face, the culmination, the breaking point, and he braced himself for whatever bad was going to happen, because something bad was certainly going to happen and it was utterly out of Turnbull's control.

The blue shirt turned to face the student's table; '34 leaned back, smiling at her success with her petty humiliations. The blue

132

shirt, for his part, said nothing. He simply reached onto the table beside one of '34's comrades, grabbed a table knife, and leapt at his tormentor.

'34's expression changed in a fraction of a second from smug satisfaction to sheer terror as the blue shirt screamed "Fucking whore!" and brought the dull knife down over and over again, plunging it shallowly into her shoulder, then her chest, then her face.

Her tablemates scattered; she shrieked. The knife was going in, but it was dull and there was more blood than actual damage outside of the rent across her right cheek. Yet the blue shirt was continuing to try and gut her there and then.

One of the males with her tried to pull off the berserk server, but another blue shirt came up from the side holding a drink tray and swung it with all his might like a scythe across the student's face, smashing his nose and spattering blood over the table. He went down to the floor, and the server continued to pound his prone, frantic victim with the edge of the tray.

Across the room, the rest of the patrons were stunned. And the other blue shirts were inspired. One server dumped a sizzling plate of fajitas into the décolletage and lap of the blonde companion of an older man in an expensive suit. Another brought a beer bottle down on the head of a bewildered Asian student; foam and blood flowed down his face. A blue shirted woman attacked another diner's face with her bare hands, clawing at her victim's eyes.

Turnbull was on his feet now, glancing over to Junior to see what his situation was. Junior was reaching for his weapon – Turnbull shook his head "No" and motioned toward the exit. A plate flew toward them and shattered on their table.

"Oh, awesome," muttered Turnbull, trying to spot a safe path out, but everyone was now on their feet, fighting, screaming, and/or panicking.

'34 had somehow escaped her chair and started running, but she plowed directly into Turnbull and bounced back, shaken and bloody, staring at him, her eyes imploring. The blue shirt was right behind her, coming at them both, his throat open to a punch. Turnbull made a quick decision and roughly pushed the girl back into the blue shirt's arms. She screamed again as the worker descended on her in a silvery blur of knife thrusts.

"Let's *go*," he said to the stunned Junior.

133

They moved, Turnbull in the lead, pushing or throwing out of the way anyone in their path. Halfway to the exit, which was choked with terrified patrons trying to escape, a wide-eyed blue shirt wielding a chair blocked their way. At his feet was the crumpled body of the student he had just smashed over the head.

Turnbull shook his head "No," but the blue shirt only saw another well-dressed elite tormentor. He charged, the chair held high. Turnbull pivoted left, grabbing the man's forearms, using his weight to throw him down to the floor. A heel kick to the sternum kept the worker down for good. Junior hopped over the wounded man and followed Turnbull into the chaos.

The front door was a no-go – it was jammed and besides, a pair of busboys was beating on the clump of escapees with potted artificial trees that they wielded like maces. On one of the waiting benches, slumped over to his left, was the three-piece suited restaurant manager; someone had shoved a fork through his right eye.

"Kitchen!" Turnbull said, turning against the flow. He pushed through the surging crowd, almost as if he were doing the breast stroke. One panicked man grabbed his left arm; Turnbull pounded his nose flat with his right fist and kept moving. The swinging doors to the kitchen were just ahead.

Junior turned in time to see at least two black uniformed PBI men with AKs out through the front window. Inside the restaurant, the blue shirt who started it all stood up over '34's inert body, panting, covered with blood. The PBI men opened fire on automatic, tearing him up, his body twitching and jerking as it was pushed backwards and to the ground. But several others, some patrons, some workers, caught rounds in the background and dropped too. Then a blur of blue shirts hit the two PBI men from the flank and they disappeared from view.

Turnbull burst through the swinging double doors and was confronted with a blue shirt cook packing an oversized meat cleaver. It flashed as the man swung it, but Turnbull dodged and the blade planted deep into one of the doors. The cook pulled on it, his arm taut and therefore vulnerable when Turnbull smashed down on the locked elbow with his full weight. The cook howled as blood spurted from his compound fracture.

134

A second cook approached, now with a long knife in his right hand and a skillet in his left. Turnbull drew his Glock in a smooth motion, aiming directly at the man's face.

"I am fucking tired of this shit," he shouted, moving forward, gun up. "Get the fuck out of my way or I will fucking end you. Three! Two!"

The cook complied, the blade and pan clanging on the floor as he turned and ran.

"The PBI is out front. They're shooting, but people are fighting them," Junior reported. "Is this the revolution? Is this it?"

"I don't know if this is *it*, but it sure looks like what I think *it* would look like," Turnbull answered. He bolted through the storage racks toward a door with an exit sign. Pushing it open, he carefully surveyed the rear alley. Nothing to see, but plenty of shots to be heard from around front. They put their Glocks away.

"Let's go," he said, running outside, followed by Junior.

They headed down the alley to the end, where it opened onto Gayley, one of Westwood Village's main arteries. The bucolic town of that morning was gone, replaced by a battlefield full of running, screaming people. Across the way, a blue shirted gardener was hitting a middle-aged man, wearing a half-way unbuttoned white shirt and several gold chains, over the head with a hoe.

A PBI trooper came up behind him and shot the gardener through the head with his AK, then moved on.

"Let's get to the car," Turnbull said. They were well-dressed so they would not attract any PBI attention, but those idiots were shooting wildly, and there was also the threat of enraged blue shirts along the way.

The chaos was clearly winding down. They ran east, sometimes against, sometimes with the flow of terrified civilians. It was a few minutes until they got to their parking structure, and it was calm inside. They went up to the second floor and found their Lexus unharmed. However, someone had thrown a trash can through the back window of the Tesla.

There was more commotion in the street out front. Junior and Turnbull walked over to the side of the building and looked down to the street below. PBI men were marching a half dozen blue shirts under guard. In the middle of the road, they halted the column and ordered the workers to their knees in a line.

135

"No way," Junior muttered.

Four PBI men behind them lifted their AKs and, on order, fired into the backs of the prisoners until all six sprawled dead on the pavement.

"Oh, shit," Junior said.

"That's insurgency, Junior," Turnbull said.

"They just shot them down right there in the open!"

"Yeah, that's how it works. You need to understand. When push comes to shove, when it gets real like it did today, when they are faced with a real threat, they are going to do whatever it takes to hold on to power. These aren't nice people. They aren't good people. They care about one thing, their own power, and when that's endangered they take no prisoners. Literally."

"So that's why you don't take prisoners either."

"I stopped playing nice back in Indian Country, kid. That good guy bullshit goes right out the window when the killing really starts."

"Okay, what now?"

"We wait," Turnbull replied. "We aren't going out on that road anytime soon anyway, and we aren't doing anything until tonight anyway. Let's get in the car and sleep."

"I wish we had at least gotten to eat."

"Yeah, I think the restaurant's going to be closed for a while. At least until they hire a new staff."

14.

It was a bad day for Martin Rios-Parkinson, meaning it was a bad day for everyone around him.

"You failed to reacquire them?" the Director asked Larsen. His aide shifted uncomfortably. Next to him stood, silently, three of Larsen's department heads, a man, a woman, and a non-binary wearing a flowered muumuu.

"They never showed up. We watched her all day. They never came anywhere near her."

"But they were there in Westwood, inside the secured sector we control, weren't they?"

More uncomfortable shifting. Rios-Parkinson turned his laptop around 180 degrees so Larsen could see the screen from the far side of the desk. It was displaying several freeze frames of grainy surveillance camera footage of Westwood Village taken that afternoon at the height of the chaos in the restaurant as it spilled outside. Rios-Parkinson tapped the screen, pointing out two vague shapes walking away from the melee.

"That would be them, correct? At least the software thinks so from their size and gait. Do you know something the software does not know?"

"There's no way to tell…"

"No, they just happen to be two gentlemen who appear to be the same ones who you have been trying and failing to monitor and who just happened to manifest in the middle of a rioting outbreak right in the middle of the Westside Sector. *My* sector, *my* responsibility."

Larsen swallowed, weighing a response. Rios-Parkinson did not wait for it.

"This is more than just a pair of intruders, more than just another pair of spies. They are here to incite. I am not having another Indiana explode on my watch, not in my city."

"No," said Larsen. He had fought in Southern Indiana, Indian Country, though you would never call it by that name out loud in the blue. Larsen still walked with a slight limp from a 40-pound homemade Tannerite bomb that a farmer turned guerilla had detonated with his .30-06 just as Larsen's armored personnel carrier rolled past down a country road on the way to shoot up an unruly town inside the Hoosier National Forest. The reds had sent in trainers to organize the populace just as the blues had almost managed to assert control over the rebellious region. Larsen was well aware of what a few operatives with combat experience could do in terms of mobilizing an angry population, especially one that had buried all of its many, many guns the minute the People's Republic announced it was banning the civilian possession of firearms.

"You need to find them," Rios-Parkinson said. "You need to do that tonight."

"Cyber Division is screening the web for likely searches and map queries. We also have the best photos we could download out to every sector gate," Larsen said.

"Yet you had them out this morning and they still got inside the sector without us picking them up."

"The pictures were grainy, with no good shots of their faces."

"Because they are trained in counter-surveillance. They are aware of cameras, and they kept their faces down, wore glasses, and they never looked at the lenses."

"We are devoting all of our efforts to finding them, Director."

"They obviously know we are looking for them. Do you need more men – I mean personnel?"

"All you can spare."

"Which would be none," said Rios-Parkinson. "We are still engaged in arresting those associated with the various unrest incidents, including the Westwood riot. If you had not shot all of the ones taken into custody at the scene, we might have gotten some information from them about how our guests managed to inspire them to murder a number of our Westside citizens in broad daylight this afternoon."

Larsen said nothing in his own defense; they both knew that Rios-Parkinson had ordered that maximum force be applied to suppress mobs. The lack of prisoners Rios-Parkinson was lamenting was a direct result of his direct order to summarily execute on the spot anyone caught engaged in "lawless rebellion against the will of the People."

There was nothing left to say on that topic, so Larsen moved on. "The team is prepared to clear the Jews' building on your order, Director. The PSF will secure the perimeter. Surveillance teams are still in place."

"Keep them back. I do not want them knowing we are watching. They are not to have any warning. But nothing happens until I order it, and I will not order it until the spies have the hard drive and we have the spies."

"I understand, Director."

"You had better. Now get out," said Rios-Parkinson. Larsen turned and walked out, followed by the man, the woman, and the other, xis muumuu rustling as xe walked.

Rios-Parkinson sat back in his leather chair once the door slammed shut. The reports were uniformly bad. The ration cuts applied to Privilege Level 5 and below, meaning almost everyone, and the impacted majority was angry. There were outbreaks of violence everywhere along the West Coast, his area. It made him feel only slightly better to know that the East Coast was doing no better, and perhaps even worse. Near Boston, a routine anti-firearms raid had led to a shootout with a bunch of rebels, leaving several PBI and PSF officers dead. The town where it happened was called Concord; Rios-Parkinson had a sense that name was significant somehow, but because his study of history had focused mostly upon America's legacy of oppression he could not quite put his finger on why.

Still, it was bad enough in his own backyard. In San Francisco, mobs of largely oppressed peoples had looted several food centers. Their irrational ingratitude angered him; the People's Republic had given them so much after liberating them from the tyranny of the United States and now they could not even take on this small sacrifice in the name of the greater good. The dozens of deaths his forces inflicted quelling that unrest were a just, measured response to these hate crimes.

He picked up the phone and called the West Coast Media Justice Ombudsperson, who was on his speed dial.

"Delores, hello, this is Director Rios-Parkinson," he said.

The Ombudsperson replied cautiously, as she always did when addressing him. "Yes, Director. How may I assist you?"

"Yes, I am going to need you to emphasize in your messaging tonight and tomorrow that this criminal looting and counter-progressive rioting is not going to be tolerated by the internal security forces. You may direct your outlets to explain how deadly force is authorized to preserve order."

"But Director," the Ombudsperson replied. "Our messaging guidance was to not mention any unrest or violent counter-progressive acts at all." This was true; the Ombudsman had been told that the subject of unrest was to be ignored, and she had duly informed all of the licensed media and journalism outlets she oversaw of this mandatory guidance in her daily messaging memorandum. The memo had instead directed that stories focus on the groundswell of enthusiasm for the new ration cuts, with emphasis on patriotic citizens who were eager to sacrifice even more to ensure the coming triumph of progressivism.

And the outlets had responded obediently. Channel 5, formerly KTLA and now called "The Voice of the Voiceless," had run a lengthy interview segment on the work of a UCLA nutrition professor regarding how an ultra-low calorie diet actually improves health and longevity. But because the professor was a Jewish male, a female student named Nasser was chosen to appear on camera to do the actual interview, which she conducted from behind her burka.

"I did not say that you should mention the unrest, only that you will explain the *consequences* of any unrest," Rios-Parkinson replied impatiently.

"Of course, Director. I understand."

Rios-Parkinson hung up and drummed his fingers on his desk.

Thanks to a phone call he did not expect, Rios-Parkinson had an appointment at 6 o'clock, but not in his office. It was across the street and down Figueroa, only a few minutes by foot, but he took his SUV anyway. It was worth the carbon cost not to break a sweat in the sun.

The vehicle turned off to the right into the ramp underground leading to what had been a massive parking lot before the climate laws ended most citizen automobile use. Fewer cars on the road made his life, and the lives of the others still authorized private vehicles, much more convenient. But what Rios-Parkinson really appreciated about the climate laws was how much control over the masses they provided the elite. Global warming, he mused, was the best thing that ever happened to progressivism.

His office had called ahead and he was received underground by staff members who shepherded him and his security goons Arthur and Sam to an elevator. Arthur hit the single button – this was an express elevator that went only to the top and the bottom subfloor. It actually worked; important people needed to go to the top floor and so what was necessary to make the elevator function was done.

The doors opened to sunlight – the lounge was light and airy, with soft music provided by a gentlemen at the piano off to the side of the foyer. The bartender stood awaiting requests before a remarkably well-stocked bar. A dozen security officers stood waiting for their principals; his own guards joined them, for the lounge was not for the likes of them. Rios-Parkinson ignored the goons and the music, his eyes flitting from one well-dressed, well-fed guest to another, searching.

He knew most of the faces, and their expressions upon seeing him ranged from fear to quiet disgust. He filed those away; he would address them later. Right now, he was searching for one man.

There, in the prime southwest corner, of course, set off by a buffer of four to five tables from the other, lesser diners, sat his guest. The *maître d'* approached, nervous but solicitous. Rios-Parkinson ignored him, making his way past the other diners and over to the man in the perfect blue pinstripe suit with the deep red silk tie.

Odd, but he had a black leather bag of impeccable quality by his feet. Normally, one of his security guards would be holding it in the foyer.

The man saw him, smiled warmly and stood, extending his right hand. Was this a provocation? Shaking hands was publicly discouraged as emblematic of unequal power relations, but among themselves the elite still performed the old ritual. No, Rios-Parkinson assessed, it was not a calculated insult, but a message that something was serious, that there was no time for the usual kabuki dances that they performed in public.

"Senator Harrington," Rios-Parkinson said, shaking the extended tanned hand.

"Director," replied the senator, sitting down as Rios-Parkinson took his own seat. "I am so glad you could meet me on such short notice."

"Well, it is always a pleasure, Senator," Rios-Parkinson lied. He knew Senator Richard Harrington of California quite well; in fact, before coming he had reviewed the special file his team had assembled on the senator. It was just like the ones he kept on all the major political figures on the West Coast, except only thinner. Not much in there of use; routine phone and electronic surveillance had not uncovered anything that might provide leverage either. Harrington certainly had an active sexual life for a sixty year old, but nothing useful there. The senator made sure to include as many men as women in his rotation so there could be no irritating claims of cisnormativity that some enemy might use to derail him.

Still, Harrington was deeply connected, and since senators were now directly appointed they had to be extremely politically savvy. Each Senate seat was like a little principality unto him or her or xes self. Harrington had negotiated his own precarious position after the Split remarkably well, for rich males of English descent – his mother had tracked his family back to the Mayflower, but he had suppressed that tidbit effectively – the People's Republic hardly seemed fertile ground to cultivate a political career. But he had managed to do it. A little sexual flexibility here, a little use of compromising information against opponents there, and he had improbably remained in the highest circles of power.

Rios-Parkinson resolved not to underestimate him.

"I am glad you suggested we meet. I am sure it is something important."

"Oh," the senator replied. "It most certainly is."

The senator reached down to his bag and pulled out a small, oval electronic device with Chinese characters and several buttons and lights. He placed it on the table and pushed the green button, which illuminated a small green light and made the object whir quietly on the table.

"Director, I assume you won't mind if I scramble any microphones that someone might have emplaced here. I'd like to be able to talk with you…frankly."

"Of course," said the Director, hiding his irritation. Of course there were microphones. They were *his* microphones, at least two at

142

every table. Often people would forget themselves and the next morning the Director would be delivered the most interesting transcripts, which he filed away for future use.

"I picked up this little item in China," the senator said. "Obviously illegal here. You aren't going to arrest me for having it, now are you?"

"Well, Senator, I am less concerned with this item than with what you might want to say that requires it. Are you planning on saying something no one else can hear?"

"I am, Director."

"Something compromising?"

"Oh, yes. Certainly compromising. But not to me."

"I do not understand."

"Well, allow me to put it in context, Director. And that context is that you seem to be losing control of the area in which you have been appointed to keep order."

Rios-Parkinson bristled, which the senator noted. He continued.

"There were almost two dozen deaths in Westwood this afternoon. Right inside the secured sector. You know, nobody notices a food riot by the hungry slobs out there outside the walls. Yes, I know they are getting more common, especially after the ration debacle, and I know you have given orders to use the force necessary to shut them down."

"We will be focusing on the economic criminals too, Senator."

"Economic criminals – don't talk to me like I'm one of those true believing fools. And I'm not going to insult your intelligence by treating you like you're one either. I ran companies before all of this. I know how to make things, how to get them to the people. The people we work with, that you and I compete against, they don't, but they still naturally accrued all the power to do so themselves. They cannot abide anyone else choosing or doing or thinking without their approval, and that's why we can't even feed ourselves anymore."

Rios-Parkinson remained calm, fascinated that the senator was saying these things to him. *Why would he do that? What did he want?*

"We could not compete with the reds after the Split, so we just stopped trying. We shut the borders and pretended the rest of the

143

country was not even there anymore. Do you think they have hungry people rioting for food in Dallas, in Kansas City, in Atlanta?"

Rios-Parkinson had read the intelligence summaries on the United States – the accurate ones, not the ones modified and massaged for consumption by those less ideologically solid than he. He knew the truth too.

Harrington leaned in. "We don't produce anything, except propaganda to stoke fake outrage so people forget they're hungry. And since we don't make anything or grow anything or pump anything out of the ground because of global warming or social justice or why ever, there's no more money coming in. We are near the end of our credit line. No more loans. Russia, China, the EU already hold everything of value we have as collateral, and they are sick of carrying us. Do you know what that means? If we don't change, we collapse, and when this all falls apart, people like you and I are going to be swinging from broken lamp posts."

"We can suppress the unrest, control it."

"With who? Your PSF and PBI thugs? Pretty soon your own people will be leading the riots. They already rob citizens in the streets outside the secure sector – don't think I don't know about that. But there is an answer."

Rios-Parkinson silently considered what Harrington was telling him. Unmet expectations and anger were powerful weapons against an ossified establishment – he knew that from having exploited them himself before the Split.

The senator continued. "Remember the free market? Well, it works. And now we are seeing what happens when you replace it with a bunch of useless college professors, untalented artists, moronic movie stars, and San Francisco chardonnay sippers who think they can personally run every aspect of a country when they know absolutely nothing about how a country works."

"There is a reason you are telling me this. What is it?"

"I need your help, and you definitely need mine," the senator said.

"What help do I need from you, Senator?"

"Good," Harrington replied, smiling. "Enlightened self-interest. That's the right question. What can I do for you? Well, I can warn you that your problems have not gone unnoticed outside your little empire of the security services."

"The riots…"

"Not the riots. Well, not *just* the riots. That has people talking, important people. No, it's come to my attention that you have managed to lose a certain item that would be of great interest to people on both sides of the border. And that there are infiltrators – spies – here trying to get it."

Rios-Parkinson froze. The senator sat back in his chair.

"Did you think you were the only one who collects information?" the senator asked.

"How did you –"

"Don't bother asking. My informer network is nowhere near as extensive as yours, but what my intelligence assets lack in sheer quantity I like to think they make up in quality. But if I know, then other people know, or they *could* know, and you cannot have that."

No, he could not have that. The hard drive's files not only set out his entire informer network – that was bad enough – but provided proof of what loyal friend, devoted confidant, or faithful lover was actually an informer. The reds obviously wanted it for their own purposes, but here in the People's Republic, there would be two kinds of people seeking it: those being spied upon, and those doing the spying.

"If someone gets a hold of it, your position becomes precarious," Harrington said. "Like a man hanging out there on that ledge while another man pounds his fingers one by one with a ball-peen hammer."

The server, a young woman in a short skirt that would not play anywhere else in the PRNA, hovered a few feet away with two bottles of French sparkling water and two cups of ice. Harrington gestured for her to approach, and she dropped two coasters on the table then placed the glasses on them and filled them up without a word, leaving the bottle. Harrington remained silent, waiting. Rios-Parkinson's eyes never left him.

"Can I bring you something else, a drink maybe?"

"Go," said the Director, and the server vanished. Rios-Parkinson leaned forward.

"And you will help me by …"

"By not telling anyone about your fuck up."

"And in return for this gracious favor?

145

"Well, nothing now. You can bank that favor. Do you know what I mean by that, since we have largely done away with banking as part of our quest for ideologically unimpeachable impoverishment?"

"So sometime in the future, you anticipate requiring my assistance."

"Oh yes. You run the security apparatus on the West Coast. I expect – assuming you solve your problems with the rioting and the spies and the missing list – that you will run the national security apparatus in the not too distant future, something I can certainly assist in making happen. National Director O'Malley is, well, you understand. Ineffective. A figurehead. But you could make that job into something more, bring the East Coast under your control, and then you would be a very useful ally for an ambitious man like myself."

"You want to be the President?"

"I do," said the senator. "And once I am, I intend to stay president for a good while. And to do that, to keep from being hanged from a lamppost whose lamp hasn't worked since 2028, I need to bring people some measure of prosperity. I at least need to ensure they can eat. And if I am seen to feed them, they will love me and no one will be able to topple me."

"So I watch your back?" said Rios-Parkinson.

"Yes, but not just when I am maneuvering for position. Once I have it, I will need to reform this dysfunctional abortion we call the People's Republic. And when I say 'reforms,' as every former communist country whose standard of living has outstripped ours, from Albania to Vietnam knows, I mean market reforms."

"They'll resist."

"They don't have any guns. You have them all."

Rios-Parkinson took a sip on his fizzy water, then put the glass back down.

"There might be loyalty problems within my organization. We have our own internal politics."

"And you have a golden opportunity to deal with that, Director. Don't tell me you have not thought through the upside of riots and spies – more authority for you to address those problems. More autonomy in selecting your subordinates. I am well aware that you and the PBI are as hobbled and handicapped by quotas and

146

regulations governing who can be appointed to what job as everyone else. If you perform, you may earn the leeway to put competent and, most importantly, loyal people in positions of responsibility. No more having to promote someone into a position you need to be able to count on just because he chose to snip his prick off and sand down his Adam's apple. And that way, when the time comes, you will lead and you can be confident that they will follow."

"So, you are proposing a long term alliance?"

"I am. Because of all the people jockeying for position in this great game of ours, you seem to be the most ideologically flexible. I don't think you believe this bullshit. Nor do I think you disbelieve it. I think you don't care about it, not even a little. I think all you care about is yourself, and that is the kind of man I can find useful."

Rios-Parkinson took another drink of his water, not looking away. He returned it to its coaster.

"And my role?"

"My second. I need what they used to call an executive officer, someone to do the things I can't. When I leave – I have 20 years or so on you – then it's all yours. Hopefully functioning so that we aren't always on edge waiting for starving people to start rioting."

"That is the long term. Short term, what do you want?"

"I want you to get your shit together. I want you to crush the riots. I want you to get your list back. And I want you to get those spies."

"I intend to. And I intend to do it soon."

"Good," said Harrington. "Oh, and there is another thing. There is a lot of talk about that red state whore you are shacked up with. It makes you look weak, and far too cis besides. You need to get rid of her."

Rios-Harrington smiled. He was well aware that what had been a status symbol was becoming a liability in his circles.

"Oh yes," he replied, "I intend to do that too."

It was near 9:30 p.m. when they left the downtown complex. Before the Split, the roads in West LA would have still been clogged even at that hour, but with Arthur driving and Sam in the front seat, the black SUV made excellent time. They ignored even the working traffic signals, and the PSF cruisers ignored them. You never interfered with a black SUV.

147

They headed across the city into the Western Sector through the same gate Turnbull and Junior had used that morning. A long line of blue shirts, still in street clothes, waited patiently at the employee entrance for admittance for the night shift. It was taking longer than usual because the guards were wanding each of them for weapons. The guards waved the SUV right through; Rios-Parkinson noted that there were clearly extra guards scrutinizing both those coming in and going out.

The traffic was much heavier inside; Beverly Hills and its environs were brightly lit and festive. People walked along the sidewalks and dined in sidewalk cafes. Musicians set up at intervals to serenade those out and about. Amanda was constantly pestering him to take her out on a Friday night; he had no interest in that. Her constant assertion of her needs and wants was something he would not miss in the slightest after he had Arthur and Sam take her away and shoot her.

She was replaceable, a fungible commodity. The man who had been ignored before all this now understood that there were plenty of women to choose from if you had the power of life and death.

They continued north on the residential streets twisting and climbing up the hills to the north. Unlike out there, beyond the sector's walls, these houses were mostly occupied. Many of these people had a reason to leave; most of those who did were quickly replaced by bureaucrats who managed to obtain residence by default in the homes seized either from the worms who left for the red or from those who failed to make their reparations payments.

They turned onto his street, just below the crest of the hill, Arthur radioed ahead that they were coming and received a confirmation from the house. They drove along the winding, narrow street until they approached his gate. It opened before them and they drove in and parked. Amanda's red Nissan was in its place. The city spread out before him, the Western Sector bright, the rest of the city – other than downtown to the east and the Airport and the South Bay Sector to the southwest – were generally dark, with only a few intermittent flickers of light piercing the black.

The house itself was spectacular, a gift from one of the worms who fled after the Split. The backyard extended down the hill

148

to a flat plateau the size of a basketball court where the pool and gardens were.

Followed by Arthur and Sam, he came up the walkway to the front door and found it ajar – typical. Amanda had likely gotten drunk and forgotten to close it again. He truly would not miss her.

Pushing the heavy door open and stepping inside, he turned his head to tell Arthur to retrieve his computer from the SUV and heard one *thwoot*, then another. He saw Arthur slump against a red-splattered wall and Sam staggering.

It made no sense, but then it all became very clear as a powerful hand locked onto his shoulder, pulled him around, and forced him back against the doorjamb.

A large black handgun pressed painfully hard into the depression at the top of his nose, squarely between his eyes. Behind the gun was an unsmiling face.

"Welcome home, asshole," said Kelly Turnbull.

15.

They were stuck in the parking structure for several hours thanks to the security operation outside, which was fine with them. No one would be looking for them, if they were in fact being looked for, *inside* of a riot perimeter. Junior took the first watch and Turnbull slept in the back seat for a couple hours. He dozed right through the occasional bursts of gunfire.

It was pretty clear that the PRNA was not going to tolerate this kind of thing, not inside a security sector.

Eventually, the blues left the streets and it started slowly getting back to normal. They waited until the people and the drivers were venturing out *en masse* again before they pulled out of the space and drove down the ramp to the street. No one ever came for the Tesla with the broken out rear window. Junior wondered if the owner wasn't lying on a slab somewhere with a carving fork through his sternum.

"We need food," Junior said from the passenger's seat as they pulled out into the late Friday afternoon traffic. Up and down the street, things were normalizing again. You would never have known that this had been the scene of a bloodbath over lunch time.

"Maybe we might do better at a drive-thru," Turnbull said. "Do they even have drive-thrus here anymore? They used to. This place has devolved. They have managed to take the long arc of human progress and bend it to run right down the shitter."

"I wish they had Whataburger," Junior said. "I need a burger."

"The name 'Whataburger' is probably offensive to someone. Maybe it's racist or some shit. Remember In-N-Out Burgers? They were amazing."

"I don't know what that is. In-N-Out Burgers?"

"It was a California burger chain. Unbelievable burgers. The blues seized them along with everything else that hadn't left for the red and that wasn't shitty. This was perhaps the blues' greatest crime. Of all the crimes, of all the shit they've pulled, I think I'm most pissed off that they destroyed In-N-Out Burger."

"You seem pretty upset about it."

"Well, if you had ever had a Double Double animal style then you might understand," Turnbull said. "You know, I lived here as a kid. I grew up here. I remember it. I mean, it was not like when my dad was a kid here in the 1960s and '70s. California was really the Promised Land back then. Plenty of jobs, roads, and dams. People were flocking here because of the opportunities. Reagan was the governor. Reagan, if you can believe it. My dad told me about it. Dad was pissed off too, because by the time I came along that was all over and California was headed downhill. The Democrats took over and the state went hard blue. All the regular people like my family were getting squeezed. The middle class, the normal people who made it a great place, they started leaving before the Split was even an idea in anyone's head. What was left were rich liberals in San Francisco and the Westside of LA, and then the poor people who either got welfare or cleaned their mansions everywhere else."

"So, pretty much like today," Junior said.

"Yeah, this didn't just happen. This has been happening. They just built walls around the rich people to make it official."

"So what are we going to do about food since In-N-Out is not an option? Because I need some food."

"Yeah, I'm not entirely sure when we will get another chance to eat if this all works out right. This time tomorrow, by sunset, we ought to be making the crossing into Arizona."

"With Amanda."

"Like I said, *ought to*. Plans just don't survive contact with the enemy. So let's do our best not to contact the enemy. We get her, we get the hard drive, we get the hell out of town and go back over."

"And maybe we won't even have to kill anyone else."

"Nah, trust me. In this business you always end up killing someone."

They stopped at a busy diner down Wilshire near Beverly Hills, something called "Hep Katz." Inside there were lots of young adults enjoying the blue take on Fifties cuisine, but there were no nostalgic photos of kids bopping in poodle skirts and pompadours. Instead, the menu, in a box right above the listing of different cheeseburgers, explained that, "The 1950s were a time of incredible racism, sexism, and homophobia that Hep Katz in no way condones. Instead, Hep Katz dedicates this climate-sensitive fare as a tribute to the men, women, non-binary, and gender unspecified individuals

151

who struggled to escape the pitiless oppression inflicted upon them by the United States of America."

"I think I lost my appetite," Turnbull muttered. "No, wait, I'm having a vanilla shake."

"Is that racist?" asked Junior after checking to ensure their blue shirted dining facilitator was not nearby.

"Everything's racist. You should know that by now. And cisnormative too. Maybe you should order a corn dog. You know, expand your horizons."

"We can't be out of here soon enough."

Turnbull was still scanning the menu. "Hey, real coffee. Things are looking up."

They dug into their food, eating it all – burgers, plates of fries, shakes, and coffee too. Both ex-soldiers understood instinctively the old truism that when you could eat, you ate. You never knew when you would get another opportunity to do so. The dining facilitator barely said a word to them and did not even ask for ration coupons. Apparently, the shared sacrifice of the masses was not shared by their masters.

It was dark when they emerged. People were coming out and there were cars on the roads – not in the numbers of the past, but certainly orders of magnitude more than outside the Sector's walls. It was Friday night, and while out there the PRNA burned, the residents of the Westside Sector were preparing to fiddle.

"Any check points getting up there?" Junior asked.

"I don't know," Turnbull answered. "I would have liked to have scouted the route and the target first. The Thomas Guide tells us where the street is, but doesn't show us the layout like a satellite map off the web would."

"We could risk going online and getting one."

"That's just asking for their cyber spooks to catch us. Then they'll know where we're going."

"They might anyway."

"Yeah, that's why we'll recon it first. But they've gotta have some security there anyway. Your sister's boyfriend is the PBI director."

"He's not her boyfriend."

"Whatever he is, she hasn't made this easy for us."

There was a checkpoint inside Beverly Hills manned by a pair of bored uniformed PBI officers, one of whom held up his palm.

"I'll kill mine, you kill yours," Turnbull said casually as he eased to a stop.

"If we have to," Junior said.

"Yeah, just don't hesitate. If we have to."

But the PBI officer was satisfied with only a glance at their IDs and their privilege levels, and he waved them past.

"See," said Junior. "You didn't have to hurt anyone."

"Betcha we have to take them out on the way down."

"You know, Turnbull, I think you go looking for trouble."

"Trust me, I don't have to look for it. Remember how *you* came to *me*?"

They stopped on a quiet residential street at the base of the hills and did a final map recon, poring over the key page of the Thomas Guide. It looked like they could park one street over and approach from the rear. What it would look like in real life could well be something entirely different, but for now it seemed like a solid 70% solution.

The Lexus took on the hill with ease, but it was a bit outclassed by the newer Mercedes-Benzes and BMWs that abounded there. Below them, Los Angeles reached out to the horizon, with blocks of bright lights illuminating the various security sectors. Otherwise, the rest of Los Angeles was in the midst of the evening brownout. Except for a few flickering lights here and there, the majority of the city was dark and inscrutable.

They parked on the side of the narrow road next to a whitewashed wall surrounding a lot that backed up against the hillside. It was in a blind spot where none of the other residences along the street had a direct view of it. Junior got out and tried to pull himself up for a look over. He could not get a solid grip on the top and ended up standing on the trunk, peering over as Turnbull provided security.

"What do you see?"

"The house is empty, I'm pretty sure. No one's taking care of it. The lawn is dead. We should check it out."

Turnbull nodded and Junior jumped down.

"Change," Turnbull said. He started to take off his suit. Junior did so as well, but Turnbull told him to wait. One guy changes, the other guy pulls security. He'd learned that lesson the hard way a decade ago in Indian Country.

"Do we want the M4s?" Junior asked, pulling on his final boot.

"If we need the M4s then we're not going in. I'm taking the Ruger, though." Turnbull already had the silenced pistol in his pocket. He came around the Lexus and cupped his hands for Junior. This time Junior got a grip on the edge and pulled himself up, then he reached back and pulled Turnbull over.

They jumped down onto a patch of dirt where the grass had been back when someone was there to water it. Brown shrubs lined the side of the dark house, a rambling ranch style that probably went for several million dollars back when individuals could still freely buy and sell real estate.

"The windows aren't broken," Junior observed.

"Either they have a lot of security or they don't need security," Turnbull said. "Let's go, around back."

They moved quickly but quietly, now communicating by hand gestures and nods. At the rear of the property bordering the target lot there was another wall, only this one was about three feet high. They could see only the roof of the house further up the hill. They would need to scramble up an embankment to get there.

But first they listened. Crickets. A car backfiring. Someone down the hill must have had a window open because they could hear a TV announcer reading the UN's latest resolution decrying "the genocidal fracking atrocities of the racist criminals of the so-called United States."

Nothing from up above.

Turnbull knelt and swept up a handful of fine dust off the ground. Then he reached over the fence and gently sprinkled it over the property line.

"What are you doing?" asked Junior.

"Looking for lasers," replied Turnbull. There was nothing. He spent several minutes just looking, satisfying himself that there were probably no cameras or motion detectors or sensors waiting to alert security that they had a guest.

Probably.

"Ok, you're in my house now. Guerilla stuff. None of that infantry hooah charge shit you learned at Fort Benning. Subtle."

"Yeah, subtlety is your middle name. Kelly Subtle Turnbull." Turnbull ignored him.

"We move quiet, slow, and deliberate," Turnbull said. "If it looks like they've spotted us, we haul ass back here. The car is the rally point. Whoever gets there first gives the other guy 30 seconds and then hauls ass, with or without him. Got it?"

"Yeah, but how do I do that if you have the keys?"

"The key's on top of the rear passenger tire. Okay, I'm going over and halfway up the embankment and then we're going to wait for five minutes. If nothing happens, I'll wave you forward and then we'll wait again at the top before we go on. Got it?"

Junior nodded, and Turnbull went over the wall. He slowly worked his way half-way up the embankment and waited. More crickets. More television announcers blaming the people on the other side of the Rocky Mountains for the People's Republic's misfortunes.

But no alarms.

Junior joined them and they carefully moved up the embankment to the ridge, then waited again, listening. From down below them somewhere, the voice of the television announcer warned that the climate change crisis was once again just a year away from reaching the point of no return, and urged the largely pedestrian citizenry to continue to reduce their collective carbon footprint.

But again, no alarms.

Turnbull slowly lifted his head over the crest. The developer had cut a large flat plain into the hill, landscaped it and dug in a large swimming pool. A few empty chaise lounges lay around the edge of the water on a patio of white stone. A stairway of the same white stone lead upwards toward the house, whose southern face was dominated by a vast picture window. There were lights on inside.

"Okay Junior, there's a big open space and a pool. The house is up some steps and there's someone home. We work around the side, then up. Follow me."

Turnbull skirted the crest, moving along the hillside slowly around to the far edge of the patio. Using the manicured bushes for concealment, he moved swiftly past the pool to the stairway. Junior came along behind.

"Don't shoot my sister," Junior said. Turnbull looked down and saw he had drawn the silenced Ruger without a conscious thought.

"I'm more concerned with security than her."

"You ought to be worried about her. She'll mess you up."

"You just calm her down because she's going to be freaked out when she sees us."

"Oh, I'm a calming presence."

Turnbull rolled his eyes and peeked around the corner. The lights were on inside the big window, but there did not appear to be anyone looking out into the back yard. Turnbull moved, taking the stone steps upward two at a time with Junior to his rear.

At the top of the steps, Turnbull came around the corner onto another patio and stopped, facing a puzzled, round-faced man in a brown suit who was about to light a cigarette. Behind him was the open door to the first floor of the house. The guy had a radio on his belt and a SIG Sauer pistol. He stood there for a moment, another kind of cig dangling from his lips, his hands cupping his as-yet unflicked lighter.

Turnbull raised the Ruger to center mass and fired two shots. The man stumbled back just a half step – he pretty clearly wore a vest under his shirt and the .22 rounds didn't penetrate. Turnbull raised the weapon and took the headshot. That worked – a red dot appeared in the guard's forehead and he fell over backwards.

Junior's Glock was out and he was covering high and to the flanks. No one was coming. Turnbull led the way inside the door as Junior knelt down to pick up the radio.

It seemed to be some sort of living room, but with a full bar taking up the far wall. There were dark hardwood stairs that headed up. There was light but no sound other than low music – some kind of jazz. Above them was a half-wall that made up the side of the upstairs room. Turnbull looked at the ceiling, trying to see if there were moving shadows. Satisfied there were none, he waved the pistol and Junior followed, covering their rear.

Turnbull moved up, step by step, the weapon fixed on the top of the stairwell. His breathing was slow and controlled. Up he went, one step at a time. A creak, a loud one. Turnbull froze, waiting. Junior had followed and was on the third step, and he froze too, swinging the Glock to cover the bar room they had just come

156

through, then the half-wall above them, then back to the bar room again.

The attack came from over the wall, and at the point in Junior's cycle when he was covering the bar room from about half-way up the steps. Had he been covering high, he might have fired. Turnbull was almost at the top when the lamp flew down toward him. Since it was thrown blind it missed him, barely, shattering on the wall and spraying glass over them both.

"Lou!" a woman's voice screamed.

Turnbull bolted up to the landing and pivoted, catching a glimpse of a wild-eyed blonde clad in blue jeans and a white t-shirt for just a moment before the heavy bookend she had hurled at him connected with his hip. The sharp pain from where the statuette's bill hit him – the bookend was made of iron and shaped like a mallard duck – broke his concentration enough to override his instinctive response, which was to have shot her in the face a couple of times. Turnbull bit his lip and charged her, though he found his left leg dragging – it hurt like hell. Behind him, Junior was rushing up the last few steps.

Amanda realized she was out of weapons and began looking around her to grab something else. Turnbull charged forward and she dodged, with Turnbull tripping over a low mid-century modern table in front of a sleek black leather couch. She ran out and around, skirting his grasp as Turnbull futilely reached out for her as she passed. Her attention focused on Turnbull, she had not seen Junior, who leapt into her path.

She saw him and her expression changed from rage to shock, and Junior smiled. Then her expression returned to rage and she ran directly at him, screeching and nails out like claws.

Junior caught Amanda by the forearms, but the momentum was too much even for such a slight woman; losing his footing on the throw rug that covered the hardwood floor, Junior went down with Amanda atop him, her hands clawing at his face as he tried to hold her back from gouging out his eyes.

"You fucking uuuurrrfff," she shrieked before the chokehold Turnbull gained by wrapping his right forearm around her throat snuffed it out. He pulled her back and off Junior, taking her to the floor and pinning her under his bulk.

157

"Damn it, pull security!" he hissed at Junior, who shook it off and swung the Glock up to engage any more security guards who might enter the room from the stairs or from one of the halls.

"You," Turnbull said. "You need to calm the fuck down!"

Amanda squirmed more and Turnbull pressed down harder. She gasped for air.

"Hey!" Junior said.

"Hey, you want her back? I'll let her go and she can claw off your face if you want."

Then Turnbull looked down into her furious eyes and said, slowly, "If you don't calm down I am going to calm you down and you do not want that. Are you going to be calm?"

She made a series of unintelligible guttural noises that, had she been able to speak, probably would have been a string of words that boiled down to a series of questions regarding his mother's chastity. But she stopped squirming.

"Calm down," Turnbull said again. "I know you're a Texas woman, but go against your instincts and stop trying to hurt me."

She made another short, abrupt noise, then was quiet and still, her dagger eyes still fixed on him.

"I'm going to let you talk. Don't scream. I just want a yes or no. Okay, we took out a guard downstairs. Are there more guards? Yes or no?" Turnbull eased up on her throat.

"Fuck you!" Turnbull pressed down and muffled most of the "you."

"Okay, that's not a yes or no. I just want a yes or no. Let's try it again." He eased up.

She didn't say anything for a moment.

"More guards. Yes or no?"

"No," she said. "Just the one asshole."

"I'm going to let you go now," Turnbull said. "Don't run. Don't throw anymore shit at me. Don't try to kill your brother again. Okay?"

"Yeah,"

"Okay, just be calm." Turnbull rolled off her, and stood up. His hip hurt like hell.

Amanda sat up and looked at Junior.

"You stupid idiot, what the hell are you doing here?"

"I'm here to get you out!"

"Yeah, I guessed that. You know how dangerous this is? You know they'll kill you when they catch you?"

"They aren't going to catch me."

"Do you have any idea whose house this is? The PBI director for the West Coast!" She stood up; there were tears on her cheeks. Junior holstered his Glock. Turnbull sat down in one of the soft, black leather chairs around the table.

"I know that," said Junior.

"And you came anyway?" Amanda replied.

"Yes," Junior replied.

She rushed at him again, and the hug he expected turned into a hard slap across the face.

"You dumbass! You have to get out of here before he gets home or we're all dead!" Now it was Junior's turn to try and restrain her.

Turnbull sighed and stood up. The pain in his hip was now a dull ache, and he was losing patience.

"Can you two knock it the hell off? We need to get out of here."

"Who *are* you?" asked Amanda, relaxing and ceasing her struggling. "Are you his assistant or something?"

"Assistant?" sniffed Turnbull. "No, I'm the guy your daddy paid to get your dumb ass the hell out of Dodge. *He's* the assistant. Now, are you coming along voluntarily or not, because if I have to tie your ass up, ball gag you and carry you out of here over my shoulder, then I need to get on with that before your boyfriend shows up with his posse."

"You won't get away. Martin can't let me go. It'd be too embarrassing. He'd do whatever he has to do to stop us. You two just need to go. Leave me here. I'll be all right."

"Amanda, you have to come. It's all falling apart out there. We've been out there. This whole country is on the edge and I can't just leave you here in the middle of what's coming," Junior said.

"Yeah, that," Turnbull said. "And also, I really want my money. In fact, *mostly* I want my money. So if you can grab your shit, I'd like to walk out of here instead of having to shoot my way out."

"We're heading to the border with Arizona," Junior said. "We have travel passes and carbon offset vouchers for all of us. We

159

get there, then we hike over. Kelly has done this a lot. You need shoes you can walk in over rough terrain, and you need a coat."

Amanda just stared, processing.

"Amanda," Turnbull said. "Go with your brother and pack a bag with your stuff. If you have a backpack, use that. Now, two questions. When does lover boy get home, and do you have any kind of food in your kitchen because we should probably stock up?"

"I," she mumbled. "I don't know when he'll be back. It could be in five minutes, it could be midnight, it could be tomorrow. I don't know. His driver always calls Lou on the radio when he's almost here. Where is Lou?"

"Lou didn't make it. No one ever warned him that smoking is hazardous to your health. Junior, keep listening to that handset. If he does show up while we're still here, we need to welcome him home. How many guards does he have?"

"Just two. Big assholes, like Lou."

"Weapons?"

"Um, not the big long ones. The guns you hold in your hands."

"Handguns?"

"Yes, handguns. I've shot guns before."

"Okay, what's Martin carry?"

"Oh," she laughed. "Martin doesn't carry a gun."

"This guy has zero redeeming qualities. Okay, you two pack and I'll check the fridge."

The radio call from Arthur came in as Junior and Amanda were in the midst of packing her clothes. Junior ran down to the kitchen, where Turnbull was finishing a chicken sandwich, and said, "Hey, they're coming."

They made a quick plan, and Turnbull handed the Ruger over to Junior, who slipped out the side door. Turnbull told Amanda to get in the back bedroom and keep quiet, then went to the foyer and opened the door slightly until it was ajar. Then he stepped behind it.

The gate started to creak open with a mechanical whir, and a vehicle entered the front, followed by the gate closing. There were vehicle doors opening and closing outside; inside, Turnbull pulled back the slide on his Glock just a hair to ensure a hollow point round was seated in the chamber.

One was.

Footsteps. He could hear them coming, several people. The door swung in a bit, and someone stepped inside. There were two noises in rapid succession – to Turnbull, they sounded like *thwacks*! There were groans and rustling, and now Turnbull was moving around the door, toward the slight man with dark hair who was staring out at his two slumping thugs.

Turnbull planted his huge hand on the man's shoulder and forced him back against the door jamb with a thud; then he planted the Glock right between the terrified man's eyes.

"Welcome home, asshole," Kelly Turnbull said.

The man quivered. Turnbull grabbed his shoulder again and roughly pulled him inside. Outside on the doorstep, still holding the Ruger, Junior stepped over the bodies of the two dead guards and followed them into the house.

Turnbull double-checked Rios-Parkinson for a weapon and relieved him of his cell phone, then frog marched him into the living room and threw him forward into one of the black leather seats. Behind him, through the window, lay the vast expanse of Los Angeles.

"Sit," Turnbull said, the Glock still pointed at the Director's face. Junior entered the room, the Ruger still in hand.

Rios-Parkinson stared up at them, his face flush with both anger and fear. Turnbull stared back.

"Did you piss yourself?" he asked, noting the dark stain on the Director's suit pants that was spreading south. "You know, it'd be almost unsporting of me to shoot you. Not that I won't shoot your sorry ass."

"What do we do with him?" asked Junior.

"I vote shoot him," offered Turnbull. "Shoot him and get out of here."

"You won't make it out," Rios-Parkinson sputtered.

"Oh good, piss boy speaks. You know, I got this far. I got into your house. I got *you*. And you're in a poor position to influence events going forward."

"We know who you are," Rios-Parkinson said. "If you surrender to me now...."

"Just...no. Stop talking," Turnbull said. "But I do have some questions and maybe, if you answer them right, I won't splatter you all over your tacky modernist décor."

161

Amanda walked in, looking first at Rios-Parkinson, then at Turnbull, then back at Rios-Parkinson. The Director scowled.

"Bitch," he hissed.

"Bastard," she replied angrily, but then a smile broke across her face as she saw his lap, and she began laughing while Rios-Parkinson fumed.

"Well, that seems to answer our willing accomplice or unwitting bait debate, right Junior? Well, I'm sensing some relationship issues here, Mr. Director, but you all can work those out by email, assuming you remain a going concern," Turnbull said. Then he turned to Junior. "You and her finish up packing. We need to be gone."

They returned to her room, leaving Turnbull and Rios-Parkinson together.

"Now that we're alone, we can have a little chat."

"What do you want?" the Director asked, straightening himself in the chair.

"For starters, I want to know how you started tracking us. No, hold on there, I can see those wheels in your head turning trying to figure out what to tell me, and I gotta tell you that I'm just not in the mood. If you waste my very limited time, I will put a round in your face, and I can tell by the smell of your used coffee that you aren't one of those guys who's not afraid to die. So let's just save ourselves the hassle, cut the bullshit, and you go ahead and answer my questions."

"We know someone infiltrated into Nevada through Utah and killed a squad of our volunteers."

"Volunteers? Okay. And?"

"Somehow you got to Los Angeles." Turnbull noted that they had apparently not pinned that unpleasantness in Vegas on him.

"Then?"

"My men spotted you in town."

"Nope. You're forgetting something. The hard drive. Right?" Rios-Parkinson looked stricken.

"Yep, the hard drive. I figure that's yours. I figure that if it gets out you let it slip away that you are massively fucked. Pretty much that? Well, from your expression I'm guessing I'm on the right track. Now, you didn't just find us. You have a source, someone who

162

narced us out to you. Who is he? Or she? Or xe. See, I spend some time over here and I start doing it too. Anyway, who was it?"

"His name," Rios-Parkinson said. "Is Jacob."

"You know, I don't think you're lying to me. And that's good. Because now I can make you a proposition. It's a good one, because you get something you really want out of it, which is me not blowing your brains out of the back of your head. Interested? Come on, I know you are."

"What do you propose?"

"Well, how about I don't shoot you for starters. But wait, there's more. Word doesn't get out about the hard drive even after I get it, which as I suspect we both know I will be doing as soon as I leave here. And you also get a safety net for when this dumpster fire of a country you and your friends ruined goes all to shit, and we both know it is going to shit really quickly."

"I will take my chances," Rios-Parkinson said, mustering all his remaining bravado.

"Stop talking. You're soft and untrained. You're not a soldier, you're a glorified prison guard. What do you think you guys have? A month? A year? Two, tops? This is all coming down, and what happens to guys like you when their little regimes fall apart? Well, we both know the answer. Bad things happen to people like you."

"What do you want?"

"I have a friend who would be very interested in talking to you. A friend from the other side. His job is very similar to yours, except he doesn't arrest people for speaking freely or protesting. But you and he could develop a very mutually satisfying relationship."

"You want me to spy for the United States, to be a traitor?"

"Yes, absolutely. You understand me perfectly. A modern day Benedict Arnold. You know who he was, right? No? Forget it. Yes, if you will work with my friend Clay, I won't kill you here and now."

"I guess I have no choice."

"You do have a choice, only the wrong one will be the last choice you ever make."

"What do I do?"

"Well, I assume through his magic he'll find a way to get in contact with you. Trust me, you can't hide from him when he wants to talk to you – I've tried. Then you do what he tells you. As for tonight, I still need to think through the logistics, but the spoiler is that you live. I don't shoot you."

Junior returned to the room alone.

"She's almost ready."

"Good," said Turnbull. "Watch him. I gotta hit the head. Don't shoot him either."

Junior pulled out the Ruger as Turnbull holstered his Glock and turned away toward the bedroom. It was down a long hallway. Amanda was zipping the day pack closed on the bed when Turnbull entered.

"Don't shut it. I gotta check it."

"For what?"

"For my own personal safety. Do you have any phones, tablets, electronics, anything that has lights or buttons?"

"No."

"Let me see. You'd be surprised how many people forget to mention shit that they can track us with." Turnbull unzipped the pack and rifled through it. Socks, a jacket, some bandages – smart thinking. A wallet.

"What's this?"

"My photos," she said. "Hard copy prints." Turnbull nodded and put it back in the pack. Then he walked to the master bath and slid the door shut behind him.

The commotion began as he was washing his hands; Turnbull heard the noise and threw the towel to the floor. He pulled the door open and drew his Glock at a run down the long hallway. At the other end, he heard a hail of gunshots and saw Junior coming up the stairs and dive onto the landing as a flurry of bullets slammed into the wall.

Amanda was standing stunned, and Turnbull pulled her to the ground.

"You hit?" he shouted at Junior, who held the Ruger in his right hand. Its slide was locked to the rear.

"He got the jump on me and ran downstairs," Junior said. "I tried to shoot him through the wall as he went down the steps, but I don't think the bullets went through the plaster, I ran after him, but he must have got the pistol off the dead guard. He can't shoot for shit, though."

164

Turnbull ran to the big window and looked out across the backyard. Nothing.

"He's in the wind. Fuck. Okay, out front. Amanda, get your keys. We're taking your car down to get ours and then hauling ass back to David's."

The trio ran out front, with Amanda dodging the bodies and Turnbull stepping on them. He slid into the Nissan's passenger seat and, as Amanda drove out the gate and down the street, proceeded to open the back of Rios-Parkinson's cell phone and slip out the SIM chip. That went in his pocket; he hurled the dead cell phone out his window into someone's jasmine bushes.

Rios-Parkinson was out of breath – he was never an athlete and this scramble out of the house and across the yard, then over walls into other yards and down the streets, was probably the most physical exertion he had indulged in since his racist PE coach had made him do laps as a high school sophomore. The house ahead seemed to be occupied, but there was a wall and an iron lattice gate. He ran to it and pounded on it; nothing. There was an intercom, and he hit the button.

"Open the fucking gate!" he shrieked into the microphone. The lights inside the house went dark and none of his pleas or threats convinced the occupants to turn them back on. Finally, he gave up and ran down the street, looking for another house that might admit him.

It was another block before he found a house with no wall. He ran up the steps to the door and pounded. There were noises from inside, and an elderly man standing behind a walker opened the door a crack.

Rios-Parkinson pushed and forced himself inside.

"I am the Director of the People's Bureau of Investigation," he announced. "Where is your telephone?"

He did not wait for an answer – there was a wall-mounted land line in the kitchen. He ran to it and put it to his ear – nothing.

"That phone hasn't worked in years," said the old man.

"Your cell phone, now!"

"It's…where is it?"

But Rios-Parkinson spotted it on an end table in the living room and lunged for it. There was a signal, but a weak one, maybe one or two bars depending on where he stood. He dialed the main exchange but, because he was without his address book feature and did not remember the individual phone numbers, he had to bully his way through the central exchange until he finally reached Larsen.

"Seal the Sector! No one leaves!" he screamed. "And take the Jews now!"

16.

They parked across the street from the eastern wall of the Westside Sector, in as quiet and out-of-the-way place as they could find, and waited. No patrols. There was a camera, mounted on a light pole. Turnbull got out of the car and walked directly underneath, then shot it with the silenced Ruger. Chances are the guys assigned to watch the feeds of all the security cameras would write this off as just another malfunction. After all, who would disable a camera *inside* the Sector? The problem was keeping people out, not keeping them in.

He got back into the Lexus, which they had driven to in Amanda's Nissan, and swung it around to the other side of the road, right up next to the wall. Turnbull left the keys in the ignition; hopefully someone would come along and remove the evidence. They climbed up onto the trunk, then onto the roof, snipped through the razor wire with their wire cutters, and climbed over the wall.

It was a long walk to the abandoned Del Taco. They moved fast, knowing they needed to warn David. Turnbull was not sure exactly what he'd do to help the people, but it was pretty clear their time was running out. They would have to go out, all 27 ½ of them.

The three of them kept to the shadows and tried to avoid arousing attention. Amanda was particularly nervous; she had rarely left the Sector and it was clear she was worried. She had reason to be; several salty looking crews looked the trio over. Turnbull's hard looks in return convinced them that discretion was the better part of predation. They moved on to weaker prey.

Other than that, there were few people out that night. Maybe they sensed something.

When the three got near to the old restaurant, they didn't go straight in right away. They watched it from the ground floor window of a deserted office building about 150 yards away. The kid, Abraham, was there all right, staying generally out of sight in the back parking lot. No one else was around. No one seemed to be watching.

"He's got a pack on," said Junior, handing back the binos.

"Yeah," Turnbull said. He scanned the surrounding bushes for signs of an ambush.

Down the street, maybe 350 yards to the east, in the direction of David's building, a pair of PSF cruisers slid into view and blocked the intersection. Their light bars went on. Four PSF thugs got out, casually standing around their vehicles.

"Awesome," said Turnbull bitterly, but he didn't move. He just watched.

"Shit, they're setting up a perimeter," Junior said.

"Yeah, but I don't see any other cruisers." Turnbull pivoted to look south and north. Nothing there. Then, from the east, the rattle of gunfire. Controlled bursts.

"What's happening?" asked Amanda.

"It's a perimeter all right, but not one around us," said Turnbull.

"David?" asked Junior.

"Yeah. Gotta be. I should have shot that son of a bitch in the doorway."

"We need to go get Abraham."

"Ah shit, he's moving."

Abraham had stared east for a moment, then paced, then began running east down the street, directly at the cruisers.

"What's he doing?" Amanda asked.

"The kid's going back to his house. Damnit!" Turnbull pointed at Amanda, binos still in his hand. "You stay here! Junior, come on!"

They dumped their packs and tore out of the building at a run, not entirely sure of exactly what they intended to do. It was clear they were not going to outrun Abraham, who was charging toward the PSF roadblock at full speed.

In the distance, more bursts of gunfire. Many more. And the dull thud of an explosion.

The kid was far ahead of them – there was no way they would catch him before he reached the vehicles, so Turnbull pulled Junior into an overgrown yard and watched.

Abraham seemed not to have a plan either. He kept running east on the sidewalk. When he was perhaps 50 yards away, one of the PSF thugs started yelling something at him. Abraham ignored it, and as it became clear that the kid was going to try to rush through the roadblock, the PSF thugs spread out to take him down. He tried to dodge, and when they tackled him, he struggled. He was shouting, but Turnbull could not make out the words. Turnbull brought up the binoculars.

They rolled him over on his face and took off his pack. One of the PSF thugs then kicked the pinned teen hard in the ribs. Another pressed a knee into his back to hold him down while zip-tying the kid's hands behind him. Two of them lifted Abraham to his feet and threw him against one of the cruisers. They patted him down while another put the pack on the trunk and started going through it.

Turnbull focused the binoculars, trying to see what was coming out of the pack in the red and blue flashes of the light bar.

The thug was looking at something, puzzled. It was small, maybe metallic.

"Is it the drive?" Junior asked, straining to see unaided. Another long burst of gunfire from the east echoed through the deserted streets.

"Maybe. I can't say for sure. But whatever it is, the blues don't seem to think it's important."

One of them opened the back door of the cruiser and unceremoniously shoved Abraham inside. The other went to the passenger's seat with the pack. After a brief conversation, the driver got in, started up the cruiser, and pulled away to the south.

"They gotta be going to the Hollywood station," Turnbull said.

"Shit, what do we do?"

"Come on."

Turnbull stepped back onto the sidewalk and started heading toward the remaining cruiser. Junior followed, unsure.

As they approached, one of the PSF thugs shouted, "Hey, turn your ass around."

"What?" asked Turnbull, slurring the word a bit.

"Turn your drunk asses around or we'll kick 'em!"

Turnbull closed to about 15 yards and the PSF thugs were imagining some entertainment. The closer one pulled out his stick and stepped forward.

"I told you to…."

Turnbull drew and fired two quick shots into his face, then pivoted and dropped the other with two rounds as he tried to draw.

"Shit, Kelly," said Junior.

"Take their vests," Turnbull growled. "And a Beretta plus some extra mags." In the distance, there was more gunfire.

"What are we doing?"

"Well, we aren't leaving that kid and the hard drive with those assholes. Everyone else is probably dead by now, but I'm not leaving that kid. We're going in to get him."

"He's in a PSF station. It's full of cops."

"Don't ever call them cops. They aren't police. They're just criminals with guns and uniforms, and they just helped the PBI kill all those people who helped us."

Turnbull had the driver's door open and was looking under the dash for a switch. There it was – he flipped it. The PSF thugs liked to be able to cut off their GPS tracking sometimes so they could do their personal business using official vehicles, so most had unofficial kill switches installed by PSF mechanics they threw a few bucks at for the service.

"You know what empties a station of PSF assholes fast? Dead PSF assholes. Now get in." Turnbull reached for the radio hand mic as Junior brought the Kevlar vests around and jumped into the passenger seat.

Turnbull keyed it.

"Uh, help, I'm a citizen and there's two PSF who are shot here. Help! Somebody shot them!"

The speaker came alive. "Who is this? Say again?"

"Uh, yeah, I'm just a citizen and there's two officers lying in the road here near, uh...." Turnbull thought about it for a moment. "Rosewood and Fairfax."

That would lead them away nicely. Then he added, "The guy who did it is a short cismale, red hair, blue jacket!"

"What is your name?"

"You gotta come quick! They're both really badly hurt. Oh no, he's coming back!" Turnbull kept it keyed as he pulled out his Glock and fired a round out the window, then tossed away the mic. Next, he flipped off the light bar, turned on the ignition, and gunned the cruiser west up the street back to Amanda.

They pulled up outside the deserted office building where they had left her and trotted inside. Amanda stood, holding a two-by-four that was splattered with red. On the ground, a dirty gentlemen groaned. His head had evidently become acquainted with the piece of wood in the not too distant past.

"He was very rude," Amanda said. "He has no social graces."

"Yep, you're a Texas girl. Get the packs. We're out of here."

They sat in the cruiser, idling, watching the police station from across Wilcox Avenue. The patrol car lot was nearly empty. On the way over, they had seen at least a dozen heading west fast on their wild goose chase after the cisnormative ginger assassin.

"It looks like they keep the impounded cars over there. I don't expect them to do an inventory of them and find one missing before we get out to the border," Turnbull said, slipping a mag into his M4. Junior started putting on his suppressor, but Turnbull stopped him.

"No, we want it loud," he said. "This is flat out urban guerilla warfare. We're done with subtlety. We're going in and shooting anyone who gets in our way. Speed, aggression, and violent execution. Remember, these assholes aren't soldiers. We are. They're just thugs with a mandate. I saw it in Indian Country. We hit hard and fast and they'll be disoriented. It'll take them time to react. By then, you will have keys to one of those cars and I'll have Abraham and the drive."

"How do I find where they keep the impound keys, Kelly?"

"You take a blue and you shove the muzzle of that M4 in his face and ask him."

"What if he doesn't tell me?"

"Then you pull the fucking trigger and then ask the next one. *He'll* tell you."

Turnbull was stuffing spare magazines into the black PSF vest Junior had liberated. Junior was staring.

"What?" asked Turnbull.

"Maybe I'm just not as angry at them as you are," Junior said.

"No, but you should be. They say the worst wars are the civil wars. Well, they're right. You know those nice Jewish people who helped us? These fuckers helped slaughter them. We laugh at their

171

stupid political correctness shit, but deep down what they are about isn't funny. We're all expendable when it comes to them preserving their power. They're just the latest people to try to butcher their way to utopia. Did I ever tell you what they did to a church full of people in Indiana who they thought were red sympathizers? I got to help pull out the bodies of people whose only crime was not worshipping socialism's false god. Now that kid and probably a lot of other innocent people are going to die unless we do what we gotta do. So are you coming?"

"I'm coming."

"You know, I didn't ask for it to be this way. I didn't ask for them to rip my country apart. But it fucking is what it is. Now let's go get that kid."

They got out and opened the rear door for Amanda. Turnbull produced the PSF Beretta and handed it to Amanda, along with three extra magazines.

"You know how to use this?" he asked.

"I may have been stupid enough to leave it once, but I'm still from Texas," she answered, pulling back the slide and loading a round.

"Shoot anyone who gets in your way. We'll be out in about ten minutes with one of those cars." Amanda nodded, got into the passenger seat and closed the door behind her.

Turnbull and Junior locked and loaded as they walked across Wilcox Avenue to the PSF station.

17.

The convoy of three SUVs eventually arrived at the home of the baffled elderly man on the ridge above Beverly Hills who had played the unwilling host to the Director of the People's Bureau of Investigation. Rios-Parkinson was livid – he had spent that critical hour trying and largely failing to organize his forces via intermittent cellular phone communication. But now, in the back of the middle SUV, he had clear comms again.

"Do you have the tracker up yet?" he demanded of Larsen.

"The techs are still working on it."

"Tell them to get it operational. And the raid?"

"We are about an hour away from being able to launch," Larsen reported. "We are organizing the PSF's perimeter and the assault element from the PBI."

"An hour?" Rio-Parkinson shrieked. "Do it now!"

"Director," Larsen said patiently. "You can't just launch an assault. You have to plan. You have to move the people and equipment into position."

"Larsen, I am warning you. Raid the compound. They are coming. The spies are coming if they are not already there and they *cannot* get the hard drive."

On the other end, Larsen scowled. Unlike his boss, he was a professional. He had run operations in the old military before the Split, and then for the blues during the bloody Indiana counter-insurgency campaign. If you did not plan, prepare, and rehearse, you failed. Even a relatively simple operation like this could go very wrong, especially when so much was at stake.

"We will move the moment we can, Director," Larsen said, trying to be soothing.

"When you secure it, you search the building. Everywhere. Tear it apart. Tear out the walls. The drive has to be there," Rios-Parkinson ordered. But there was a doubt in his mind. What if it wasn't?

"Understood," Larsen replied.

"And take the main one alive, this David Kaplan. Get him to tell you where he hid it. Remember, I want not a word of this to become known. So kill the rest."

The convoy was speeding east toward David's compound when Larsen called back to report.

"We have entered the compound and engaged a number of the subversives already."

"Have they resisted?" Rios-Parkinson asked.

"No," said Larsen. "They have no weapons."

"Execute your orders. And find the drive."

The convoy flew past the PSF perimeter and onward until it reached the crush of PSF and PBI vehicles surrounding the apartment complex. Rios-Parkinson's new ten-man personal security team – it was all male, in defiance of the strict rules designed to stamp out phallocentrism in the security forces – exited the vehicles before their boss, ensuring it was safe for him to come out. They wore black uniforms with modern vests, and each carried a new M4-style carbine with optics. No second hand Chinese-made AKs for them.

Larsen approached as Rios-Parkinson got out of his SUV. His boss's suit was a mess – it looked like he had spilled coffee on himself.

From inside the complex, there were bursts of gunfire and occasional screams. There was the dull thud of an explosion.

"Director, we have secured most of the compound with no casualties to our forces. A few of the subversives have locked themselves inside apartments. We are eliminating those one by one." More gunfire erupted inside, and another explosion. Apparently they were using grenades.

"What have you found in the cleared areas so far?"

"Nothing yet," said Larsen. "No hard drive. And we have not found their leader yet, this David Kaplan. He doesn't match any of them." Larsen pointed over to a row of covered bodies lying on the sidewalk, at least a dozen of them, with pairs of PSF tactical personnel carrying out several more. Dark, thin rivulets seeped out from underneath them and drained into the gutter.

There was more shooting from inside.

"Let me look at the dead ones. Our spies may be among them, but I doubt it. We would have casualties of our own if that were true."

They began walking toward the field mortuary, the security team roughly clearing lesser PSF and PBI personnel from the Director's path. A female wearing PSF tactical gear pulled back the tarps, exposing the faces of the dead, one after another. Several men. Several women. Some kids. And Jacob, shot through the windpipe, his eyes wide and afraid.

"What did you find?" Larsen asked; he had been coordinating the final assault on the top floors.

"No one important," Rios-Parkinson relied. "The spies are not here. If they did escape the sector, they could not have done it with a vehicle so they likely did not get here before your forces did. They are still in Los Angeles, and without the hard drive. Find them."

There was a commotion around them that the Director did not immediately understand; his security men brought their weapons to the ready position. Now people were pointing upwards. Rios-Parkinson looked up too.

A man stood on the edge of the rooftop above them. Rios-Parkinson could make out a skullcap. Larsen glanced at his tablet's screen.

"I think that's David Kaplan," he whispered.

"Get him," Rios-Parkinson said, and Larsen turned away, shouting orders into his radio.

David stood on the edge of the rooftop for a moment, his eyes closed, his mouth moving as if he was speaking. Was it…a prayer? Rios-Parkinson watched fascinated – the man really believed all his superstitious nonsense.

David tumbled forward, rolling in the air, hitting squarely on the spiked fence. The crowd gasped – there was no question of him having survived.

"It has to still be in there. Find it," Rios-Parkinson said, staring at the body. But Larsen had the radio to his ear, listening. He put the radio down.

"There has been a reported shooting of two PSF officers somewhere to the west, near Fairfax and Rosewood. It's a confused situation, but all units not engaged here are responding."

"It has to be them," said Rios-Parkinson. "Send everyone available. Seal off the entire area for a dozen blocks. Go house to house. Kick in every door. Find them. And kill them. No prisoners. Do you understand me?"

"Absolutely, Director."

Rios-Parkinson savored the feeling or relief, the feeling of victory. They did not have the hard drive. He would find it. And he would find them.

But Larsen was overcome with a deep unease, and against his better judgment, he shared it. "There's a story about the Jews. They were surrounded on a hilltop by Romans. There was no way out, so they killed themselves rather than being taken alive. It was called Masada."

Rios-Parkinson looked at his deputy with a measure of disgust.

"So?"

"I was just thinking that the Jews, well, they're still around. And the Romans...they aren't."

Rios-Parkinson's face was stony and blank. "Just find me the hard drive."

Turnbull and Junior crossed Wilcox toward the PSF building, which looked like it was probably an edgy harbinger of the not-too-distant future when it was built in the 1960s. It had gone downhill considerably since, and had been partially rebuilt after the post-Split rioting had destroyed some of it. The old Los Angeles Police Department signage was all pulled down, replaced with the words "People's Security Force" on the dirty brick face. A central stairwell led up to the public entrance where a dim light shone.

"Put in your plugs," Turnbull said, jamming the plastic baffles into his ear canals. There were some people wandering about – none uniformed – but the two men in what looked like plainclothes carrying weapons and wearing old, black plate-carrying vests that had "PSF" spray-painted on the front and back in yellow drew little notice.

They reached the sidewalk and Turnbull charged his weapon. Junior did the same.

"Don't come back out the front if you can help it," Turnbull said. "Find the keys, head to the south side, come out in the lot."

"Okay."

Turnbull checked his watch. "It's 10:43. If I am not out there in the impound lot at 10:53, you take your sister and get the fuck out of here. Don't come after me. If I'm not there it's because I'm dead."

"Okay."

They turned up the steps to the public entrance. Inside, a blue sat at a counter typing something, taking no notice. A few sad, dour people sat on bench seats lining the foyer.

"Hard and fast," Turnbull said, and pushed open the front door.

The PSF officer looked up and Turnbull opened fire with a burst into his upper chest. He spilled backwards out of his chair. The attackers rushed forward, heedless of the civilians screaming and taking cover around them.

Behind the counter was an empty work area with two doors. One read "IMPOUND OPERATIONS" and went off the rear. The other read "AUTHORIZED PERSONNEL ONLY."

Junior leapt the low barrier and went to the dead officer's work station, looking for, finding, and then pushing a green button. There was a buzz, and Turnbull, weapon up, pulled open the "AUTHORIZED PERSONNEL ONLY" door. It opened to a long hallway occupied by three PSF officers who were rushing forward, one with her Beretta out, two more struggling to remove theirs from their holsters.

Turnbull squeezed off a burst one-handed, then rushed through the door and raised the weapon to his ready position, firing again. The walls erupted with geysers of plaster and dust as the first officer staggered back under the impact. Turnbull fired again, at face level, and the other two went down as well. There were doors along the hallway which turned left at the end. Turnbull charged down, trying to cover any angle of potential attack. A blue with a mug stood stunned in an office as he passed; Turnbull fired again and he went backwards and crashed over a desk, blood and coffee mingling on his stomach. The M4's bolt locked back and Turnbull seamlessly replaced the magazine, hundreds of training iterations in the close quarter battle houses at Bragg paying off.

Despite the plugs, his ears were ringing. He reached the end of the corridor and sliced the turn left 15 degrees at a time. Another long hallway, and two more PSF officers were in it. He fired and could make out the center mass impacts on the first one. The second got off a shot, then a second with his Beretta. They were wild – Turnbull had no idea where they went, glad only it was not into him. His next burst caught the shooter in the upper chest, neck, and face.

There was a sign – just what he was looking for. It said a number of things, but he paid attention to "CELLS," "EVIDENCE LOCKER" and "ARMS ROOM." The arrow for all three pointed down the hall. Weapon ready, Turnbull moved out.

Junior let go the buzzer and stood back, looking for a telephone box. It was there, in the rear of the front office. He raised the M4 and shot it to ribbons. No more calls, in or out.

Then he raised his weapon and kicked open the "IMPOUND OPERATIONS" door, finding no one inside. On the wall was a mounted key box. Someone had lost the key to it long ago, and jimmied the lock with a screwdriver. Letting his M4 hang by its sling across his chest, Junior started flipping through the two dozen sets of car keys and the paper labels clipped to them. There was a hell of a lot of firing going on elsewhere in the building. He stepped it up.

The labels told the color, make and model, and Junior was indecisive for a moment until he saw one marked "RESERVED FOR LT WINFREY." He looked over the label. It was an old brown Ford Explorer, a 2018. Perfect. If the lieutenant was going to steal it for himself, it was probably good to go. He took the keyless remote and put it in his pocket.

Weapon up, he went to the door that led back into the front office and pushed it open gently. Two PSF, pistols out, were screaming at the civilians, who could not seem to respond coherently. Junior took a deep breath and went through the door.

The PSF officers' eyes went to him before their weapons did, the last tactical error of their lives. Junior put a burst into the farthest one, then pivoted to the second PSF officer as his Beretta came up and squeezed the trigger. The 5.56 mm rounds stitched the blue from navel to neck, and he arced backwards, muscle spasms causing the dead officer's trigger finger to squeeze off a couple of rounds into the wall before he fell dead on his back.

The half dozen civilians on the floor of the foyer shrieked in terror.

"Get the fuck out! Out!" Junior yelled. After a moment, they rose as one and crowded the front door as they sprinted for the street.

Junior returned to look at the dead officer's desk. There was a public address microphone, just as they had expected, probably used to page people to the front. Junior keyed it.

"Attention Hollywood station!" – there was a burst of rifle fire somewhere in back – "We are under attack by racist terrorists! They are dressed as uniformed officers! Repeat: They are dressed as uniformed PSF officers! Engage them whenever you see them!"

Junior threw down the mic and hit the buzzer. At the same time, he stretched to reach for the door, just barely grabbing the handle and pulling it open. Gun up, he went inside where Turnbull had been.

That guy squatting behind the desk in the office off the second hallway was actually putting up some resistance, Turnbull admitted to himself as he sat on the dirty linoleum floor pulling a fresh mag out of his vest and inserting it in his M4's well. Three more shots from a handgun slammed into the closed door across from the open doorway to the office where the gunman lurked. Turnbull could try to leap past the doorway and just bypass the guy, but you don't want an armed and determined enemy behind you.

"Fuck it," he said and leveled his carbine at the dirty, light green-painted wall about 18 inches above the floor in the general direction of his nemesis and fired off the entire 30-round magazine. Wafting fingers of smoke and a cloud of pulverized plaster rose in the hallway as he tossed away the empty mag and replaced it with a full one. There was a slight groan from the office, then nothing. Turnbull got to his feet and kept moving toward the arms room.

A few yards ahead, a uniformed PSF officer, clearly wounded, stepped out of an office, firing back into it. There was a moan, then silence from inside. The officer was unsteady and fell. Turnbull noted two chest wounds. Inside, sprawled on the linoleum floor, was another uniformed PSF officer. The thug with the chest wounds had killed him.

"Nice job, Junior," Turnbull muttered.

He pressed forward, scanning for targets, until he came to the arms room. Someone had opened it up, because the door was wide and the light was on. A PSF officer stood outside yelling something – it was hard to hear through the ringing and the plugs but it sounded like "Rifle!" Turnbull lit him up and charged into the open door. Another officer was fumbling with keys to unlock a rack of M4s; he dropped the keys to try to draw his pistol, but Turnbull shot him too. Alone, as he reloaded, he looked around the room.

"Fucking A," he said, delighted.

Turnbull let his M4 fall across his chest, supported by its sling, as he grabbed a canvas bag off the shelf. He ignored the AK ammo and helped himself to some of the loaded M4 mags sitting in a cardboard box on the arms room clerk's desk.

Then his eyes alighted on something even more interesting.

It was a wooden crate, the top pried open, with the words "Grenade, Fragmentation, M67." Someone had spray-painted on the top "Tactical Squad Use Only."

"Oh, hell yes," he said, stepping forward.

But from behind, a voice, "Come on, man, get me a fucking AK or M4! I need a rifle!" It was a PSF officer, with two tear drop tatts below his left eye, fearfully looking back down the hall.

"Well, the M4 is technically a carbine."

"What?" replied the blue, incredulous.

"The M4 is a carbine. Ah, whatever." Turnbull drew his Glock in a smooth motion, double tapped him center mass, then finished him with a round to the forehead. The blue dropped, and Turnbull went back to gathering up hand grenades. After all, in all his adventures, he had never found himself unhappy about being too well-armed.

There were three dead PSF officers in the hallway as Junior moved down it, weapon up. There was much more shooting from the back of the building – pistol shots too. Apparently someone was fighting back. He pressed on, looking for a sign to direct him. There was one at the intersection with another long corridor, which was likewise occupied by several dead thugs. The impound lot was through a door to his right. Gun up, he pushed it open. There was a short corridor ending in a windowed steel door. The windowed door opened to the outside. And by the door was a control box that read "GATE OPEN/CLOSE."

Hitting the button, Junior went through the door into the night air, standing on a concrete patio from which a few stairs led down to the impound lot. The 12 foot high chain link fence was opening with a low grrrrrrrr. There was the barest hint of a siren in the distance; he could still hear occasional shots from inside, but the brick exterior walls muffled the sound. Outside, on Wilcox, people were gathering. They just stood there, watching, quiet. For now.

He hit the keyless remote button and there was a beep and a flash of lights. The Explorer. He headed down the stairs.

Down the hall from the arms room, Turnbull took one of the grenades out of the bag and pulled the pin, throwing it underhanded back inside. Then he ran and covered his ears. Before leaving the arms room he had made sure to smash every bottle of gun cleaner on the shelves, so the bone-shaking explosion of the Composition B in the grenade was complimented by the flammability of the cleaning fluid. The arms room erupted in flames, with the remaining ammo almost immediately beginning to cook off.

He headed toward the small cellblock where they held short term prisoners before either letting them go with a beating or transferring them downtown for more extensive abuse. In the cell room was an unarmed, dumpy PSF officer cowering behind a counter – no guns in the cellblock.

"You," Turnbull said, M4 leveled at her head. "They brought in a kid tonight. Where is he?"

She stuttered something incoherent, terrified. She was used to cuffed and cowed prisoners, not this.

"Listen, I will fucking shoot you. Where's the kid?"

She continued to stutter.

"Shit," he said. "Okay, we're going back in there. Open all the cells."

She stood, her jaw quivering.

"Do it! Three, two…."

She leaned forward and hit several buttons. Somewhere back behind her, through the door marked "CELLBLOCK" there was clanging and whirring. Turnbull grabbed her by the shoulder and pushed her through.

It smelled like a sewer had shit another sewer back there. There was a row of a dozen cells, and all the doors were wide open. Some of the inhabitants were stepping tentatively outside, looking around. There was not a one that did not look like he or she had been worked over.

181

Turnbull shoved the officer forward and covered her with his carbine. "Abraham! Abraham, come out! We're leaving!" The other prisoners stared, numb.

Down at the end, a young boy's head peeked around the corner. He had a black eye.

"Remember me, Abraham? We're going. I'm taking you out of here."

Abraham blinked, then started to approach.

"Come on, run, we gotta go. All of you, you're free! Get out of here! Go! Before this place burns down!"

But the prisoners seemed less interested in leaving than in the guard. They surrounded her, silently, and she began to babble and step backwards. They kept coming.

Abraham reached Turnbull and he took the kid by the upper arm and pulled him out the door. The last thing he saw was one of the prisoners raise her fist and bring it down on the guard's face. As he turned and pushed the kid out into the hallway, he could hear her incoherent screaming through his plugs.

Junior opened the door of the brown Explorer and jumped into the driver's seat. It started right up – the lieutenant had good taste in what he stole from other citizens. It even had a full tank of gas – probably courtesy the PSF's own pumps – and the range indicator estimated 413 miles, which should be more than enough.

He pulled it out of the stall and over to the gate. Leaving it to idle, he got out and ran around to the fence to wave to Amanda up the street to come on over. The cruiser's engine turned over, and Junior turned around to head back to the Explorer.

The buckshot hit the ground low in front of him; his left leg was technically struck by three ricocheting pellets. The gunner was a PSF officer with an ancient Remington 870 about 50 yards up in the dark of the road kneeling to take the shot. Limited practice had limited his effectiveness. If he had been better trained he might have come close to taking off the leg entirely, if not killing him outright. Still, Junior was now on the ground tangled in his carbine's sling and trying to draw his Glock.

Around them, a growing audience of civilians watched from the darkness.

The PSF thug smiled as he stood up and racked another double aught shell into the chamber and prepared to empty it into

Junior's head. He got two steps before the cruiser slammed into him at 30 miles per hour, snapping his femurs and fracturing his skull on the light bar when he flipped over the roof.

Amanda braked and the cruiser skidded to a stop. She got out of the cruiser, Beretta in hand, and walked back to the shattered officer, who lay groaning in the middle of the road, bloody, his legs at terrifying and impossible angles.

"You shot my brother, you fucking dick" she screamed as she raised the pistol and shot him again and again, until the slide locked back on the empty gun.

Satisfied that the PSF officer was off to his final reward, she turned and ran over to Junior, who had managed to stand upright, sort of. Putting her arm around his shoulder, she helped him to the idling Explorer and put him in the rear passenger seat so he could cover the station door with his M4 through the open window.

On the street, shadowy human shapes swarmed over the dead officer.

Junior checked his watch. It read 10:50 p.m. And the sirens in the distance were getting more numerous and louder.

Turnbull took a vest off a dead thug and put it on Abraham and warned the kid to keep behind him, but to always remain close. The Evidence Room was at the end of another corridor; he had seen it going to the cellblock. Smoke was starting to fill the station. There were still occasional gunshots. A PSF officer came up in his blind spot, looked at the pair, then simply decided – for whatever reason – to continue on his way. Someone had gotten very lucky in that encounter.

The Evidence Room door was closed, and it looked reinforced. A grenade might not take it down. Turnbull approached slowly, weapon up, covering each room he passed. Inside Detective Room C were four desks, and on one was Abraham's backpack.

Turnbull charged in. Two detectives had taken cover inside behind a desk in a corner. They had no intention of going out to look for trouble, but trouble had come to them and they fired their Berettas. One's rounds both went off the mark, but the other managed to hit Turnbull in his vest an inch left of his front Kevlar trauma plate just before he squeezed the trigger and emptied an entire magazine into both of them.

183

"Shit," said Turnbull. He knew what a broken rib felt like. He also know what a gunshot wound tearing through his flesh felt like, and at least this didn't feel like that. He dropped the empty mag and seated another.

It occurred to him that his hip still hurt. That's what he got for pissing off a Texan girl. He looked at Abraham.

"That's your pack, right?"

Abraham nodded.

"Please tell me the hard drive is in there."

"It was."

"Look."

Abraham unzipped it. "It's here."

"Take the pack and let's go. Stay behind me." Turnbull moved to the door, but the kid didn't budge. He was staring at the dead detectives.

"He's the one that hit my face," Abraham said.

"He's not going to hit anyone's face any more. Now we have got to go."

The smoke was getting very thick as Turnbull led the kid toward the impound lot exit. There was a lot of yelling now, and some more shooting. Down the hall, shadows appeared – people, but not PSF. Turnbull held his fire and the intruders, already carrying spoils, rushed past them as if they weren't even there. The civilians were looting the station. Good, he thought. Harder to figure out just what we were doing here.

They found the exit to the impound lot, and Turnbull went out first. A brown SUV was idling at the gate. Shadowy figures were rushing by, swarming the cars, lurking at the foot of the stairs to go in the door when the big man with the big gun got out of the way.

"Kelly!" Junior yelled, waving from the window.

"Come on," Turnbull said, pulling Abraham outside and down the steps. Before the door shut and locked, several civilians had come up, pulled it open and rushed inside.

Turnbull ran around to the driver side and put Abraham in the back next to Junior, then jumped behind the wheel. He hit the gas, accelerating into the street past the dead officer and dodging the civilians running across Wilcox to join in the chaos.

"Abraham, this is Amanda. Amanda, Abraham." Turnbull said.

184

"Where are we going?" the boy asked.

"We're taking you out of here, like I promised your father."

"He's gone, isn't he?" Abraham asked.

"Yeah, he's gone. I'm sorry."

Turnbull turned right on Sunset, entered the freeway, and headed east. They said nothing for a long time.

18.

"They found two dead officers in the street just a half mile from here," said Larsen, puzzled. "Their cruiser is gone. They were part of our perimeter operation."

"And nothing to the west?" asked Rios-Parkinson.

"No, we flooded the zone with personnel. Nothing."

"Why would they draw attention to themselves by shooting two officers here and getting on the radio pretending to be a regular citizen telling us it happened elsewhere?"

Larsen shrugged. "They wanted to draw us away?"

"But we were never going to be drawn away from this raid by a couple of dead PSF," the Director scoffed. Larsen shrugged again.

Rios-Parkinson took a few minutes to change out of his soiled suit and into a tactical PBI black utility uniform. He felt it was good for the men to see him like that – it might inspire them, though he had absolutely no tactical training himself. Then he waved over a sergeant.

"Get me a gun," he ordered.

Adjusting the SIG Sauer on his hip, he admired himself in the SUV's window. He had never fired a SIG before taking Lou's from his corpse tonight and turning it on one of the spies before it ran empty. The big spy had called him weak and untrained. The Director of the PBI intended to prove all that irrelevant.

He would not let some racist, sexist, red brute take away everything he had earned.

Larsen trotted over to him.

"Have you found it?" Rios-Parkinson asked.

"No, nothing," Larsen replied. "But we are getting strange reports from the Hollywood PSF station."

"What kind of reports?"

"Gunfire. We can't reach anyone inside."

"That's the PSF station for this area. What would be...?" Rios-Parkinson paused. "They would take anyone arrested around here there for booking?"

"Yes," said Larsen, confused.

186

"You usually secure the outer perimeter with two vehicles per location, correct?" asked Rios-Parkinson, although he knew the answer.

"Where was the other car when they killed those officers?" asked Larsen.

"Perhaps it was transporting an arrestee who has something they wanted," said Rios-Parkinson. "Get my team together. Get everyone back to the Hollywood station! Now!"

The SUV convoy pulled up parallel to the station on Wilcox. The security team got out and set a perimeter around the vehicles. There were scores of civilians still running around in the shadows, fleeing as several dozen cruisers with lights flashing descended upon the scene.

Flames licked out of the building's roof top. A pair of civilians were carrying a couch out the public entrance in the front.

Larsen came to the window of the SUV as Rios-Parkinson stared at the disaster.

"It appears from witnesses that a terrorist group burst in and attacked the station by surprise. Most of the officers were out in the field looking for the shooters. They must have taken out a dozen PSF, sir," Larsen said, slipping back into military mode. Rios-Parkinson let it pass. That military mode might come in handy in the coming hours. He could deal with Larsen's moral and character flaws later.

"What do the central server records say?"

"They arrested several people tonight. The one who fits best was male-identifying, cisgender, not a person of color, and flagged as Jewish. Age 14. John Brown, obviously a false name. It says he was disturbing the People's order and disobeying the People's will, which could mean anything."

"The arresting officers?"

Larsen jerked his head toward the burning building. "I don't think they made it."

"And what was he carrying? What did they take into evidence?" "It says a backpack, $353 dollars, and 'electronics.'"

"Electronics?"

"That's all it said."

"Did David Kaplan have a son?" "There's a birth record of an Abraham Kaplan, but he never registered in a school, was never in the Young Progressives, never joined any of the voluntary committees on racism or gender justice or climate change like he was required to."

"Let me guess. He was born around 2020."

Larsen nodded. "That's right."

"Then they will have the hard drive," Rios-Parkinson said, unable to fully conceal his fear.

"But we have the tracker," Larsen said.

"Is the system working again?" Rios-Parkinson asked, hopefully.

"They say it will work, but you were very clear – do not start it outside your presence." "Listen," Rios-Parkinson said. "Get it transferred to your tablet and encrypted. You have to be the only ones who can track them. No one else can know. And we will follow them and we will get back the drive ourselves. Do you understand?"

"Yes, sir," Larsen said, again slipping into old habits.

"And have our forces clear this building. Find out what you can from whoever they catch, then eliminate them. I want to demonstrate that the culprits have been caught and punished."

Larsen nodded. He called over the PSF senior leaders and gave them their instructions. Their forces began to surround the building. Next, they would go in and retake it. And woe to whomever had not yet escaped with his lucre.

Larsen next directed the drivers of the SUVs to the gas pumps in back of the station to top off. Then he proceeded to contact the techs at headquarters about transferring the tracking program to his tablet, and to his tablet alone.

Early Friday morning on old Interstate 15, the traffic was sparse. There were a few cars roaring out to Las Vegas on spontaneous trips, the kind only those wielding Privilege Levels of 7 and up could plausibly explain at the frequent checkpoints. By Barstow, they had hit four of them, the bored PSF guards scanning their passes and then waving them through to keep heading out across the desert. The stars were subdued and obscured through this part of the journey, since the dozen coal plants that at least intermittently powered Southern California had been located out here in the middle of nowhere. They were out of sight, well off the freeway off in the desert, the better to avoid raising uncomfortable questions about why the government was essentially eliminating private vehicles from the non-elite citizenry in the name of climate sanity while it was also pouring many tons of carbon into the air every hour of every day.

They had switched seats after taking a rest break in the abandoned town of Victorville. Turnbull had pulled the Explorer off the road and behind an old, abandoned fast food place.

"See," he said to Junior, pointing out the two untrimmed palm trees growing at a weird angle that created an "X." "This was an In-N-Out. Now I'm going to go take a leak. See if that spigot still works. We need some water."

They continued down the freeway, having filled several discarded plastic bottles they found lying about, with Abraham holding a flashlight from the front passenger seat while Amanda tried to dig the buckshot pellets out of Junior's leg with the forceps from the medical kit.

"How about a pain pill?" Junior hissed through clenched teeth.

"Nope, need you fresh. Have a Motrin. And give me one. Damn rib hurts like a motherfucker," said Turnbull. "So does my hip. Thanks, Amanda."

Outside Barstow, they passed a broken down sign for Fort Irwin Road.

"Ugh," said Turnbull. "If the old US Army had a rectum, Irwin would be it. It's all gone now since the blues decided they didn't need a real army."

"Shit," Junior said, wincing as Amanda bandaged his leg.

"You were always such a baby," she replied.

"Will you be able to walk?" Turnbull asked.

"I think so, as long as it's not too far."

"Yeah, well I'm driving this to as close to Utah as we can get, off road if necessary."

"What, we're going back the same way we came?" asked Junior. "We don't do that."

"I know. Amanda's boyfriend Rios-Parkinson may be a hack, but he probably has one or two real soldiers working for him, and they are going to tell him that there is no way we will ever go back out the way we came in."

"Do they know we're coming?"

189

"Nope. But once we cross the line, Meachum will pick us up and vector in some of his guys to check us out and they'll bring us in. Now all we gotta do is get there."

They got through the Vegas checkpoint without a problem shortly before 4:00 a.m. and drove through the heart of the city on the freeway. The Strip was so bright it cast shadows in the desert. The rest of the town was a black hole; the power went off overnight, and the masses were left to swelter while the elite partied in icy comfort.

About 20 miles out of town, they ran into stopped traffic that extended over a ridge to their front. The high flyers had all turned off in Las Vegas. This was mostly trucks and locals. And the line of vehicles was simply not moving.

"I'm going forward to see what's up." Turnbull tossed Amanda the remote. "I'll be ten minutes, tops." He got out and crossed over the median and the westbound lane into the dark of the desert.

He moved out about 100 yards from the freeway and climbed up the ridge parallel to it. He did not stop at the top of the ridge, but instead crawled over top, sliding down a few yards to the military crest where he would not be silhouetted against the sky on the ridge line. The line of vehicles descended down the hill maybe a quarter mile and stopped at a roadblock of four vehicles with blue and red light bars, probably PSF.

But the PSF officers were not doing anything. Turnbull watched them through the binos. They were just standing there, walking around their vehicles, not checking documents, not interacting with the people they had halted, nothing. The westbound lane was open; every once in a while a truck passed through going toward Vegas. But eastbound was completely stalled – and there was no indication anyone was in any hurry to get it restarted.

What the hell?

It was maybe an hour and a half until dawn. He took his binos and turned them toward the desert. There was a little bit of moonlight, maybe enough, he decided.

Fifteen minutes later he was back at the Explorer.

"What is it?" Amanda asked from the driver's seat.

"It's a problem. Get in the passenger seat." Turnbull said, going to the back of the vehicle and opening the rear hatch. Inside, he opened the access panels to the rear lights and pulled the bulbs out of their sockets, then shut the hatch again. Behind him, a trucker watched him curiously from his seat above the road. Turnbull gave him the stink eye, and the driver averted his gaze. He didn't see anything. This was none of his business.

Back in the driver's seat, Turnbull killed the headlights, cranked the ignition, and engaged the four wheel drive, then pulled a hard left over the shoulder and into the median and across the westbound lane and then into the desert. The brown Explorer soon disappeared from view. With the bulbs gone, he was able to brake without flashing his red lights. Slowly, but faster as his eyes adjusted to the moonlight, he drove north around the far spur of the ridge.

"The freeway turns north. If we go east here maybe five miles, we hit it again way past the roadblock," Junior said, squinting at the map by the light of a small pocket flashlight with a red lens.

They passed the roadblock lying a mile to their south; there was no reaction as they bypassed it. No one was looking out into the desert. Turnbull pressed on, concerned that they would be making the crossing well-past dawn. And the fuel indicator was dropping much faster than he had hoped.

The SUV convoy roared through Las Vegas at 80 miles per hour. They were making up lost time. Larsen convinced Rios-Parkinson to refuel in Baker to ensure they had gas for the entire conceivable route. The station had been closed and two of the ten PBI tactical team members had had to kick in the door of the gas station's proprietor's trailer to convince him to fuel the vehicles.

The tracker now indicated that their quarry had left the freeway.

"This can't be right," Larsen said, looking at the screen on his tablet. "They were sitting there on the road for 20 minutes a mile south of the roadblock and now it's showing them north of the freeway, off-road, heading east."

"They are bypassing the block," Rios-Parkinson said. He had ordered the PSF to seal I-15 outside of town to the east, where no one who mattered would ever be at this hour. Then the tactical team could easily take them trapped in traffic and no one would ever know what happened. A few civilians might get killed in the crossfire, but that was acceptable. Except these bastards were refusing to cooperate – again.

191

"I don't get it," Larsen said. "He's a professional, obviously. But it looks like he's heading to cross in Utah. He's going out the way he came in."

"So?"

"So professionals don't do that," said Larsen. "I don't understand."

"Maybe he is not as professional as you think," Rios-Parkinson said, dismissively. But Larsen had been inside the PSF station, and he had had personal experience in Indiana with the kind of people who were able to conduct operations like that. He clutched his own M4, and he began to be afraid.

Turnbull wheeled the Explorer back onto the 15 and accelerated northeast. There was almost no traffic in their direction, and only a few occasional vehicles heading west. The sun would be up soon. Turnbull hit the accelerator and pushed it to 90. The fuel economy dipped, but he had few options with daylight coming.

They drove for almost a half hour before the gas station where he and Junior had eaten their first meal on the blue side came into view. He passed it and then, down the freeway out of sight, turned left and again crossed the westbound lane to head north. Using the nav system on the Explorer, he made some rough calculations of where he needed to go and headed in that direction.

"Kelly," asked Junior from the back. "Let's assume that roadblock was for us."

"I already do."

"Okay, so if it was for us, then your idea about going back the way we came was totally wrong."

"Looks like it."

"So why didn't they grab us at the roadblock?"

"Not enough of them, maybe," Turnbull opined.

"So that's got to mean that there are more coming from the west. I mean, we haven't seen any bad guys from the east."

"What's that tell you?"

"They are behind us, following."

"Except we went off-road again, and they don't know that."

"Maybe," said Junior, but he sounded unconvinced.

They drove on, using dirt tracks where they could and flat washes where there were no trails. The going was tough, and the sun was beginning to rise in the east.

Turnbull looked at the nav system and decided it was time to turn east up a dry arroyo that jostled them with rocks every few seconds. It was slow going, but steady.

The fuel reserve warning had been lit for a half hour, and it estimated four more miles until empty.

Fine. Four less miles for them to walk out.

Leaving about five or six miles to the Utah border.

The Explorer did not run out of gas; the indicator said there were two miles left in the tank. Instead, the terrain simply became impossible for a vehicle. There was a low ridge ahead, the summit at least a mile ahead, and the Ford was just not going to make it over the rocky terrain.

"Everyone out," Turnbull said. He took his M4, his pack, and his ammo bag, and put on his PSF vest. Hopefully no one would read the letters "PSF" and shoot him. Junior hobbled out with his weapon slung around his neck, unsteady but game to give it a try. The hard drive was in his pack. Abraham was solemn, and Amanda looked happy to be out of the SUV and in the fresh air.

"Let's go," Turnbull said, leading the way up the rocky incline.

A half mile in, they had to rest. Abraham, the city boy, was having a hard time with the exertion. Amanda's frequent gym workouts had her in better shape. Junior was obviously in pain, and blood was seeping out from under one of Amanda's bandages, but he didn't complain.

"Everyone drink water," Turnbull said. The sun was now rising well above the horizon, and the evening chill was gone. They were sweating. It was only going to get worse. Up ahead was a low ridge running north to south, its west face covered with rocks and brush.

They took another break on the military crest of the hill, finding shelter out of the sun 20 feet below the ridge line. It was a good position, concealed in a small clearing behind vegetation, with sightlines back toward the abandoned Explorer and both north and south along the face of the hill.

Turnbull had gone ahead a bit to scout, moving carefully up and over the crest. There was a three mile wide valley on the other side, full of rocks and scrub trees, then another low ridge. Somewhere beyond that was Utah. At this rate, it was going to take them most of the day to get there.

Turnbull kept low coming over back west over the crest to link up again with the group, making his broken rib ache and hip hurt. They were still in the small clearing behind a clump of bushes. Inside it he found the group intently staring back towards the east.

"You got the binos?" Junior asked. "Look, there, by where we left the vehicle."

Turnbull brought up the field glasses. Three black SUVs. At least 10 guys in black tactical rig, maybe more. Long weapons. And another one who didn't quite fit with the toughs.

"Shit. Amanda, your boyfriend's back and I think we're in trouble."

"How did they find us?" she asked.

"Yeah, I was just wondering that too, Amanda. How *did* they find us?"

"What are you saying?" Amanda demanded.

"I'm saying they know exactly where we are. Are you sure you didn't forget to mention a cell phone, or maybe a tracker in your keister? Something like that?"

"Kelly!" said Junior.

"Fuck you," Amanda hissed.

"Give me your pack."

"I don't…."

"Give me your fucking pack." Amanda threw the brown backpack at him. Turnbull unzipped it and dumped it out in the dirt. There was a sweater, some food, her thick photo wallet. Turnbull grabbed the wallet and opened it. Photos of the Ryan family, her dogs, a trip to Hawaii before it became off limits to Americans.

And a small gray metal disc.

"That sneaky bastard," Turnbull said, holding it up. "Your boy really didn't trust you, did he?"

"What is it?" she asked.

"A tracker, a pretty primitive one. New ones are a lot smaller. They can even have microphones so they can listen in on your conversations. This one's just good for a location. But that's good

194

enough for government work." He slipped the tracker into the pocket of his jeans.

"What do we do?" asked Junior. "They're coming."

"*We* don't do anything. You three beat feet east. They will be following the signal until they figure out I'm not you guys."

"There's a dozen of them," Amanda said. "And there have to be more coming."

"No, there won't be any more. They'd be here now. No, your boyfriend wants to wrap up us loose ends personally and quietly. It's just these guys."

"They still outnumber you a dozen to one," said Junior.

"They aren't soldiers. This isn't their house. It's mine. Now, you get going. I'm going to hold them off. It should give you enough lead time, but don't slow down, no matter what. You gotta get this cargo out, Junior."

"I have the drive. I'll get it out."

"I mean them. These two. They're the cargo. You get them out. You keep my promise for me, okay?"

Junior nodded, and handed over three 30-round magazines.

"Keep them," said Turnbull.

"No, you take them. If it gets to the point where I'm shooting it out with them, I've already lost."

"That's probably true." Turnbull took the spare mags. "Now get the hell out of here. Tell Meachum's guys I may be coming east running, so don't shoot me. Stay low over the crest of the hill, and when you hit the other side, haul ass."

"Bye, Kelly," Junior said. "See you tonight."

"Sure," said Turnbull, sounding unconvinced.

The trio scrambled up and over the hilltop as Turnbull remained in the space inside the clump of bushes, watching his pursuers begin moving his way. Whatever movement formation they were in, Turnbull didn't know it. It wasn't a wedge, it wasn't a column. It was a clusterfuck. But it was still a clusterfuck with a lot of M4s.

They were at least 20 minutes away, but coming fast. They would only get faster as they acclimated to the rocky terrain. Turnbull took the suppressor out of his pack and screwed it on. Then he took a few other items out of his gear. He had time enough to prepare.

195

Time enough to welcome these bastards to his house.

Rios-Parkinson staggered and fell on the sharp rocks. No one laughed, but he *felt* like they were laughing at him. Not that any of them were doing much better. They had only gone a few hundred meters and already most of his tactical team was drenched with sweat. Perhaps black uniforms and black-covered Kevlar helmets were not the best choice for desert operations.

Larsen held the tablet and kept checking it.

"Where are they?" Rios-Parkinson demanded.

"Still there. Right up there just over the crest of the hill from where they were resting when we got here, not moving much. A little, back and forth, but they are pretty much sitting there, maybe out of the sun behind a bush or something."

Rios-Parkinson grunted. "Can they see us?"

"They could if they looked back over the hill," Larsen said with disgust. His attempts to cajole the others into something like a tactical movement formation and to use the natural cover had simply been ignored. "But if they had, they would have moved by now."

Most of their force was ahead of them, picking their way forward through the bushes and over the rocks. Larsen and Rios-Parkinson held back, with a pair of tactical team members hovering nearby, weapons ready. Their radios, hooked onto their vests on the left shoulder, buzzed and crackled quietly.

They approached to about 200 yards from the crest, slowly moving forward. By now, they had spread, quite without consideration or coherent plan, into a skirmish line with a frontage of about 150 meters.

"This is Alpha team leader. We're moving up the left and we'll come over and take them from the flank, over."

Larsen keyed his mic. "Affirmative."

On the left, the Alpha team leader waved his men forward, then dropped out of sight. A high pitched wail of pain echoed over the desert.

Rios-Parkinson looked stricken, his head swiveling back and forth until Larsen pulled him down flat on the rocky ground.

"Oh God, I'm hit, I'm...I'm fucking shot!" cried the Alpha team leader.

Bravo team responded – the five of them rose as one and unloaded on the face of the ridge, firing long bursts. The remaining Alpha members joined them, their M4s tearing off long bursts in their general direction of travel. Lines of impacts scored the ground as bits of rock face disintegrated and puffs of dust erupted everywhere, in no particular pattern or order.

They stopped shooting when their weapons ran dry. At once, everyone seemed to be shouting "Loading!" as they slammed in fresh mags.

"Cease fire!" yelled Larsen into his mic. "Does anyone see a target?"

Again, the Alpha team leader cried out, "I need a medic, oh God!"

They had no medic.

"Did we get him?" Rios-Parkinson asked, his voice revealing his fear.

"I say again, did anyone see any of them?" shouted Larsen into his radio.

No one answered.

"Help me, oh fuck, fuck! It hurts. I need a medic!" the wounded man screamed.

"This is Sawyer," came a voice from the radio. "I'm here with Collins and he's hit bad in the gut. The bullet went right under his plate. He's hurt bad, over."

"Oh, mother fuck!" Collins screamed.

"Sawyer, you get Sanchez and you haul Collins back to the vehicles and wait for evac, do you read me? Tell him to put pressure on the wound while you two carry him out, over?"

"What if he shoots us while we're carrying him, over," asked Sawyer.

"He's not going to shoot you when you're leaving, Sawyer. Out."

Rios-Parkinson looked over at one of the two team members near him. It was obvious that Collins's screams had shaken them.

"I told you he was a professional," Larsen said. "He stayed behind to delay us."

"Your professional only wounded Collins," protested Rios-Parkinson dismissively.

"He *wanted* to wound him. Now we're down Collins and the two guys carrying him out, and the rest of our men are pissing themselves!" Larsen returned to scanning the ridgeline.

Rios-Parkinson frowned, but said nothing. What could he say? He had no idea what to do. But he could not defer to Larsen. *He* was the Director.

"Get them moving," Rios-Parkinson hissed.

Larsen stared back, the patience draining from his face, but he keyed the mic.

"Bravo, I want you to take two men and move slowly – *slowly* – to that spot under the crest where they were holed up. Everyone else, provide overwatch. Watch for movement, especially on the crest. If he tries to go over it will silhouette him and you take him down. All copy? "This is Bravo team leader, copy, over."

Rios-Parkinson watched as two black clad team members began moving forward in short rushes, then falling and taking up concealment behind bushes or rocks every few steps, at which point his partner moved out. They were heading straight up the middle. The rest of the force scanned the face of the ridge with their optics, looking for movement, a shadow, a shaking branch – anything that would reveal their enemy's position.

"Those two will clear that rest position they were in and see if anyone is still there. From that position they can dominate north and south along the ridge," Larsen explained.

"Yes," Rios-Parkinson said, as if he fully understood.

Larsen halted the two men about 10 meters from the rest position, telling them to look and listen. After a couple of tense minutes, they called back that they saw nothing.

Larsen had them hold fast but remain vigilant. Then he used the radio to order the rest of the team to move rapidly forward toward the ridgeline.

"Come on," he told Rios-Parkinson, who staggered to his feet and tumbled forward behind Larsen, waving his SIG pistol uselessly in his right hand. For his part, Larsen moved quickly and confidently, staying up no more than three to five seconds, then falling behind whatever stunted tree or large rock was closest, M4 up and ready.

Rios-Parkinson stumbled along behind, his throat parched, reluctant to fall fully on the ground like Larsen, instead crouching and panting between rushes. Larsen took his final position some 40 to 50 yards east of where their quarry had holed up, covering the ridgeline with his carbine. After thirty seconds, Rios-Parkinson caught up and collapsed beside him, panting. He had no canteen; instead, he had stuffed a plastic one liter bottle of French sparking water into his cargo pocket. Lying there panting, he pulled it out and opened the twist top; the pressurized mineral water, shaken by his exertions, sprayed it all over him and Larsen.

Rios-Parkinson threw the damned bottle away with all his strength; it flew a dozen feet and the contents spilled out on the desert floor. His mouth was still parched. Larsen said nothing, returning to his observations.

They waited, at least five minutes, until Rios-Parkinson finally spoke.

"They could be getting away. We must *move*."

"But the tracker says they are right over the crest, maybe 35 meters east on the other side. They are *not* moving."

"Tell the men to go forward *now*."

"If you go too fast, people die. There is a professional out there. He is waiting for us to make a mistake."

"He is waiting for the rest of his group to escape with my hard drive," Rios-Parkinson said. "He is a professional, but there are nine of us. Get them moving *now*."

Larsen looked down at the dirt, considering, but a split-second before his pause could have been considered defiance, he relented. He keyed his mic.

"Bravo, you two, *slowly*, move forward and occupy that rest position. If anyone's still there, take him or her out, over."

"Look for any gear, anything they abandoned," Rios-Parkinson said. "Tell them."

"And look for anything they left behind. Out."

The two PBI troopers advanced, first one moving ahead five yards, then the next, always with the other in overwatch. Ahead, behind the clump of bushes where the trackers said their quarry had rested, there was no movement. At the edge of the bushes, the pair came on line, and silently counted down from three. On zero, they burst through the vegetation into the small clearing, sweeping it with their weapons.

199

No people, but lots of tracks and disrupted dirt. They had been here. And a small brown backpack was leaning against a shrub.

"We got a day pack here," said the team leader, advancing.

Rios-Parkinson keyed his radio first. "What is inside?"

The PBI officer picked it up. There was something in it, something heavy, and there was resistance, but he tugged hard and the resistance suddenly disappeared.

Larsen's hand flashed to his mic, desperately shouting. "Don't touch…!"

The pack came free and the PBI officer saw that two 18 inch lengths of OD green 550 cord were tied to the trunk of the shrub. At the other end of each were tied two round metal rings that were now falling to the ground out of the underside of the backpack.

The two frag grenades detonated about a foot from the first tactical team member and about three feet from the second. Their respective distances were immaterial; both were blown apart.

Rios-Parkinson and Larsen watched slack-jawed as the clump of brush detonated, showering them with dirt, rocks, bits of vegetation and, likely, their two former companions.

"Fucking idiots," Larsen spat. He turned to Rios-Parkinson. "He's waiting over there for us, just waiting for us to come over. So the way we get him – the *only* way – is to hit him from the side and front simultaneously. So I am going down there" – he pointed south – "and I am going to slip over and come at him from his flank."

Rios-Parkinson stared, confused.

"His side. I'll come at him from the side and when I radio you, you send the other five guys over the crest spraying full auto. He'll get one or two of them, but the others can pin him down and then I'll be able to close in and take him out. Do you understand?"

Rios-Parkinson nodded.

"Tell me, what are you going to do?" Larsen said, no respect at all in his voice.

"I – you, you are going to go down there and sneak over and come at him from the side. When you call me, I send them all over firing automatic. They pin him down and you close in and finish him."

Larsen nodded. "When I call, the *second* I call, you send them all over."

200

Rios-Parkinson nodded again, a cold fury welling up inside him at the insolence, the lack of deference, the contempt in his deputy's voice and manner. If Larsen survived this encounter, there was no assurance that he would survive the one coming once they returned home.

Larsen bolted toward the south, and Rios-Parkinson called over the surviving members of his team to give them their new mission.

Turnbull had kept Amanda's backpack and now he took a knife and cut two small slits in the back. Next, he cut two lengths of the OD green 550 parachute cord and tied the ends to the trunk of a bush. He took out two of his M67 hand grenades and unbent and straightened the pins so they would pull out smoothly. Then he ran each 550 parachute cord line through a hole, slid the grenades inside the pack, and tied the ends of the cords to the metal rings. Carefully, he zipped up the bag and leaned it back against the bush, ensuring the 550 cord remained hidden.

No one who fought guerillas for a living would mess with such a tempting find before checking it out very carefully, but maybe guys whose job was shooting civilians would.

He turned and scrambled low over the ridge, taking care not to silhouette himself on the crest.

The little valley was down a steep grade, with about 25 yards to the line of bushes and shrubs. He went straight downward and found a tree whose branches swayed slightly in the dry breeze. Using his hundred mile an hour tape, he attached the tracker to a branch. It would not sway much, maybe a foot or so, but on their tracker it might look like it was moving around a little, like it was on a person shifting around in a hiding place.

He then went north about 25 meters to get off the centerline and started looking for a position with good concealment to keep out of sight. Ideally, it would have cover too – that is, protection from small arms fire, but the rocks were too small and the bush trunks too thin. His best protection was going to have to be remaining hidden.

He moved through the brush as quickly as he could, favoring the broken rib and his sore hip. He considered several spots, finally choosing one about a yard back from the brush line under a shrub with a nicely shaped "V" in its trunk that would provide support for his M4 as he covered the crest of the ridge. Turnbull dumped his backpack there, along with his water bottle.

Next, he went farther east and broke off several branches with small leaves, then brought them back, using them to obscure the position a little more. Another branch he put down flat on the ground in front of the "V" – it might help keep down the dust when he fired.

Going out and around, careful not to trample any of the vegetation, he viewed his hide site from the perspective of the hilltop, where they would be coming from. Merely okay – not particularly good, but his time was limited.

Next, he looked to the right and left of the position. There was a dry wash running generally parallel to the ridgeline, and it would provide a high speed avenue of approach for an enemy right into his sides. This was why being alone sucked – there was no one to cover his three and nine o'clock. He figured he had about ten minutes to create a field expedient solution to defend his flanks.

Finishing that, he moved another 25 yards north and slowly crept up the eastern face of the hill, pausing to pat dust into his face to at least try to help subdue any shine from his skin – it was already scorching and he was sweating.

He found a small pile of rocks near the top, probably the best he would be able to do, and carefully peered around them toward where he had come from.

The enemy was closing in, though they were moving slower than he had estimated. They were out about 200 yards, still in clusterfuck formation. They were fixing on the clump of trees where he and his group had rested, and on the tracking device that was taped to a bough directly to the east over the hill. Turnbull was off center to the north. They were not looking at him.

He hoped.

He counted twelve guys in black tactical rig, with about eight of them spread across an uneven 100-150 yard wide frontage about 225 meters or so from the ridge. All carried M4s with optics, and they were scanning and panning with their weapons as they advanced. Behind them another 25 yards were four more PBI guys. Two had carbines up. Another was looking at a screen – that had to be the tracker operator. And then another was stumbling along without a long weapon. Rios-Parkinson? Turnbull figured the

Director had to be in a helluva a lot of trouble if he was coming out personally to fix it.

To fix *him*.

Turnbull observed them as they came forward. He noted who was giving hand signals and verbal cues, and who was listening and obeying. It looked like the eight guys in the skirmish line were divided into two fire teams – it was easy to peg the team leaders. The closest one was second in on the right from his perspective.

The school book maximum effective range of an M4 is 500 meters, but this was not a school, nor was it a maintained Army rifle range. It was hot and there was dust. His broken rib hurt like hell. He was using a close quarter battle sight, plus he would have to move fast – no loitering in order to set up the perfect shot. And he was not merely shooting center mass. He knew right where he wanted to hit the team leader.

All this meant that the guy had to be closer than Turnbull would have liked. He waited until his target was at just over 150 meters.

At that point, Turnbull carefully swung the M4 around the rocks and took aim through his optic. A dot danced on the black of the team leader's body armor. The team leader was waving his men forward as Turnbull dropped the dot to the lower abdomen, mentally adjusting for the round's downward flight trajectory, and exhaled. At the bottom of the exhale, he squeezed the trigger, gentle and steady.

The carbine cycled smoothly, and the weapon barely flinched from the recoil. The sound of the action clacking was louder to him than that of the round itself – the suppressor dissipated the hot gasses, leaving only a *thwack*. The enemy was too far away to hear anything at all.

The impact was only a couple inches off from his aim point; the round came from the side as much as the front, so it entered into his target's belly below the protection of his vest and proceeded to tear across his gut. Turnbull watched the target fall as if his legs had been swept out from under him. He was pulling the weapon around when the man began screaming, then yelling obscenities. Turnbull had pulled completely back off the crest by the time the remaining team members opened fire for what seemed like a full minute.

He ran back to his hide position as best he could – lying on his stomach had been agonizing thanks to his broken rib – and took up his position with the M4 in the "V" of the trunk, sighted to the crest of the ridge. He figured he had a few minutes at least until they sorted out the mess and evacuated the wounded man. That would take at least a two-man carry.

So now, he was only facing odds of nine to one.

He remained sighted along the ridgeline. From his position, he could see and cover about the 100 yards straddling the centerline of the enemy's avenue of approach to the tracker he had taped to the tree. He waited, breathing slowly and steadily. The pain in his left side morphed from a knife sticking into him and twisting to something more like a mace pounding on him every time he was forced to breathe.

The shade kept some of the sunlight off of him, but the air was already wicking away the moisture in his nose and mouth. He took his water bottle and had a swig.

The grenades went off – he saw the explosion's cloud of dust and debris rise right in the middle of his field of fire. "Sorry about your pack, Amanda," he muttered. He could not believe these guys were so dumb.

If he was lucky, he got three, maybe four.

Which meant, best case, the odds were now five to one.

Rios-Parkinson cajoled and threatened the remaining five PBI tactical team members in a low voice, which only made it more threatening. He had briefed them on their task, and warned them to be careful not to kill his deputy as he crossed their axis of advance. He then put them in a line, about three meters apart, just under the crest and ordered them to wait for his command to go over the top. He ordered each to set his selector switch to "Auto."

All of them silently calculated whether his personal chance of survival would be better fighting against whoever was on the other side of that hill, or defying the Director of the People's Bureau of Investigation. Each chose to go with having a fighting chance of surviving this ungodly misadventure. Each chose to charge over the top when the call from Larsen came.

Larsen low crawled over the ridge about 200 meters south of their positions, then slowly worked his way down the eastern face on his belly through the brush line down to the dry wash that ran parallel to the hill to the east. In the sandy soil of the wash, he got up into a squat and observed north. The guy had to be up there, somewhere. Larsen was almost certain the round that took down the Alpha team leader had come from the north side. Carefully, deliberately, he began working himself north along the wash, scanning the brush for signs of the enemy. After all, if it had been him ambushing the PBI team, that's where he would have put himself.

At about where the tracker was reading, Larsen paused and observed. Nothing. No one. It was a diversion. The tracker had to be over there in the bushes somewhere.

If he hadn't run away, the enemy had to be to the north. And in Larsen's experience, sons of bitches like this guy never, ever ran.

He went another five meters, gun up, ready to engage. The guerilla had to be close – Larsen could *feel* him up there ahead.

Speed, aggression. Those were his allies. He checked and confirmed that his M4 was set to "Auto."

His left hand came off the fore grip to key his mic; Larsen had muted his speaker before coming over the top so that Rios-Parkinson would not get him killed by sending some damn fool radio traffic.

"Go. I say again, go!"

Rios-Parkinson looked up at his five men.

"Go! Go now!"

They stood up as one and charged over the crest as Rios-Parkinson watched them from the safety of the west side of the hill.

Out of nowhere, five black shapes crested the ridge, silhouetted against the morning sky. Turnbull sighted on the first one who appeared in his optic – it happened to be the south most one. He squeezed the trigger twice, the first round kicking up a puff of fabric and dust over the target's chest plate, the second slicing through his neck and out the back after severing his spine at the C2 level. The man fell like a black bag of Jell-O, his carbine flying out of his grip, his body rolling down the hill.

The other four opened fire on full automatic, initially randomly. Yet whether they had heard a sound or seen dust or simply guessed well, they began to direct their streams of lead in Turnbull's general direction as they charged down the hill.

Turnbull shifted his aim. This time the dot came to rest over the face of one who was screaming something – you couldn't hear anything over the roar of the guns. Turnbull squeezed, the M4 kicked, and the man's black helmet flew off to the rear, along with a healthy portion of the back of his skull. He managed to take two more perfectly normal strides, still firing his weapon, before he collapsed in a jumble of his suddenly limp arms and legs.

Larsen was charging now at full speed, not yet firing, but seeking a target. To his left, the other five had crested the hill, one dropping before he got a meter over. Yeah, the enemy was here, somewhere ahead.

Larsen pressed forward. Rounds were shredding the brush ahead of him. The enemy *had* to be there.

A round took most of the head off another man in black, but that left three. Three targets for the enemy to focus on while Larsen came up unseen from the side. He ran faster, his eyes scanning the bushes to his left.

A shape, there, amidst the hurricane of lead from the survivors. The enemy.

As he ran across the wash, he brought the M4 up to follow his eyes, which were locked onto his target. He felt something catch his legs, just for a moment, before it gave. He took another step, distracted, and his eyes turned downward.

550 cord, stretched across the wash. He had run through three trip wires which were now tangled around his legs and trailing little metal rings.

"I'm a fucking idiot, too," he thought as the three hand grenades detonated.

The trunk in front of him exploded in a cloud of wood chucks and splinters. Turnbull shut his eyes tight. Rounds hit the dirt right before his position. There were sparks in front of his face as rounds tore into his M4's receiver assembly. He crawled backwards. There were three more coming.

This was it.

The grenades in the wash's south approach exploded each within a split second of each other. They were 40 feet away, but he felt the concussion and so did the three shooters, at least for a moment. His ears roared, and he rolled over on his stomach, the pain from his rib like a bayonet in his kidney, and began to crawl back toward the wash.

The closest one fired again, one round striking his rear trauma plate and shattering it, the second slamming into the plate's left edge, driving a piece of it down into the back of his ribs, breaking them too. Turnbull collapsed on his belly with a grunt.

It felt like a dozen bayonets jabbing his kidney.

The shooting stopped for a moment and Turnbull rolled onto his back. It hurt so bad it actually stopped hurting for a moment, as if his brain simply could not process that sheer volume of hurt. The bastard who shot him was pushing in a fresh mag as Turnbull drew his Glock with his right hand and raised it.

Instinctively, he ordered his left hand to come and join the grip. But his left hand simply declined, and lay flopped on the dirt. One handed, Turnbull fired. The round hit the PBI officer's chest plate. He fired again, then again, both into the chest plate. He continued firing, losing count, the man in black staggering backward, until it occurred to Turnbull to try shooting him in the face, which he did and which worked.

Turnbull scrambled to his feet, dizzy, his ears ringing, seeking the other two targets. One was lying on his face 25 yards away. Turnbull stumbled west, up the hillside. The other one lay on his back, headshot. Had he shot them? Had they shot each other?

Where was Rios-Parkinson?

Turnbull staggered up the hill, forcing one foot forward, then the next, pushing himself upward. He spit out a coppery, salty wad of red blood. Lung puncture from broken ribs. He didn't have much time. But that didn't matter now.

That little fucker had to die.

The pain came back and, unimaginably, it was worse than before. He gasped, nauseous, the pain fighting to dominate his mind and force him into a fetal position until it might fade. But the pain was wrestling with his desire to finish the job. In agony, Turnbull crested the hill and fell to his knees, the blood spurting out of his mouth and over his chin as he coughed and sought to regain his breath.

A little man in black, down there, running west, back to the vehicles.

Turnbull lifted the Glock and fired as best he could aim. The man kept running. He fired again and again, one handed, until he squeezed the trigger and nothing happened and he realized the slide was locked back on his empty gun.

Down below, Rios-Parkinson was still running.

Turnbull fell face first onto the rocky ground. He coughed, and blood splattered the dirt. Something grabbed his shoulder and turned him on his back; it hurt way too much to cry out.

A bear hovered overhead, blocking out the sun.

No, a man.

"Kelly, Kelly, you still with me?"

"Shoot him," sputtered Turnbull, "Shoot him, Meachum."

"I can't," Meachum said. "Orders. I was supposed to stop you from doing it too. Looks like I almost blew that."

"Shoot him," Turnbull said. Meachum's face was spinning now.

"Nope, Clay would not like that one bit," Meachum said, before saying more words that Turnbull at first could not understand and soon could not hear at all.

19.

"I'm guessing I'm in a hospital," Turnbull said to Clay Deeds, who put down his tablet when the patient began stirring. A variety of machines surrounded his bed. There were a number of lines running into his arms. It hurt to breathe.

"St. George Combined Hospital. You are in the civilian side. Prettier nurses. You're welcome."

"My people?"

"All out. All safe. All in Dallas for debrief. When you get better, that's where you'll be going."

"If," said Turnbull. "If I get better. I feel like shit."

"The doctors say you'll be fine. And you need to be fine. *We* need you."

"Ha!" Turnbull began to laugh, but it hurt too much so he stopped. It wasn't that funny anyway.

"I think I know what you want to ask me," Clay said.

"Meachum could have taken the little bastard easy, Clay. The son of a bitch massacred two dozen people who worked for you."

"You're right on both counts."

"So why not?"

"Because he's compromised, thanks to you."

"I don't understand."

"You. Not just bringing out the hard drive, but your little discussion with him about working for me. You compromised him. And we can use that. That was some solid initiative there, Kelly."

"How do you know about that?" Turnbull asked. "I did it when everyone else was out of the room, so they couldn't tell you. So *how* did you know?"

Clay smiled, proud of himself.

"You bugged me. You son of a bitch, you bugged me."

Clay continued to smile.

"How? Not my clothes, I could change those. Something I'd always – my Glock. You *bugged* my gun?"

"Yes, and not just bugged. Tracker too. Fascinating technology. The transmitter is actually inside the metal of the slide, which acts as a microphone and an antennae. Funny thing, we assessed that it would keep operating only until you fired maybe nine, ten rounds. But we all thought, you know, what are the chances that he'll even have to draw it? Then, of course, you reminded us that you are Kelly Turnbull. You fired a lot more, and it kept working. Out of curiosity, is there anyone you met in the blue who you didn't shoot?"

"Give me a second. I'm thinking. Nope."

"See, I know you and you will always, always have your gun. We followed you the whole time. And we listened in. By the way, I hope those intestinal issues from the food over there clear up. Sometimes we heard more than we really wanted."

"That's how you knew where we would be coming out."

"Yes, we had to protect you and, since you gave us the opportunity to turn the future Director of the PBI, we had to protect him *from* you. So once you said where you were going, we vectored Meachum's guys in to pick you up and bring you across."

"So that little bastard gets to live because he's useful."

"Kelly, he's more than useful. He's critical, and I will own him. You know what's happening over there. When the People's Republic finally goes, it's not just going to take the blues down the drain. It might well take us in the red too."

"What are you going to do with him?"

"We'll approach him, let him choose between us exposing him or working for us. You got me his SIM chip, so I'll probably just call him. What do you think he'll choose?"

"Whatever saves his miserable skin."

"That's our assessment too. He's going to be very useful."

"Useful for what, Clay?"

"Above your paygrade, Kelly"

"Is it above yours?"

"There's not a lot above mine," Clay replied. "Think of letting him live as a necessary sacrifice. I sure do."

"How does someone get morphine around here? And maybe a cheeseburger?"

"I'll summon one of the lovelies on the nursing staff," Clay said, walking to the door. "Get well soon. We need you."

"I'm retired, remember?"

Clay smiled again and opened the door.

"Of course you are," he said. And then he was gone.

20.

It was about noon that the alert on Turnbull's phone went off. There was a car coming onto his property. He had his Kimber .45, and despite the pain in his side – diminished but not yet gone – he could still be a helluva problem to anyone stupid enough to make him theirs.

From the porch, he watched a tan, late-model BMW 6-series roaring up the road and kicking up a cloud of dust in its wake. It pulled in front of his house and stopped. The driver turned off the ignition and opened his door.

Turnbull looked down at his dog, who lay on its side on the wood slats.

"Nothing?" he said. "Really, nothing? Not a bark, not a growl?"

The mutt yawned.

Junior Ryan stepped out of his car, a white bag in one hand and a six pack of something in the other, and strolled around his ride and up to the porch. The limp was still there, but less pronounced. Junior was packing a Glock, just like the one he had carried into the blue. He stopped at the foot of the steps, looked up, and smiled.

"Shiner Bock, huh?" observed Turnbull.

"Yep," said Junior.

"What's in the other bag?" "Well, since there's no Inside-Outside where I could get you a triple animal burger, I did the best I could."

"That's In-N-Out, and it's a Double Double animal style. Oh, forget it. What do you got?" "Whataburgers," Junior replied. "Double meat with cheese combos. After all, we are in Texas."

They sat at the table on his porch, eating and washing it down with the Shiners. The dog finally woke up enough to beg for fries.

"I heard the kid's getting adopted," Junior said. "Orthodox family in Dallas."

"Good," said Turnbull. "So, how's your sister?"

"She's going into the Army."

"You're kidding. Going for citizen, huh?"

"Yeah. I pity the drill sergeants," Junior said.

Turnbull chuckled. "That whole defection thing, that'll probably keep her from being an officer. The security clearance problem."

"I don't know about that. She spent a lot of time with Clay's people after she came out debriefing about what she knew. Apparently she had a lot of interesting stuff to say. Clay can work wonders for people who help him. He can make things that happened unhappen."

"Like our little adventure," said Turnbull. "That seems to have unhappened."

"This is the first time I've talked about it except with Clay's people. Not even with my dad."

"Well, get used to it. Not talking about things gets to be a way of life," replied Turnbull. He took a swig of Shiner. "I hear you're working for Clay now."

"You heard that, huh?"

"Yeah. You sure you want that life?"

"Somebody's gotta have that life, right?"

Turnbull sighed. "Yeah, I guess with things how they are. The news says it just keeps getting worse over there, but it hasn't fallen completely apart just yet."

"From what I see, it could go any time."

"What gets me," Turnbull said, sitting back, "is that it didn't have to be that way. The country didn't have to choose to rip itself in two."

"But it did," said Junior. "I never really understood what it was like before the Split, not like you. I mean, I was just a little kid. But maybe I can help fix it, you know. Help make it like it was before."

"Shit, I never took you for an idealist, Junior. Don't you have rich kid shit you could be out doing?"

"Yeah, in fact I do. But I think I'll do this instead."

"Okay then" said Turnbull, raising his Shiner Bock. "To America. As it was. As it should be. As it might be again."

Junior clinked his bottle and they drank. They didn't say anything for a few moments. Turnbull took a bite of his Whataburger, then tossed his eager dog a fry.

"So anyway, Kelly, I need to ask you something," Junior said.

Turnbull chewed for a moment and then eyed him.

"What?" he said, picking up his beer and taking a swig.

"Well, Clay asked me to run something by you. Just an idea. Something important. Something only you could do. And this time, it's going to be easy, a cakewalk. Now, you wouldn't be going back in alone ...."

Junior paused upon seeing his friend's expression.

Kelly Turnbull swallowed before he spoke.

"Stop talking."

About The Author

Kurt Schlichter is a senior columnist for *Townhall.com*. A stand-up comic for several years, Kurt was personally recruited by Andrew Breitbart, and his writings on political and cultural issues have been regularly published *IJ Review*, *The Federalist*, the *New York Post*, the *Washington Examiner*, the *Los Angeles Times*, the *Boston Globe*, the *Washington Times*, *Army Times*, the *San Francisco Examiner*, and elsewhere.

Kurt is a Twitter activist (@KurtSchlichter) with over 71,000 followers, which led to him writing *I Am a Conservative: Uncensored, Undiluted, and Absolutely Un-PC*, *I Am a Liberal: A Conservative's Guide to Dealing with Nature's Most Irritating Mistake*, and *Fetch My Latte: Sharing Feelings with Stupid People*. All three e-books reached number one on the Amazon Kindle "Political Humor" bestseller list. In 2014, his book *Conservative Insurgency: The Struggle to Take America Back 2013-2041* was published by Post Tree Press.

Kurt has served as a news source, an on-screen commentator, and a guest on nationally syndicated radio programs regarding political, military, and legal issues, including *Fox News*, *Fox Business News*, *The Hugh Hewitt Show*, *The Dr. Drew Show*, *The Larry Elder Show*, *The Dennis Miller Show*, *Geraldo*, *The John Phillips Show*, *The Tony Katz Show*, PJTV's *The Conversation*, *The Tamara Jackson Show*, *The Delivery with Jimmie Bise, Jr.*, *The Dana Loesch Show*, *The Point*, the *WMAL Washington Morning Show with Larry O'Connor*, *The Derek Hunter Show*, and *The Snark Factor*, among others. Kurt appears weekly on the *Cam and Company* show, and averages four to five other media appearances a week.

Kurt is a successful trial lawyer and name partner in a Los Angeles law firm representing Fortune 500 companies and individuals in matters ranging from routine business cases to confidential Hollywood disputes. A member of the Million Dollar Advocates Forum, which recognizes attorneys who have won trial verdicts in excess of $1 million, his litigation strategy and legal analysis articles have been published in legal publications such as the *Los Angeles Daily Journal* and *California Lawyer*.

Kurt is a 1994 graduate of Loyola Law School, where he was a law review editor. He majored in communications and political science as an undergraduate at the University of California, San Diego, co-editing the conservative student paper *California Review* while also writing a regular column in the student humor paper *The Koala*.

Kurt served as a US Army infantry officer on active duty and in the California Army National Guard, retiring at the rank of full colonel. He wears the silver "jump wings" of a paratrooper and commanded the elite 1st Squadron, 18th Cavalry Regiment. A veteran of both the Persian Gulf War and Operation Enduring Freedom (Kosovo), he is a graduate of the Army's Combined Arms and Services Staff School, the Command and General Staff College, and the United States Army War College, where he received a master of strategic studies degree.

He lives with his wife Irina, and his favorite caliber is .45.

CPSIA information can be obtained
at www.ICGtesting.com
Printed in the USA
BVHW051200090521
606888BV00018B/1853